SUKARI’

It's just you and me alone, my son.
Please stay close by my side.
We journey together, to face the unknown.
With no longer protection of a pride.

Scars of my past, lay deep inside.
We had to leave everything behind.
You now give me reason, a purpose to live.
New beginnings I promise you, I'll find...

ADAM NEALE

Cover design and illustrations by: Adam Neale

Character designs:
'Legacy' – Mark Wickham
'Tefnut' – Kirsi Mikkonen
'Shujaa' – Nathalie Thunholm

All contributors are credited in the acknowledgements.

Published by: KDP
First Print
Paperback Edition

Your Journey...

To Lydia

A Neale

From The Author

The first thing you should know, I don't know what I'm doing! Well... almost.

Although I have had many years of writing experience, this was mainly short paragraphs when roleplaying on internet forums (they were the days). But now, it's the first time I have sat down and written a whole novel, which I soon learned is a completely different experience. One thing I found out, as I wrote, I looked back at chapters and knew I could either do better or add more depth. This inevitably turned into a vicious yet rewarding circle of self-learning with many, many, many... many edits and rewriting. However, it has got me to where I am now. I'm writing a "From the Author" of all things! This is one lump of text I thought I would never be doing. But please, take my writing with a pinch of forgiveness, I'm new! I don't have the funds for an editor, so this has all been written and proofed solely by me.

With that part of my lack of self-confidence put aside, I would like to say I'm proud of this story, its rich plot, the rollercoaster of emotions it will put you through and the unexpected twists and turns you will have to endure. If you enjoyed it to the end, then you will see it in a completely different light if you read it again with the knowledge gained the first time around. It's been as much of a journey for me as it has for Sukari. I hope you enjoy it just as much as I had while writing it.

As mentioned earlier, my writing stemmed from a more casual and social form. It was on a forum I was an administrator of, a site dedicated to creating roleplays with like-minded people. This forum was inspired and dedicated to Disney's 'The Lion King'.

This novel is <u>not fan fiction</u>. It has no connection whatsoever to the film and its characters. The entire works are completely original by me, along with certain characters and lore by people that I have credited in the Acknowledgments. It's a standalone story but takes place after one of the forum's longest running roleplays which ended.

Of course, it draws inspiration from the film in terms of anthropomorphic lions set in Africa, but that's it. I have also implemented certain lion characteristics and behaviour that exist in the wild. I learnt this either from studying videos, in real life, or reading books by pioneering professionals in lion behaviour and rehabilitation such as George and Joy Adamson, also their assistant Tony Fitzjohn.

As you will notice while you read, I also love drawing! Though before this novel I only did so now and then as I didn't have much drive or inspiration. However, once I had done a few for this novel I couldn't stop and knew I had to do one for each chapter! The illustrations you will see throughout the story each have an aspect I haven't drawn before, be it a pose, expression, or action. I have learnt so much in terms of anatomy and shading, that it has been an adventure in itself. As you look at each one, I hope it gives you the visions I have tried to portray. I would like to think that drawing *so many* illustrations (like my writing) has improved my confidence and ability.

I have been on as much of an exploration in discovering my strengths, learning new things, and solving problems, just as much as Sukari has in her endeavours. I hope I can take you along and transport you to my little fictional corner of Africa, and we will watch everything unfold together.

"*Asante!*"
(*Thanks*)

Adam

Prologue - Fear

"Welcome to this land, my little one. You won't understand my words, but from a bereaved parent to their newborn cub, I just want to say... I'm sorry. I wish your beginnings started under brighter circumstances. However, I promise my unconditional love and protection, sacrificing anything to shield you, from what will lay ahead... alone."

It's a cruel, challenging, dangerous, and brutal place. If you turn your back at the wrong moment, it kills you. One wrong decision, one bad move, can cause a chain reaction making your life a living catastrophe. It's truly where the quickest, smartest, strongest, or largest survive. It is host to several thousand forms and species of life. From the endless bush, flora and fauna painting the low grounds, to the almighty Baobab trees towering over the lands. From the tiny, helpless African wild pups poking their heads out from their burrow, to the lions patrolling, tracking their many prey that majestically sweep across the land. This also makes this one of the most beautiful and diverse places in the world. This is the wilds of Africa.

If you imagine yourself as a buzzard, flying high above the lands, watching the world go by down below, what would you see? What events could unfold?

A lost lion cub perhaps? Chased away by a grown rogue male lion and now alone, defenceless. You as a buzzard would take interest in this because you know what could happen. Soon enough the cub is being stalked by a hyena, it didn't take long for the hyena to ambush it, quickly sinking its extremely powerful jaws into the cub's neck, breaking it like a twig. You wait patiently for the hyena to consume what parts of the cub its belly needs to survive. After all, it has every right to survive as any other animal in these lands. The same goes for yourself, who would swoop in later to pick off what flesh remains.

It reminds you of a cub that was a lot luckier in the life it was dealt so far. You had landed on a branch and could see movement in some dense bush below. There lies a lioness, cradling and curling around her little fluffball of a cub, giving it tender licks with the proudest of smiles. You watch with a sense of awe at the sweet playful interactions between the mother and her cub. Then after a short while, she stretched out, exposing her belly for her cub to have his morning feed. That was your prompt to turn around and fly away to give her some privacy. Still, it made you ponder on how precious life is, and how precious that moment must be for her, being the sole life support for something she had created.

You then remember you have seen this lioness before, back when she was pregnant, you could tell by the abnormal sway in her stride. She was straggling behind her group and being stalked by a lion. It soon pounced towards her; claws bared with a killer intention. Maybe she had crossed his territory? Luckily, another lion had come to her aide, protecting her just in time. Thanks to that lion, she had lived to see another day, including her cub snuggled up inside.

Not all fights end well though. You remember when you saw a lion laying on the ground, motionless, covered in scars, blood, and battle wounds. This one seemed to have not only lost but had been made sure he was finished. His body now lays at the bottom of the food chain, ready for you and any other scavengers to feast on. What was his life like before it ended? Full of love, friendship, family, and honour? Or was his death justified? Imagine all the things he had done or could have done in his life. But all that now... just gone. Nothing more but a body. Still, more food for you though.

All these happenings lay a story behind them, more so they all share one crucial thing; this is how nature works. It gives and sustains life, but can just as quickly take it away.

However, something not so natural has been cast over this land. It's living in such a fear, that it is unbalancing all animal's way of life.

Fear cannot be touched, seen, or heard, and it lives inside, controlling you. Fear can only be felt and, like a virus, can be spread, shared, and absorbed effortlessly. Fear is the most potent weapon for an animal to wield if you desire power over these lands. If animals fear you, then you are untouchable.

'Legacy' is that fear. A lion of mass proportion. Ironically, nature gave him the gifts of everything that makes a lion a king predator, even deadlier. His claws are twice as long as they are sharp. His jaws bear teeth that can sink deeper than any other animal, even that of his own kind. His mane is extremely thick, giving complete protection to vulnerable areas such as his neck and chest. In his self-twisted mind, his extra 'gifts' were given to him for a reason. Not only to be the dominant lion of his pride but to make sure every other lion and pride in these lands only answer to *him*.

In the past, many brave lions and lionesses have tried to overthrow him only to suffer a terrible fate. The more lions that died, the more others feared him. This in turn, fed Legacy's self-confidence that he was undefeatable. Legacy's pride, influence and fear spread across the land like wildfire, consuming it piece by piece. If he came into your territory and you gave him what he wanted; be it food, a worthy lioness, or a lion, then he would *let* you surrender and live under his rule. If you refused, you would be made an example of.

Legacy had one issue that had to be dealt with, which was 'wanderers'. These were lions or lionesses that had no pride, no territory, and no future. He saw them as lowlifes with nothing to contribute to the land. This also meant they had little collateral to give to *him*, this for Legacy was a problem. Furthermore, they were scattered and dotted all over the land, like annoying flies that are impossible to swat. They could easily vanish, only to reappear. So, he used a spy, his son, for his twisted idea to cleanse this 'problem'. To him, it was all a hunting game.

His son had the opposite demeanour of his father. He looked extremely friendly yet could hold his ground. He had partially inherited the gift of his dad's claws and jaws too. Legacy in his dark twisted mind did sometimes wonder if his son's inherited gifts could be the only ones ever to be able to kill him! His son would travel far across the lands, finding and gaining the trust of these wanderers by posing as one himself.

He would gather them up over time, with the promise of comfort and defence in numbers. When he felt there were enough, they would all by 'coincidence' come across a perfect place to live and settle with a substantial shelter, good vantage points and an abundant water source nearby. This was his den but to them was 'their luckily found home'.

Soon after, he would convince them he had 'sighted' Legacy and they all needed to flee, instead, he led them right to him. Legacy would give them an ultimatum, they either work for his pride to contribute to his cause, or be killed.

This is where we meet Sukari, a wanderer, along with her partner and a group of others. Unfortunately, their fate two months prior was almost sealed by the same scheme Legacy trapped them with. Her partner, Sheek, fought hard but unfortunately lay defeated and motionless from trying to protect them. He gave enough of his life for them to escape.

Without Sheek, Sukari travelled bearing their unborn cub, with the only company she could trust, the remaining group. She had the comfort of protection in high numbers, but deep down she knew it couldn't last.

A lioness close to giving birth has the instinct to be alone and far away from others. If anything, she should already be alone, but she was fighting hard to delay it. However, she felt conflicted and concerned about many more instincts that could endanger her cub. Not instincts of her own, but of others that surround her. She soon needed to make choices that would change how she lived her life forever. Though she knew she would have to tread carefully.

She questioned her past, present and future, she needed to survive and search this land for her answers. She knew all too well that this dangerous yet breathtaking place had every ability to give herself and her cub a forever home. However, it could just as easily kill her.

For the future of her cub, it was worth fighting for.

Though Legacy was relentless.

1. A Mother's Instinct

As much as a lion or lioness wants or tries to resist, its inner instincts always lay deep inside. When certain situations arise, they come to the surface, controlling, or altering the lion or lioness's unique personality, making them who they normally are... different.

Hunger can make them kill the most innocent of newborn prey without the guilt of taking a life that has hardly been lived.

When they embrace one another, be it in a play fight or holding onto each other. If one were forced to pull away, their claws would naturally unsheathe and dig in like they were prey trying to escape, even if their bond of friendship or relationship were strong.

A newly dominant male lion of the pride will intentionally kill any cubs not of his bloodline as they are seen as a threat, regardless of if they are cute, playful and submissive. Furthermore, this will bring the lioness back into heat so she can produce cubs for the new dominant male. Thus, his own bloodline continues.

All this and many other scenarios are real examples of how instincts can control a lion or lioness in unexpected ways, contradictory to their normal personality, actions, or beliefs.

Sukari had been fighting so hard, but she could no longer. She is now a lioness with her single newborn cub, Anthi. In this situation of being a wanderer, she was glad she only had one, as it was easier to manage. This little fluffy ball of new life was her only living proof that her mate Sheek, used to exist. This cub meant even more to her than anyone could imagine because of this.

The more she nursed and cradled their little creation, the more a deep urge inside her grew that she had to be alone. It's a natural inevitability of any new mother lioness.

It didn't feel right being surrounded by other lions and lionesses; her motherly instincts were growing with each passing moment. She didn't want these thoughts to control her normal loving and social nature, but it was becoming inevitable.

Apart from Tefnut, her other unrelated friends and acquaintances overwhelmed her mind. Tefnut being the half-sister of Sheek meant she was family, now the only family Sukari has left. Tefnut had supported Sukari through her entire sorrow, pain and struggle from losing Sheek, a debt Sukari could never repay and was forever grateful for. They were also the best of friends when they were cubs. Her heart said she couldn't even imagine leaving her, but her brain made her think the opposite. She now needed to be alone with her newborn until it was the right age to be reintroduced to the group. If that were to ever happen though?

This 'group' as she called it, was all she knew for a long time. It wasn't a pride. It consisted of lions and lionesses, either wanderers, orphans, exiles, or rogues. They were the misfits that never had a place in life, constantly moving around the lands with the hope of never feeling Legacy's fear. She had seen members of the group come and go. They joined to seek strength and survival while others gave their lives to protect it. Each member had imprinted a bit of their life on the group over the years.

From a mothering lioness's view, this group consisted of many male lions. Naturally, this now could be viewed as a threat to Sukari and her cub. Her mind was being moulded and flooded with a mix of maternal hormones and instinct; she could not help telling herself that Anthi was not safe among them. Regardless of how loyal they are with good intentions; how will she know in the future? Their instincts could betray them. Her confidence in their good nature could betray her.

As much as Sukari had been through with the group, a bond of friendship does not last in this kind of world. We all grow up and go our own ways eventually; regardless of how deep that friendship goes, it's nature's law. Of course, she would miss them terribly, and she loved them in many ways. However, it all comes down to the most crucial thing; as selfish as it may be, it's her own bloodline survival.

Sukari's eyes opened softly. She immediately looked down to see the blurred outline of Anthi. She waited a moment for her eyes to adjust to the little ball of fluff to come fully into focus. She smiled warmly as she just gazed at him sound asleep. Tefnut must have placed him back between her paws while she was sleeping.

Raising a brow at herself, she thought, what was she even doing handing her cub over to Tefnut to cradle at such a newborn age? In her heart, it felt right at the time with Tefnut being related to Anthi's Father, but her brain was now telling her otherwise. Sukari winced and gritted her teeth as she battled with her inner emotions and actions, some coming from her heart and some from her brain. She felt like she was changing rapidly, and she couldn't stop it. What instinct does to an animal can be a gift for survival or a bond-breaking curse.

She opened her eyes again when Anthi made little chirps as he exhaled, at once soothing her inner battle a little. She soon reminisced that Sheek was a terrible snorer. She hoped that these cute little chirps didn't turn into that in the future! That's one trait Sukari didn't want him to of inherited. She could already imagine him all grown up with a lioness of his own, and the disapproving look on her face while she tries to get some sleep! Sukari faintly chuckled to herself at the thought.

Peering through the branches and leaves that surrounded her birth den, she felt the night had become cold, and a layer of mist hung low over the area. It was the opportune moment to do what was needed. The darkness would hide her, and the low mist would dampen her scents left on the ground. Mist also meant no breeze, so her scent couldn't be carried far through the air. Anthi being a newborn would hopefully mean he shouldn't make too much noise. She just had to be gentle to not wake him up too much.

Sukari slowly rose from the spot she had made warm with her body heat. Anthi felt the lack of warmth from his mother, making his body shiver a little. She at once felt guilty letting her little furball feel cold, but she knew it was with her best intentions. She gently picked up Anthi by the nape of his neck and then sat down. She held him close to her chest, cradling him with her paw, letting him listen to her soothing heartbeat while being wrapped in a blanket of new warmth.

"There there Anthi, I'm sorry we have to go, but don't worry, we will find another place. We will be warm and safe once again. I love you," she cooed, followed by tender licks around his ears. She Knew Anthi wouldn't understand her words, but what mother doesn't talk to her newborn?

She looked up from Anthi and towards Tefnut who was still sound asleep. Her eyes soon filled. She blinked, and tears trickled down her tear duct and onto her cheek while her nostrils began to block. She continued to gaze at Tefnut's peaceful slumber. She wanted so badly to hear her voice once more. However, she knew if she woke her, she would have to explain her reason for leaving, then Tefnut may protest and explain many reasons as to why to stay.

Then again, Tefnut was naturally a solitary animal, so maybe she would understand Sukari's reasons to leave? She could embrace her once more, feel her warmth, and hear her voice before leaving. Sadly, Sukari couldn't take that chance, and it was ripping her soul apart. Her Instincts were pulling her away, but her heart was still trying to cling on.

"I'm sorry Tef, I'm so sorry. I hope when you wake..." she whispered as tears started to flow down her cheek, tapping onto the ground. "...and you find me gone, you understand. I hope we meet one day again but under different circumstances... and you won't be angry," she continued with a developing tremble.

Sukari doubted herself. Would they meet again? This group, she felt, had a curse of living in constant fear, fighting, and dying. There was the possibility that Legacy, the main culprit of these atrocities to still be alive. Sheek had injured him severely, sacrificing his life in the process to protect the group. Legacy fled with his final fate unknown from his injuries. But she could still feel the fear.

How far away Sukari intended to get away from this place was unplanned but vast. She wanted a completely fresh start in her life without the slightest worry of even a hint of Legacy. She strongly felt that this would indeed be her final goodbye.

She gazed at Tefnut, still fast asleep, and it continued to hurt her heart. She *had* to go now. She picked up Anthi by the nape and stood up. However, she couldn't resist her emotions and leaned forward. She ever so lightly pressed her muzzle on Tef's cheek. She just wanted to feel the warmth from her only family; one last time. Anthi had the same idea as he sensed Tef's warm fur brush against him. Half asleep, he stretched out his paw and touched Tef's muzzle, which in turn twitched. Sukari saw this out of the corner of her eye and withdrew her small embrace. "Anthi, you little cutie, yet I'm so sorry you have to say goodbye like this," she whispered through her teeth gently, with a warm smile.

She took a couple of steps back. Thankfully, it seemed her own and Anthi's little gesture didn't wake her up. It had been a busy day for all of them, and every moment Sukari stayed here was getting increasingly painful. She closed her eyes tight shut and turned her back. "Goodbye, my dear... dear friend," she whispered.

Her paws silently padded the ground as she crept out of her den and into the open. She knew at least one group member would be awake on the lookout while the others slept. Due to the mist surrounding the area, she could not see anyone, which fortunately also meant that they couldn't see her either. They could be lying anywhere. She didn't want to risk bumping into the elected lookout for the night. It would all be down to sound detection alone. She stood completely still for a moment to pick up the faintest of sounds, anything to give away who was awake and where, so she could slink off in the opposite direction.

Her body stayed motionless. Even though her thoughts consumed her mind with the guilt of what she was leaving behind, she knew she still had to go, regardless that they had all been through so much together as a group. Safila, now a fully grown lioness, Kisima and Anmani are on the way to almost getting to adolescent age. Mlinzi and Mkuki were the newcomers; though at first sceptical, she accepted them as they seemed decent. However, Sukari's motherly instincts had made her grow highly protective against unknowns. It was nothing personal. She just wanted what was best for Anthi. Aramile was now turning to be an old male, just like Sheek. As much as she admired him, she knew that he had a massive interest in her, even admitting it himself. What if now he made an advance on her since Sheek, the dominant male, was gone? She didn't want that attention or risk, now with her new beginnings with Anthi.

Sukari took a further moment to mourn the other members and close friends who had their lives cut short. Mino, Desmani, Pulsar and Jenna. Sukari then said her goodbyes in her head to the remaining living members of the group. Would

Tefnut explain the reason for her departure to the rest of them? In a negative way or good? She hoped it would be the latter.

Her ears were still perked up for any sounds. She soon enough heard an old-sounding yawn coming from ahead of her, that of Aramile. With that information, she turned back towards the den and veered off to the side. Suddenly she caught a glimpse of two figures lying together by the base of a tree not so far from the birth den. After focusing on them, it was found to be Anmani and Kisima, curled up and by each other's side, keeping each other warm. It seemed as if they were playing lookout on Sukari's birth den. This made her smile yet made her heart ache more. They looked so cute and content together and showed they had become the closest friends. She was sure they would grow up to look after each other. She knew she wouldn't be there to watch them flourish. She winced as another tear dropped down her cheek.

With one final soft sigh through her nose, she started to walk away from the area, tears still dropping on the cool dewed grass. A few tears fell onto Anthi himself, soon soaking into his fur. Anthi let out a little chirp and stirred in his sleep. His tiny body was so sensitive to everything that touched him; he must have felt his Mum's tears.

"This is it Anthi, time to find a new home and a new life..."

Sukari's search had begun. She didn't look back.

2. Empty Night

Sukari started her walk with Anthi dangling from her muzzle, still fast asleep. Time passed by before ending up having to tackle some steep inclines and large boulders. She chose this challenging path on purpose, being a less obvious route to take with a cub in her mouth, making sure there would be a lower chance of her being followed or tracked. She wanted to avoid any awkward explanations or goodbyes. This caused Anthi to swing from side to side and bobble up and down. Still, this didn't stir him from his slumber.

"All that time rolling around in my belly must have been exhausting, huh Anthi?" she thought to herself, cracking a faint smile.

After tackling these obstacles, she now had a height advantage and could look over to the land ahead, the moon and stars shining off the tops of the trees and hills, then being consumed by a soup of mist underneath. She gazed at this natural display of beauty and tranquillity. Her tail flicked with an odd slight spark of unknown excitement in what lay ahead. This could be dangerous yet also could be the start of a more promising future life. She changed her heading and went for the smoother-looking path that disappeared into the mist down below, she would be blind by it, but in a way, it would be the safest.

She soon started to feel isolated as she was consumed by the thick soup of water vapour on her descent, meaning she could hardly see in front of her. No help would come in time if something now happened, such as being attacked by something hungry. She'd already taken this risk into account before leaving, and she had to go regardless. Still, a feeling of vulnerability travelled through her mind and body. She kept herself calm by reassuring herself that if she couldn't hear, smell, or see any predators, then neither could they! The mist was doing its job by lessening the chance of crossing paths with undesirables.

More time had passed, and she had spent a good part of the night walking. She was now long gone from the group and the farthest she had ever been from them. The air around her soon started to feel colder, the dew from the grass soaking into her paws and spreading up her legs. Her muscles began twitching intermittently, the beginning signs of shivering. Anthi started to whimper slightly from the cold and had begun to wake up. The whimpering soon turned to little growls; the cold was getting to him. It was not suitable for such a newborn to be in this situation, but being back where they came from wasn't a good one either in her mind. She just didn't expect it would turn *this* cold.

"Hey hey hey," she hushed softly through the sides of her muzzle, trying to comfort him.

Sukari knew his growls would attract attention, she tried to calm him down, but his growls grew louder. He started to wriggle around in protest, and his paws were flapping around, trying to grab her muzzle while his own muzzle suckled the air. He must be cold and hungry! Sukari's heartbeat started to race, getting increasingly anxious about the noise he was making. She made cooing sounds to try and soothe him as she picked up her pace, hoping to come across anything that would resemble somewhat of a temporary shelter to address Anthi's needs. Her anxiety grew as she could hardly see anything that lay ahead. Her breathing increased, and her heart started to race as Anthi consistently continued to protest louder.

SNAP! Sukari jumped as she stood on a small old branch lying across her path. She was so focused on looking ahead that she paid less attention to what lay below. She winced at her stupidity and looked down. A few more branches lay in her path. She carefully placed her paws in-between them as she continued to walk, making sure she wouldn't make the same stupid mistake again.

This night luck was on her side. She could see a large dark shape in front of her coming into view. She slowed down her pace and approached it with caution. She had come across a large boulder with a hole dug out underneath. Looking at the size of the hole, it seemed like a den made by an African wild dog. She briefly placed Anthi by the side of the rock. She then stuck her head inside, checking for any fresh scents. The burrow inside smelt unoccupied and looked like it was just large enough for her and Anthi, although the entrance was naturally too small for a lion.

Using her claws, she started to dig around the entrance to widen the hole just enough so she could squeeze her body through. Being only built by African wild dogs, it was a little cramped, but most importantly, it was empty. The past occupants must have grown up and left it abandoned.

Sukari poked her head out of the entrance and dragged Anthi inside. She curled up slightly to try and regain some body heat. Anthi soon enough lay right up against Sukari's stomach, shuffling and digging himself in as deep as possible, instinct present even in the youngest of lions for a need to keep warm. Sukari curled around him more to muffle the noises he continued to make. Soon enough, the growls started to fade, and his body stopped wriggling around as much. He then began to calm down overall. Sukari stretched her head over and started licking him to give him extra comfort.

Now that Anthi was cosy and warm, there was another matter to deal with, he was hungry! Luckily, that wasn't a problem for him, though

Sukari momentarily thought about what she would do when her own stomach started complaining. She pushed this thought aside and concentrated on the more important matter of the two. She didn't have to do much to direct him, though he was already off shuffling downwards from her stomach, rubbing his muzzle on her skin, trying to find that all-important food source.

His eyes were not at the stage of opening yet, so he had to rely on feeling alone. Soon, he struggled, yet Sukari watched on rather than help him. This is not to be mistaken for neglect, she cared for him immensely, yet she didn't want to do *everything* for him. He had to learn fast about self-nursing. Hard times potentially lay ahead, and there may be times when Sukari may be asleep, weak, or injured, and he would have to feed himself. Every little bit of practice early on helps. Anthi continued to struggle and soon started to protest again by making unwanted noise. Given the situation, she was just about to lean over and help him this time around, though soon, to her amazement, Anthi then found her teat and latched on.

Sukari lay on her side and released the tension that had shrouded her body from walking and finding emergency shelter. She huffed a sigh of relief through her nose. Anthi was now almost silent as he suckled, making the odd chirp now and then but nothing too loud that would carry through the air. Sukari continued to calm down little by little. She was in a near-perfect shelter, warm, cosy and keeping Anthi quiet. She agreed that this would be a wise place to stay for the rest of the night. She couldn't bear thinking about being out in the cold again, making Anthi uncomfortable. Staying here until morning may bring other risks, but the benefits of staying outweighed the risks if she continued walking tonight.

The most powerful bond between a mother and a cub was nursing. It cements the connection between them. Sukari lifted her head and watched in awe as her hungry little furball filled himself. This was only the second time she had nursed him, and it still felt surreal being a mum and to such a cute, tiny, and helpless creation at that. Without her, her cub would perish. This sense of responsibility grew with every moment. She gazed at Anthi for a while, giving him tender licks on his back and head. She then lay her head back down on the ground, letting Anthi continue his feeding undisturbed. The knowing of creating this life from inside her own body, which now provides him with essential food for living outside of it, is something only a mother can describe. A mother's milk makes the newborn grow strong quickly, so in normal circumstances, he can be introduced back into the safety of the pride and father. In Sukari's case, Anthi had to grow up strong and quick for self-survival in a life of just the two of them. No pride and no father.

After laying and letting Anthi feed, Sukari's eyes grew heavy. Her birth the previous day had been exhausting, and she only had a small nap before waking up in the middle of the night. She had now made a decent head start on her journey and found a proper, safe place to rest. Her body began to go into a more relaxed and sleepy state. She lifted her head and looked down towards her son, who had now finished feeding and had curled up into a ball close to Sukari's warm, soft belly.

"Feeling better now, huh?" she whispered and chuckled.

Sukari's muzzle opened wide as she took a good long yawn with her eyelids half-closed, itching to close fully. She needed sleep, but as much of a blessing this den was, she started to feel a little paranoid about where she was and who could be potentially around. Under normal circumstances, a lioness can choose a den better when there is a clearer view of her surroundings, but of course, tonight she couldn't. There could be a hyena pack just over the next hill for all she knew.

She suddenly had an idea, sparked from a fond memory as a cub. It may not be completely adequate, but it gave a better sense of security. She slowly shuffled herself to the burrow's opening, ensuring not to disturb Anthi. She squeezed herself out and headed towards the branches she came across just before finding this place. She needed to be quick as she would get too worried about her son being alone for too long. As she found out earlier, newborns can be unpredictable, and predators can be even more so.

Once she found the branches, she went back

and forth, picking a few up each time and placing them all around the entrance. Hopefully, if anything comes near and wants to investigate the hole, they may make a decent snapping noise when accidentally stepped on like she had discovered, much to her distress. This branch idea wasn't perfect, but it would give Sukari enough warning to grab Anthi, sprint out the entrance and run, hopefully taking the approaching animal by surprise. This was better than the animal sneaking into the burrow undetected and trapping Sukari, with nowhere to run. Newborns are an easy ball of meat to snatch. Indeed, Sukari could fend off one animal in this burrow, but all it takes is for a pack of them to turn up, and she would not be able to defend herself and Anthi from all of them.

With the branches in place, Sukari now had a better sense of security. She went back inside the burrow to be greeted by an awake Anthi. He must have felt her absence by feeling slightly chillier once more. Surprisingly, this time he wasn't making any noise. Many baby animals have this instinct to keep quiet if the mother isn't present. Sukari was glad and surprised that Anthi had done this. A new mother doesn't know *everything* from the start. She picked him up by the nape of his neck, now noticing the plump belly of a well-fed cub. She then placed him between her two front paws, cradling him closely to make him warm again.

"No wonder you were complaining earlier. You sure were hungry!" she cooed softly, chuckling to herself.

Anthi lifted his nose into the air, making short little sniffs. Sukari lowered her muzzle, intending to give him a lick goodnight. However, as soon as her muzzle lowered, Anthi beat her to it. His little tongue poked out and licked the very tip of Sukari's nose. Her eyes started to water up with a heartfelt smile. She closed her eyes and embraced him as a deep soft rumble vibrated in her throat. The sound and vibration gave Anthi a soothing lullaby of sorts, soon making him take a big yawn, ending with a little squeak.

She then began to hum an actual lullaby, a particular soothing arrangement of soft notes that she remembered as a cub. It's now the first time the melody has been passed onto her *own* cub. She couldn't remember the origin, but she had always carried it in her memory. Other bittersweet memories were attached to it though, and she couldn't help but choke up in places. However, this didn't stop Anthi from drifting off, soon into a gentle slumber.

She gave him one last lick on his head with her continued warm smile.

"Goodnight," she whispered.

Sukari gazed out the entrance into the night. Under the mist, she could not gaze further upon the stars or the moon like she used to with Sheek. Now it was just a plain blanket of nothingness. Even the sounds of the nocturnal insects and small animals were not heard either. The cold mist must be keeping everything sheltered away, just like they both were. The whole night outside was just silent, cold, and dark. It felt lifeless. It was an empty night. Yet inside, the burrow was full of warmth, love, and life.

Sukari lowered her head over her paws with Anthi tucked and curled up in between. She curled her body into a ball to hold as much heat as possible for them both. Her eyes soon closed and she swiftly drifted off to sleep.

Even though the night was empty, the bond between mother and son could not feel any more full.

3. Legacy Of Two Sons

"Do you want to rest soon?" Pulsar turned and asked Sukari. She then nodded in agreement.

"Somewhere cool and shaded would be nice," she replied.

Sukari's dream had taken her back to when she was a wanderer, having been exiled by her pride in her young adulthood and destined to live her life alone. Before all this, since she was a cub, she had been best friends with a lion called Sheek. They both grew up to their adolescent ages together, developing a strong bond of friendship and a kindling love.

Unfortunately, this was not to last, as Sukari was chased away from her pride by her father. He stressed he was instead ordered by Legacy to kill her after leading her away, far from the pride so there were no witnesses. They both ran together when hearing Legacy's roar. After a time, he eventually slowed down and let her continue alone before telling her she could never return home or ever try to visit Sheek again, her life depended on it. She knew he resented his actions and she had nothing but great respect for him. After all, he wasn't her blood father but he had treated her like his own daughter. He was all she knew as a father throughout her entire growing up, after losing her mother.

She had now been wandering for a couple of years, depressed and alone with no hope for the future. It wasn't until she had come across this friendly and unique-looking lion, Pulsar, that things started to turn a little brighter. He bared an extremely dark, almost black pelt with a mighty blonde mane. Their paths crossed, and they got talking. Being sceptical of strangers, she didn't reveal much at first, stating that she was just trying to survive. Pulsar then offered his company for a while, which she accepted. They were both starving, and hunting for a large meal was more effective as a team of two.

They ended up travelling together for several days, both enjoying some much-needed companionship (and that extra bit of protection) and became quite acquainted. Sukari started to share more about her life and past events by this time. She explained how she was exiled by her pride and was never allowed to see Sheek again, not even having the chance to say goodbye. Pulsar gave her some comforting words, that Sheek could have left his pride too and now looking for her perhaps?

Sukari wanted to hope so but stayed pessimistic on the matter. Pulsar's ears, however, had flicked at the name 'Sheek' being mentioned from the start, though she didn't think anything of it at the time.

Pulsar offered to help her if she didn't mind him sticking around for a while longer. Two noses, two pairs of eyes and ears are better than one. He assured her that *if* Sheek had run away, he would endeavour to help her find him. 'All wanderers help each other out,' he explained. Sukari now started to feel a bit more hopeful for her future, because even if she didn't find Sheek, she had made a decent friend.

One day, they both approached the base of a steep hill. On the summit was a large Baobab tree. It's not the most common of sights and a perfect place to rest in the shade, all whilst having an unobstructed view of the surroundings. They were about to ascend when a lion appeared from the summit. Sukari's heart skipped, she recognised him immediately, it was Sheek!!!

Sukari was about to relive one of the happiest moments in her life, the time when she was finally reunited with him. However, her dream suddenly faded, forwarding two years later when things had turned so much darker, changing her life forever.

"Sheek? How could you... HOW COULD YOU!" she raged, letting off a thundering roar in disgust and betrayal. Sheek slightly winced as it shot through him when approaching the group. Along with him was his father, Legacy.

The group were already aware of Sheek's family connection with Legacy. Especially Sukari, as they both grew up together. However, they always believed that Sheek was against Legacy's ideologies. He had, after all, abandoned his pride, vowing to keep as many lions as possible away from Legacy's grasp and power. Now it seemed this wasn't the case. He had intentionally led them directly to him!

"Sukari, it's not my fault you all were blind by my intentions. Do you think I could ever betray my own father? I would like to keep my head on my shoulders!" he almost scoffed.

It seemed he had to force a confident smile while glancing up at Legacy like he was looking for his approval, to which Legacy just gave a soulless wide-eyed stare in return. Sukari's mouth was frozen open in fear and anger. Since cubs, the lion she loved and soulmate, was all along aiding Legacy, not against him like he had led her and the group to believe. He had made it so convincing! All that time being apart from each other in adolescence, this is what Sheek was doing all this time.

"Sukari, as much as I love you, my father's demands come first," he proclaimed, trying to act smug and proud.

Sukari's eyes filled with fire and her muzzle twitched, baring the points of her teeth. Not ever would she think that Sheek would be a traitor. He had been a sleeping spy all this time, ready to wake when called. Sukari's eyes, full of anger and upset, stared piercingly into Sheek's own. Yet she could not help but sense his eyes were saying something different. They hinted at the eyes of regret and fear. Sukari knew him since he was a cub, she knew he had a soft heart and could easily be persuaded and his ideals moulded. He was brainwashed, she needed to bring him back, and there was only one thing she could mention to try and snap him out of it.

"Well! After you came back from your search for Desmani and Mino, I was going to tell you something. However, after you found them dead, and we all needed to 'run away', It wasn't the best time. The following days running away never were..." she explained, her throat tightening and her voice croaking. Sheek raised a brow in reply and his forced smile now flattening. "I'm... pregnant." she mewed.

Sheek's eyes immediately widened, and he took a few steps back with his lower jaw hanging. He knew she went into heat a month ago, but it didn't seem entirely successful at the time. So, this had come as a big shock.

"I'm... going to be... a dad?" he trembled.

"No... NO!" "Thanks to you, if I choose to join Legacy, our cub will be killed the moment it's born. I'd rather he kills me now," she growled with a heartbroken whine. "*If I somehow* escape tonight, my cub has no father... not you!" she tried to shout but broke intermittently into a whisper as her throat tightened even more.

"Don't worry Sukari, my dear," Legacy

grinned. "You will have food and constant protection by my pride. You will also have plenty of chances again to be a loving mum, by my pride." he teased in a soft yet sinister voice.

"WHAT?" Sheek gasped with his eyes wide open, "DAD! If I ever brought her back, you promised-"

"Well, *you* promised *me* lions a year ago! You should be grateful I have been forgiving for how late you are!" Legacy interrupted with a vicious snarl.

Sukari couldn't bear to look at Sheek any more, turning her head and closing her eyes, tears being pushed down her ducts and over her cheeks. Her breathing was heavy and rasped. The visions in her dream went dark, then silent.

Sukari was re-witnessing a fateful night, the night that Sheek had betrayed the group, though he was not entirely to blame. He had been brainwashed into doing his father's bidding. That night it was discovered he had a double life. One was a 'friendly protector' that would do anything to keep his 'friends' safe and happy. The other was obeying his father's orders. He had done this many times to gain the trust of wanderers, then after a while he would lead them to Legacy, forcing them to join Legacy's pride or be killed.

However, these wanderers he rounded up were different. There was a bond that Sheek hadn't felt before compared to the others he betrayed in the past. While in their company, he got reunited with Sukari and fell back in love. This, along with going through many bright times and dark times with the group, sharing moments of fun and joy, sharing times of sorrow when members passed away, and watching scared cubs grow into confident young adolescents. It bonded him and them, closer than he could ever imagine.

Over time, his duties towards Legacy were pushed to the back of his mind, and he started to live an actual life of his own with the group and felt genuinely happy. He knew he was digging a hole deeper by being late handing them over to Legacy, knowing the later it became, the greater chance he would be hunted down. If Legacy found Sheek had bonded with the group instead of doing his job, he would have gone on a rampage and killed them all. A connected group is harder to brainwash in Legacy's eyes. It was incomprehensible, but so was Legacy.

If Sheek handed them all in on the guise that he was still doing his job, at least the group would be given a chance to survive by serving Legacy. Their lives wouldn't be perfect, but they would be alive. It was the only way.

However, due to Sukari's apparent failed season in heat, he had never considered her falling pregnant. He now couldn't bear the thought of their cub being born just to be killed by Legacy straight after, and the complete soul-crushing grief Sukari would endure. Now knowing Legacy was going to break his promise and use her as a breeding vessel, it was too much guilt to bestow.

Sheek's mind cracked. What had he done? He stared at each group member, all returning expressions of disgust and upset from being betrayed. He had been trained to block his emotions when this moment came. It worked fine for the earlier groups, but this bond had become too great. Guilt was flowing through him.

While Sheek was in thought, Jenna suddenly tried to attack Legacy in retaliation, and Sheek was too late to stop her and let out a harrowing protest as she pounced. He knew her fate was already sealed the moment she leapt.

One swipe of Legacy's extra-long claws sliced straight through her neck like grass. She was the first one. Sheek found her when she was a cub and was the beginning of his 'group'. He promised to keep her safe. At first, it was a lie due to his ‘other' life, but it had grown into a genuine promise over time. He took a great shine and a bond formed, she looked up to him as a father, and he watched with pride as she grew up. Now she lay dead because of him. He pawed the side of her head and gave her a nudge with his muzzle. Her lifeless body flopped into her own blood from his betrayal. He was now getting too sick and angry from his actions, causing the innocent to perish.

Sukari's dream vision returned. Sheek was no longer standing beside Legacy. He was instead facing against him! His claws were extended, and his body leant back and ready to pounce.

“Legacy, I cannot live the life you expected of

me, be it my life or yours; one will end, and it ends now!" he growled.

Sheek half turned his head to the group while keeping partial eye contact with Legacy. "I'm sorry for what I've done. If you have any trust in me left, use it now and get out of here... RUN!" he begged. "I have made terrible choices in my life, and now it's time to make peace with myself and my actions," his voice trembled.

A tear appeared in Sheek's eye, he knew this new path he was taking would have a high chance of not ending well for him, but at least his conscience would be clear. He made an almighty roar and pounced on Legacy, avoiding his counterattack as he inflicted on Jenna. Sheek knew Legacy's fighting tactics as Legacy taught them to him! He pinned him down hard and dug his claws deep into his chest. Being a little longer than average, they pushed through Legacy's thick thatched mane that was protecting it. His paws soon absorbed the blood that flowed.

Sukari gasped at Sheek's actions and his change of heart. She knew this would be a definite death sentence if he lost this fight, and it was proof enough that his good intentions had taken over from his father's brainwashed ideologies. She leapt a few steps towards the two with her claws bared. She would not let Sheek fight this alone.

"Sukari, STOP!" Sheek demanded and turned his head towards her. "Lead the group away. You have a cub inside you need to look after; take care of it," he demanded, though his voice was breaking. Sukari stopped in her tracks. It was then that she heard the gentle voice of Tefnut.

"You have to, Sukari, I know it's not easy, but you have to think of your cub. Sheek is giving it and all of us a chance to escape. If you stay, that will never happen," Tefnut begged. Sukari's paw trembled as she tried to take another step closer towards Sheek and Legacy. "Try to understand, we cannot stay... you cannot stay!" Tefnut spoke again, slightly more demanding. Sukari retracted her paw and placed it back on the ground.

"Sheek... I..." Sukari managed to squeak from her throat. It was becoming all too overwhelming. He couldn't hear anything from a retaliating roar being displayed by Legacy.

"GO... NOW!" Sheek yelled, turning his head fully towards her. Just as his attention was diverted, it was Legacy's chance for his move. He tucked his hind legs under Sheek in a trained place on his ribcage. He then pushed hard with all his strength, a loud harrowing pop, crack and crunch followed, thundering from Sheek's chest. He was then catapulted high into the air before landing with a crashing thud, then slid across the ground.

"SHEEK!" Sukari cried, before suddenly feeling a paw wrap around her shoulder, pulling her away from the confrontation. Her vision went dark again.

The next thing Sukari's vision showed was her being carried away on Tefnut's back, fleeing from the fight. She could make out Sheek was on the ground in the far distance, Legacy not to be seen. Sukari rolled off Tefnut's back and ran towards him. She was halfway there when Legacy suddenly came into view, appearing from the tall grass in an attempted ambush, using Sheek as the bait. Sukari stopped in her tracks after Sheek took an almighty surprise leap through the air. Her jaw dropped, raising her paw and she cried out, knowing Sheek was jumping to his demise.

Sheek felt agonising pain pulsate from his chest and rush around the rest of his body, however, he kept focused. While mid-air above Legacy, he twisted his body and then extended his front leg to deliver a massive slice from his claws deep into Legacy's neck. Sheek's claws, though extra-long, were still a fraction shorter. Legacy's mane quickly soaked up the blood from the massive gash and rapidly turned red. Were Sheek's claws long enough to effectively penetrate Legacy's neck sufficiently for a fatal blow?

Sheek thumped back onto the ground with an agonising roar, rolling a couple of times before lying motionless. Legacy breathed and grunted heavily, standing over him, blood seeping and running down his mane. He simply grinned demonically.

"You have played your move, now time to make mine." he scoffed.

Sukari now full of anger and upset, charged towards Legacy with no care for herself. She watched as astonishingly, Legacy retreated and out of sight, she could only assume he knew he was too injured to fight, leaving a trail of blood behind. She heard a faint calling of a name as he ran into the distance... 'Kikome'. His final fate was unknown for now, but this meant he had backup.

Sukari stood by Sheek's motionless body and slumped helplessly beside him. An awful wheeze escaped Sheek's throat. He gazed upon Sukari with his powerful green eyes that strained to stay open, yet shone right through her. Sheek's eyes were a soft spot for Sukari, and she loved them, and they always made her heart melt. Sheek slid his paw across the ground with one final ounce of strength and gently lay it on top of Sukari's belly.

"Remember..." Sheek coughed painfully, with blood starting to trickle down from his muzzle and onto his mane. "You always liked the name Anthi."

After his words, Sheek closed his eyes once more, and it was the last time she saw them. Sukari buried her face into his mane, muffling the long, loud shattering mournful cry that came from her. She placed her paw on top of his, holding it tight. She then felt another warmth, embracing her from behind. It was Tefnut.

Sukari Suddenly burst wide awake, breathing heavily. She looked around her, and she was still in the burrow. However, the night had started to fade, and the sun was beginning to rise. A beam of light signalling the start of a fresh new morning shone through the hole and onto herself. Her paw still felt warm from holding Sheek's own, but it was instead the warmth coming from Anthi. She lifted her paw off him. The beam of light glowing over his face made him stir in his sleep and stretched his little front paws out. A satisfying night's sleep was shown by a little warm smile across his muzzle along with a squeaky yawn. Suddenly something caught Sukari's attention. Anthi's eyelids opened ever so slightly for a fraction of a moment before closing again.

Usually, newborn eyes are fully open from around four days after birth, and Sukari as a new mother was none the wiser. But what caught her attention even more so was the colour of Anthi's eyes, the same beautiful shade of green as Sheek's.

Sukari uncontrollably started to cry. She had let out many tears since that night but never cried as much as when she saw Sheek's eyes for the last time, and she had now seen them again, through her son's.

The whole dream reminded her how much pain and suffering Sheek had endured protecting her and the group that night. Sheek was on the verge of being a traitor but redeemed himself. He had saved her and all the group that night from a life sentence of slavery or even death. Instead, he had paid it with his own. Now Sheek's personal legacy had a chance to live, that of Anthi.

4. Death For A Life

Anthi started to get agitated by the sound of Sukari's crying, and he began to squirm around, letting off his little chirps in protest. Sukari lowered her head, giving him a couple of licks for comfort.

"I'm sorry," she sniffed, flicking away her tears. Calming down and composing herself, she let Anthi return to his slumber. "Just a bad dream," she whispered.

Sukari stretched out her legs, all her paws touching the confines of the burrow. It was *just* the perfect size for her. She had quickly grown accustomed to this place. It was cosy, and it kept her warm and well-sheltered. She wanted to stay a bit longer, but she knew she had to make more progress. This place would have been a perfect permanent hideaway for herself and Anthi, but she felt it was still too close to her past.

With her past in mind, she couldn't help but think that far away, her group would also be waking up too about now. Tefnut would open her eyes to see an empty spot beside her. She could hear it in her head, all of them now calling out her name, worried, confused and upset that the group had shrunk once again by two more. She hoped they would come to terms with her departure. They should understand that Sukari, like any new mother, would need solitude when caring for her newborn. The difference that would worry them is she didn't say goodbye, even more so when they realise she hasn't returned after a few weeks.

Sukari pushed these thoughts to the back of her mind and shuffled to the burrow entrance, peering outside. All the scents had returned, the insects were making their noises, and the other animals made their calls. The mist had lifted, and the sun was warming up the ground. She slowly squeezed herself out of the burrow and scanned the area with her eyes, ears and nose while intermittently glancing back at Anthi, still enjoying his sleep. Besides the *lovely* aroma of animal dung in the air, nothing looked, smelt, or sounded out of the ordinary or dangerous... until.

A large deep rumbling growl was heard, so powerful it vibrated through her whole body. She flinched out of surprise for a split moment before realising what animal made the growl. It was her! More specifically, it was her stomach. She hadn't eaten the day before she had given birth. Since then, her body had been running on energy reserves and the pure will of needing to continue alone. This had only gotten her so far, now her hunger had caught up, and she needed to eat. She couldn't let herself starve in her current situation. Under normal circumstances, it wouldn't be much of an issue as a lion or lioness can go a long time without a decent meal. However, she needed to keep up her health to provide proper nutrition for Anthi. What she makes for her cub is currently the only thing that would keep him alive. If she became malnourished, her milk might not be as effective or abundant.

She leapt onto the boulder above the burrow and then began to scan the landscape, looking for a decent-sized prey that she could kill. It soon became apparent that nothing decent was around here, just tiny animals scurrying around on the ground or meatless monkeys and birds in the trees. Her stomach demanded a more fulfilling meal, so she knew she needed to hunt further away.

Another reason for leaving was soon apparent. She noticed a small tuft of dampened matted hair on the rock where she sat, that from a lion. Her heart skipped a beat. Although this could be old hair from anywhere and anytime, she still felt uneasy about its origin. She had to tell herself that she would have already been found if a lion had been around here last night. Still, she felt it safer to leave. This little burrow had been a cosy and lifesaving den for last night, but now it's time to move on.

Sukari turned and shuffled back into the burrow, grabbing her half-asleep cub by the nape before pulling him out. His paws were flapping in protest of being deprived of his cosy spot, and she noticed the tiniest of a claw poke out when he did so.

"Oh, a little fighter this morning, are we?" she mocked jokingly whilst he hung from her muzzle, letting out a yawn with a disgruntled expression. They soon started to make their way across the plains.

Time passed, and the sun started to climb into the sky. She continued walking while keeping her eye out for a meal. Her stomach continued to complain and rumble, the vibrations once again travelling through her body. She then heard the unmistakable sound of a giggle coming from Anthi. Not only he had now fully woken up and not as moody, but it was the first time she had ever heard him make such a sound; her heart immediately began to melt.

"Oh, Mum's tummy grumbles are amusing, are they?" she said sarcastically yet warmly. "First, it's you that makes a fuss in my belly, then when that matter was taken care of, you find it *hilarious* when something else causes it!" she rolled her eyes to herself, though growing a smile.

After another while of walking, the scenery eerily seemed to be getting more and more familiar. Sukari shook these thoughts out of her head and continued, thinking it was just her memory being mistaken.

She passed over a slight incline, and her eyes lit up. Her thoughts of the familiar-looking place were soon taken over by the sight of a small herd of

Zebra, one of which was laying down near some bushes a little isolated from the others, still resting from the previous night, perhaps? This seemed too easy, yet there wasn't an entirely safe area to place Anthi while she went hunting. She wouldn't and couldn't let this opportunity pass, she had to make an on-the-spot decision.

There stood a tree nearby with dense leaves and branches that she could climb and hide Anthi perfectly, but she was too concerned he may roll over and fall off. Her stomach took control of her judgement and instead placed Anthi down in a patch of long grass at the base, hopefully enough to hide him a little. A slight crack from one of the tree branches sounded above and some birds flew away. She must have just startled them. Hopefully, Anthi would keep quiet like he did last time when she was absent from last night's burrow. She took a few paces away before turning her head back momentarily with a sense of worry and guilt. However, she knew this needed to be done, she had to start her hunt.

She kept herself low to the ground, keeping herself as flat as possible to blend into the long grass. She took an extended circle around the herd, ensuring her scent would be carried behind her by the slight breeze. Her pace slowed as she approached closer to the single zebra, taking tiny steps at a time not to alert the rest. When she got close enough, she lay down flat and peered through the blades of the grass with her eyes locked onto her target. Lionesses typically hunt better as a party made of a few or several. Some of the hunting party would chase the target prey while the others would lay down in wait and ambush it. Most prey can be quicker and more agile than lionesses, darting and taking sharp turns to avoid being caught. In comparison with her situation, she had a lesser chance of a kill. She had to be patient yet quick, and have a bit of good luck, to be successful.

She lay in wait, debating whether to pounce and hopefully take the zebra by surprise or hold it out until it gets up and hopefully walks closer towards her direction. She waited for a little while but soon became anxious about her son's well-being.

Soon, the inevitable happened. Another large deep growl rumbled from her stomach. She winced and gritted her teeth. The zebra's head perked up immediately and locked eyes with her. In a desperate moment, she pounced with all her strength and sprang towards it with both front legs stretched out and claws bared, but it was too late. The zebra had jumped up, turned around and extended its rear legs, delivering a powerful rear kick and striking one of her front legs. Sukari roared out in pain, however still adamant, she sunk her other set of claws into the rear of the zebra, but it slipped away with only a deep laceration to show for it, no way near enough for it to be a fatal blow.

For a split moment, the zebra astonishingly turned and challenged Sukari by raising its hind legs and crying out an ear-piercing warning call. Sukari's eyes widened in astonishment. "*Why would a zebra even try this?*" she thought. Another roar and a swipe knocked the zebra down onto all four legs again. She tried to wrap both her paws around the zebra's shoulders so she could go in for a bite to the neck. Unfortunately, her front leg still throbbed with pain which meant she couldn't hold on. The zebra slipped from her grasp once again, though this time ran away with the rest of the herd.

Sukari Slumped down onto the ground, defeated. There is nothing more humiliating than being bested by its prey. Though this could happen, she didn't want this meal; she *needed it.* She coughed up the dry dust that had settled in her throat; flicked up from the confrontation. Breathing heavily after her failed attempt with her front legs spread out, she growled in anger at her failure. She lay for a few moments panting until she regained her breath.

Her self-confidence in being a successful mother dropped rapidly. Not only she had failed a hunt, but she was now injured. How could she provide for Anthi now, let alone herself? She will soon begin to starve, and milk for her cub will be the first thing to run dry. Anthi would starve and die.

Suddenly she heard a faint call of distress. She perked up her ears to try and pinpoint it. She slowly stood up, pain shooting up her injured leg. She winced and sucked air through her teeth, trying to endure it. The only thing on her mind is she may have another opportunity for a meal... if the sound was what she hoped it was. She limped over to the origin of the distressful call. It was coming from the bush where the zebra had laid nearby. She poked her head through an opening between the small branches, and there lay a newly born zebra.

It all made sense now. The zebra she attempted to kill was resting because it had just given birth to this new life, and it had challenged Sukari to try and protect it from her.

Sukari's brows softened for a moment, taking pity on the poor defenceless fowl. But a helpless prey and a hungry lioness, unfortunately (for the prey) will mean only one outcome. Especially if a lioness has a cub to tend to as well. Her survival instinct set alight inside her; her softened brows soon lowered, her eyes narrowed, her teeth bared and glistened with saliva. She promised herself she would make it quick. With that, she sank her teeth straight into the neck of the fowl, biting down as hard and as quickly as possible, feeling the fragile frame of a spine crack like a twig and the windpipe pop. The fowl was dead before it knew what even happened. Sukari kept her jaw latched on tight, dragged it out of the bush, and slowly limped towards where she had left Anthi. It wasn't the big feast of a meal that she had hoped for, but it was adequate for her needs and would keep her healthy for a few more days.

Thankfully Anthi was still where he was placed and not making a sound. Sukari put her kill on the ground and lay down by his side. She scanned around the area to make sure she hadn't gotten the attention of any other scavengers. Except for the aroma of dung again in the air, everything looked clear. She stared at the lifeless fowl, the fire inside her dying down now as she had what she needed. A glimmer of guilt then came across her. She had to eat a new life that hadn't lived, to save another, that of her son. She shook away her inner thoughts and started chewing and crunching away at her kill.

Since introducing a life of her own, the taste of a freshly killed animal was a welcome yet bitter ironic one. After a short while, there was hardly any evidence of her kill left. Even the bones were gone as they were small, thin, and turned into mush with her powerful jaws. Just blood that had soaked into the grass remained which she licked as much off as she could, then did the same to her blood-soaked paws and muzzle. She then lay flat on the ground but facing Anthi, who had curled up by her stomach and happily chirped away, as if being patient and waiting for his mum to feed herself first for a change.

She noticed the healthy look of her now slightly distended stomach. She knew it could have been more if it wasn't for it giving her position away in the first place! However, what mattered was that she had fed, and it would keep her going.

Sukari tried to keep her injured leg moving by flexing it at intervals, not letting it seize. She occasionally licked it to soothe the pain, which helped slightly. Thankfully from experience, it didn't feel like a break, and that would have had disastrous consequences! It should feel better in a couple of days, just in time for her next kill. She shivered at the thought of if it were to have been a broken bone. She now knew to be a lot more careful in the future and not to let herself get so hungry again! She had a duty of care for Anthi but also for herself too.

During her thoughts, she felt a slight tug from her teat. Anthi had now started taking his turn for his meal. This solidified the assurance that he was fully self-dependent in doing this himself if Sukari hadn't had the strength or consciousness to help.

Sukari scanned the area as Anthi fed, with the gentle hum of her lullaby playing in her throat. Now her mind was at ease from both of them not going hungry, she had time to take in the surroundings, and it started to feel increasingly familiar. The contours of the hills, the surrounding bushes, flora and fauna. It eventually hit her where she was. A mournful squeak escaped her as she took a quick deep breath in realisation. She had inadvertently stumbled across where Sheek would've handed the group over to Legacy, therefore where he and Legacy had fought. This was the final resting place where he laid his life to save her and the group.

She wasn't surprised that she couldn't see any remains of him, plus it would have been too distressing to look at.

A fully grown lion's body would attract a lot of scavengers, and everything would eventually be taken. However, this didn't upset her. If anything, it did the opposite. It's the knowing that his flesh and bone, now no longer being used by himself, had kept other animals large and small, nourished and alive, feeding their own families too. Even animals that may be rival carnivores like hyenas, jackals, and African wild dogs (thanks to them, she had a safe shelter for the night) have a right to live just like she does. It's all just down to survival. Sukari has eaten an animal, and other animals have eaten Sheek. It's a naturally evolved perfect cycle of all animals that live here.

Sukari had to remind herself that her son could have easily met the same fate as that zebra's newborn. If she wasn't on her best guard today or injured badly enough, anything could have found him. He was not adequately hidden and would have been an opportunist snack with Sukari gone. Even other lions have been known to eat their own species if desperate enough.

She realised another thing being in the area where she had last seen Legacy. She was surprised that she had ended up back here after all this time! Sometimes you travel around randomly, so much in fear, that you can potentially end up back where you started! She felt too uneasy about this place and needed to move on. Though, this time, she would try and keep more focused in future.

5. Lost

Three months went by for Sukari and Anthi. During which a routine had formed. Sukari would find a suitable den for them both, stay there for a few days, then move on. During this time, she would either hunt or luckily come across scraps of meat that were just left behind, she assumed from predators.

Over these three months, it quickly became apparent that this whole solitary search for them was a lot more complicated than she imagined, but she couldn't give up. For her and Anthi's sake, she had to keep going and get further away. In the hope that a perfect place existed for her search to come to an end.

Sukari constantly felt unsettled, and she had the urge to always continue. One explanation could be that she wasn't established in an actual lion pride, so she didn't have a strong enough presence to claim her own territory. There was always a more substantial presence of other prides that she had to avoid. Even though a lone lioness may be welcome into a new pride, her cub would not, as the dominant male would see her male cub as a future threat and kill him.

Sukari already knew this, but reality hit her a few days ago when she awoke one morning. She stepped out from the cover of long grass and dense bush as her den for the previous night. Two lionesses immediately stood before her, who abnormally straight away showed no hostility, instead they kindly just informed her that she was on their territory. Instead of showing defensive aggression before fleeing like she has had to with previous encounters, she took this hospitable opportunity for a civil conversation.

Along with apologising, she soon learned that the lionesses were not hostile because they had a more worrying matter to deal with. One of the lioness's cubs had been missing for the last three months, and they had come home to rest for a couple of days before heading back out again on patrol one more time.

Assuming Sukari was an alone wanderer and taking pity on her, they surprisingly asked her to join them on their last search before giving up. They planned to go back to areas that had shown promise of finding the female cub. They explained there was a scruffy, rogue-ish-looking lion of interest. He seemed to look like he got around a bit in an area where their cub's scent was lost, so that was the first place to go back to see if there was any new information of her whereabouts.

The lionesses show pity towards Sukari and

asked her if she would like to join and help them, it would give them a reason to take Sukari to their dominant lion and ask for her to be part of their pride. They would be confident he would accept because of her help, regardless of if the cub was found or not.

Sukari was touched by their kind gesture, but Anthi then appeared behind her with a sleepy yawn just at that moment. Both lionesses' faces then suddenly dropped. They knew what Anthi's fate could be and soon apologised to Sukari for getting her hopes up. They sympathetically suggested she leave for the sake of her cub. Sukari nodded thanks for their brief act of kindness and understanding before picking up Anthi and turning to go. As she did so, one of the lionesses spoke up.

"First-time mum?" she asked curiously with a flick of her ear and a glint in her eye while taking a step forward. Sukari turned her head, replying with a gentle nod and a slight sway in her tail. "It must be hard for you in the situation you're in, but from one mother who was stupid enough to let her cub go missing... to a mother like yourself with everything you are tasked to endure alone."-She lowered her head and took another step closer, brushing her head against Sukari's shoulder-"You're doing great," she said with a slight tremble in her voice.

Sukari's throat immediately tightened, and she had to hold back her emotions. It was something she needed to hear, yet never expected such kind words from a stranger, now being at a loss of her own. With tears quickly developing, she simply smiled warmly and briefly spoke.

"I dearly hope you find your daughter, and we meet again in brighter times," she strained with a whisper as her throat tightened more. She then briskly turned and walked away, continuing her own path once more.

As friendly as the lionesses were, she could not help but notice something about them, an ember of fear flickered in their eyes. Sukari had a feeling deep down that Legacy and his influence may still be alive. With this in mind, she preferred to continue her journey of wandering, to find somewhere that felt far enough from him while also a place without competition from other prides. But how far could his fear spread, and was she seeking too much?

A few days after the event of the kind lionesses, the wet season had started. The sky was a constant shade of grey from the heavy clouds, and the hardened ground had turned soft and, in some places, waterlogged. Sometimes the lands would experience severe downpours. Other times it would subside to light rain, even stopping for a day or two but replaced by highly humid air. It was a testing time for both Sukari and Anthi, but at least he was old enough now to walk on his own and less sensitive to elements. The timing of this was a welcome convenience now him being a walking, talking and energetic ball of fur.

Splish... splash... splosh. Anthi happily jumped

from puddle to puddle dotted along the trail that Sukari led. He was keeping himself entertained as these "walks" tend to get boring quite quickly for his short cub-like attention span. Mud splattered all over his paws and all up his legs, the tuft of his tail also soaking up the muddy water as it dragged and swished along. Sukari turned her attention to him when she heard his antics, rolling her eyes but not without a faint smile. She just couldn't help the amusement.

"Well, someone is sleeping nowhere near me tonight!" She teased.

"Pfft, I'm boooored. All we do is walk and walk and walk. Something fun needs to happen," Anthi whined. "Besides, I'm all growed up now. I can sleep all by myself," he boasted, puffing out his chest. A flash of light suddenly flooded the land along with a sharp crack of thunder. Anthi's hair quickly stood on end. He pounced underneath Sukari as she continued to walk, amused by his sudden change of opinion about needing his mum. "Heh, that was nothing!" he trembled.

Anthi slowed his pace back down, now walking behind Sukari again, eyeing up her tail dragging along the ground. He grinned with a subtle, playful growl. Soon enough, he pounced on it and held on, letting himself be dragged along the slippery mud. Sukari rolled her eyes again, but this time more irritated than amused. She stopped and sat for a moment.

"Come now Anthi, not long now, shelter is up

ahead, and we can then rest," she assured.

"But then afterwards, it's the same old routine. Why can't we... aaaaahhh!"-Sukari had turned, grabbing him with her mouth, Anthi doing his usual protest by flapping his legs- "Muuuuum!" he whined with a look of disapproval across his face. He soon admitted defeat and let his legs hang, mud and rainwater running down and dripping onto the ground. "Wait 'till I'm even biggerer, won't be able to carry me then... humf," he grumbled, crossing his forelegs.

"Mmhmm." Sukari just hummed in agreement, not listening to his whining. Her attention was more on the trees that poked out just beyond the hills in front of her. This would be the only safe bet for decent shelter and protection before the light disappeared entirely. It was quickly being consumed by the increasingly heavy rain and the fast-approaching night.

Sukari ascended the hill, her paws slipping intermittently as the once-solid ground had now turned into thick mud. She used her claws to try and gain more traction. She eventually reached the top, but her heart soon sank for two reasons.

The first being that the hill had hidden what lay between them and the trees. A river cut across that had swollen to an enormous width with a strong current.

The second reason is she recognised this place. After three months of travelling, avoiding other prides and detouring around territories, she somehow got her bearings mixed up at some point.

She had been here before, though a place deeper from her past. She took a long deep sigh and clawed the mud, trying to contain her frustration and self-stupidity. She placed Anthi back on the ground. Anthi's eyes widened with a look of amazement.

"*Awesome*! That river looks like it's in a hurry!" he joked. "So... the top of this hill has an epic view and all, but it isn't very sheltery. Are we staying here?" he questioned with a raised brow and tilted his head up to his Mum. Sukari sighed and motioned her head slightly towards the trees beyond the river, trying to hide her disappointment.

"It would be over there, but it would be dangerous to cross that river. We will have to move on and find somewhere else." Sukari sighed. Anthi looked at his Mum's sad expression, and his heightened spirit soon sank to her level. Knowing there isn't an end anytime soon and the current boredom, the elements were starting to bother him.

"But... I'm getting tired... and a little cold." he croaked, his head hung down, his ears flattened, and his little body started to shiver. Sukari looked down at him with her heart aching a little. As much as she needed Anthi to keep strong and be tough, she couldn't help but sympathise with him this time. Knowing she had been going around in circles from her past, she needed to rest in some comfort to ease her mind. There was a slightly dangerous option, which was to cross the river. Sukari stared at it, gauging it in her mind, looking at the speed of the water and the distance across. Meanwhile, Anthi curled underneath Sukari, using her as his personal rain shelter. She pondered for a moment in thought, soon remembering the words from the lioness... "*You're doing great.*"

Sukari had been through and learnt a lot these past months travelling. She wouldn't let this line of water stop her! Her self-confidence rose enough to tell herself that this river was crossable.

Sukari slumped down on the ground, lightening the mood, playfully squashing Anthi with her underbelly.

"Muuum, stop iiiit!" he said with a muffled voice and giggling.

"Well, I can't see Anthi anywhere..." she joked, turning her head each way.

"*Muuum, I'm heeere!*" Anthi carried on with his muffled laughs.

"So it looks like I'm going to cross the river alone to that lovely, sheltered area of trees," Sukari continued. Anthi paused his laughing, then wriggled his way out from under her.

"We are crossing?" he questioned excitedly, tippy tapping his paws on the spot, now having some optimism for a decent night's sleep away from the rain. Sukari nodded confidently and slowly stood back up.

"It will be cold, but it will be worth it for a sheltered night."

"Totally worth it!" Anthi said, getting hyped

up, bobbing his shoulders and head up and down. Sukari picked him up by the nape of his neck and placed him on her back. He then wrapped his paws around his mum's neck as wide as his legs would allow him. Sukari then paced down the other side of the hill before she got any second thoughts, her paws trying to keep traction on the decline but slightly slipping now and then. The mud got increasingly worse near the end, and her paws gave way. Even using her claws was not making a difference. They both slid all the rest of the way down.

"*Weeeeee!*" Anthi gleefully cheered with a big smile while Sukari looked terrified. The duo slid from the mud into the raging river with a splash. They submerged underwater for a brief moment before Sukari kicked hard, eventually surfacing with Anthi still grasping on.

"You OK, son?" Sukari yelled over the sound of the racing water.

"That... was... awesome!" Anthi laughed while Sukari mentally shook her head in amusement. He did have a confident spirit; she gave him that.

"Just hold on," she tried to demand, but not without an escaping chuckle. She felt Anthi's paws press tighter around her neck, reassuring her that he would be safe. Sukari continued to work her legs as hard as she could, the cold water wrapping around her body, the rifts of the strong current bashing her side. Anthi closed his eyes tight and kept holding on, water lapping over his body, trying to force him from his mother, his little claws twitching and trying to resist not using them to grip tighter. Sukari had managed to get halfway, and the other side of the riverbank became welcomingly into view.

Suddenly she was hit with a tremendous force. A large tree log being carried by the water had slammed straight into the side of her head and neck. Anthi instinctively, out of hesitation, dug his claws into her for a lifesaving grip, but it was not enough. The log pushed Anthi clean off Sukari's upper back, Anthi's claws cutting through her skin before he was taken away.

Sukari let out a roar in pain from the log and Anthi's actions. Her head started to spin, and her vision became blurred, and she could just make out Anthi being pulled away by the current before soon disappearing. All she then heard was the distant cry of her Son, soon drowned out by the noise of the rapid water.

"ANTHI!" she cried out before succumbing to the blow on her head from the log, then blacked out.

6. A Rogue Encounter

Night had now taken over the lands. The rain subsided to a drizzle, filtering through the dense trees and bushes, settling as droplets on the branches and leaves. A lone figure of a lion was pushing through them as silently as he could allow himself. Being extremely thin made it easier. Hearing a faint roar from a lioness at the beginning of the night, he didn't want to draw any attention. There could be a slim chance it was *her*. After what he did to her daughter some time back and not telling her, he couldn't look her in the eye again. Even though the roar was faint and sounded like it came from a great distance away, he wasn't going to risk it and just wanted to get back to his abode. The roar itself was oddly unique. It came in bursts of three, all different lengths. It went on for some time before eventually dying down, signifying she had stopped for the night.

Today, he had been scouting around for any scraps of meat left over by another predator. He had only found a tiny morsel, the first in many days. It was two mouthfuls at most, and he felt that it disappeared into nothing the moment it hit his stomach. In general, food was a luxury, and his fragile body was the big giveaway for that.

His ribs stuck out under his skin which rolled around as he walked. His stomach was non-existent, just an empty concave stretch of skin as an underbelly. The malnourishment had affected him all over. His mane was thin and matted against his body, his pelt was dull and losing its original deep colour and nothing majestic shone about him. Scars all over his body showed he must have had many confrontations with other predators - even lions, over scraps of food. This included a terrible, nasty laceration to his nose, which looked like it had just freshly healed, but still left him with a permanent deformity.

His eyes stared soullessly ahead, knowing that he would be returning to his den on a practically empty stomach once again. He had gotten used to this hunger, but things were now getting desperate. He was getting weaker each day. In the back of his mind, he felt that one morning he might not ever wake up. For a moment, he thought this could be a blessing. However, he had to continue living if his body allowed. It was in his instinct.

While in thought, he realised he had reached the river. He stared in disbelief as it had swollen three times its size since crossing it this morning.

There was no way he was strong enough to cross it now. With a frustrated growl escaping his throat, he slumped down onto the ground, baring his teeth while clawing the soft earth beneath him. He couldn't get back to his home the way he came, and he would have to take the long way around. The only welcome occurrence was that the clouds had broken a little, letting a slight glow of moonlight pierce through and illuminate the water. The shifting light patterns on the water's surface were a calming sight. The lion's eyes started to flicker as fatigue from being on his paws all day began to settle in.

Suddenly his eyes caught sight of something on the water drifting past him. It looked like a small dead animal of sorts. He leapt up and waded into the river. Swimming a small way for this 'snack' was a very welcome risk. His paws on the riverbed soon lifted as he started to float in the deeper area. His eyes locked onto his target as he swam towards it. His legs were already aching as his muscles had wasted away over time. He heard a disturbance in the water nearby like another animal was present, but he ignored it. His target was almost within reach, and he wouldn't let anything stop him.

Soon he opened his mouth and grabbed the little body before making a quick turn back to the side of the river. He climbed out onto the bank and shook his body to rid his pelt of water whilst already panting heavily and out of breath. His eyes shone with slight relief that he finally found another snack to tend to his needs. It was small but better than nothing and may help keep him alive longer. He glanced back over the water to see if whatever was in the river would make itself known. He didn't see or hear anything. Whatever it may have been was either negligible, afraid, or both.

He opened his jaw and let the body drop to the floor with a slight thud. The still glowing moonlight illuminated the body, which gave the lion a surprise glimpse of what it was, a lion cub! He first thought if this cub belonged to the same lioness he had heard from earlier. He soon dismissed this thought, he has had his fair share of experience knowing the sound of when a lioness calls out for her cub, and that odd roar isn't one of them. In any case, this cub seemed to of drowned. The lion's stomach made a long whining growl, and his mouth started to drool. It wasn't the first choice of meat to consume, but the cub was lifeless anyway. The body would just be taken by something else, so why not him?

Suddenly the cub's chest started to pulse and twitch. Soon enough, it made a retching gurgle and coughed up a lungful of water. The drop to the ground had assisted his natural reflex in clearing his lungs and windpipe. Even though this was a good thing for the cub, it would seem to all be in vain. The lion stood over him with his teeth bared. Cub or other prey, this was still a potential meal for him. No way could the cub ever survive on his own anyway, and this lion needed this lifesaving meat. The hungriest lions can eat their own species if they are desperate enough. The lion would be doing the cub a favour anyway by putting it out of a long slow death of attempting self-survival, killing it quickly instead.

Anthi took a few deep breaths after choking up the remaining water. He came around out of consciousness, groaning from his recent ordeal. He half-opened his eyes to see a blurred pair of adult lions' paws in front of him with claws bared. He scanned his eyes from the paws and up its legs. He lifted his head slightly to gaze upon the face and eyes of a menacing-looking lion hovering his head over him. His canines showed a snarl and a low growl rumbling from his throat. The sound vibrated through Anthi's body. The lion quickly lowered his head towards him with a huff and soulless eyes, a wide-open jaw equipped with a complete set of teeth and a gaping throat.

"No... NOOOO!" Anthi croaked. He was too weak to move or shout, and all he could manage to do was shut his eyes and prepare for the worst. He heard another hunger-induced low growl and felt teeth sink around his neck. In the shock of knowing his fate of being killed and eaten, plus still recovering from almost drowning, Anthi passed out.

A lot further upstream, Sukari lay unconscious and washed up on the bank of the river. Luck must have been on her side tonight. Her eyes started to flicker as she regained consciousness, hearing the rustle of bushes nearby as if something had sprinted away. Instead, she assumed and wanted to believe it was just the wind or a small critter. Her eyes immediately widened, and she struggled up to all her paws. She didn't know the length of time she had been on the bank but hoped it wasn't too late to find her son. She looked around to get her bearings. She was back on the same side from where they had tried to cross, but a lot further downstream. This was shown by how she could still see the hill they had come from far in the distance.

Calling out her son's name would have been pointless; words don't carry through the air as strongly as something like a roar. A lion's or lioness's roar can be carried through the air for a great distance, and it can be heard even by animals that are a dot on the horizon. She composed herself, took a deep breath and gave an immense roar as deep as possible, three consecutive bursts but different lengths. This may attract unwanted attention, but she didn't care for the risk. She wanted her son back! She hoped that Anthi would hear it.

Her roar pattern was unique, identifying to Anthi that it was her. She taught him this in case they got separated. The roar also served another purpose, hoping it would work; she would just have to wait and see. She continued her calling for a while as tears rolled down her cheek. She started to pace downstream a fair distance, with her nose taking in every scent for any hint of Anthi coming onto the bank. Her only concern was if he may have washed up on the other side, that's if he washed up at all. With her mind playing on this, her roar started to break down and croak as upset and guilt started to take over.

She felt so stupid for her impulse decision to cross the river, the regret soaked deep into her soul, and the roaring soon turned into a quiet sob. She had failed her only mission as a mother to keep her cub safe. She gave up her calls for the night. If Anthi was alive, he would know how to keep himself safe, and she would continue her calls in the morning. She let out one more roar sequence hoping someone else would answer it, but a reply never came.

Anthi started to come around from his passing out. His eyes opened slightly to see the ground beneath him moving. He felt teeth gripping his neck, but surprisingly in the harmless part of his nape while his body swayed slightly from side to side. He wasn't being eaten; he was being carried! He started to flap his legs around, trying to grab hold of the lion's mouth.

"Let me go! Let me go!" he growled. The lion huffed in reply and continued to walk, ignoring his demands. "If my mum finds you right now, you are DEAD!" he yelled. The lion menacingly chuckled at his brave remarks. He dropped Anthi on the ground, making sure to place his paw over his tail so he wouldn't run off.

"*You* would already be dead yourself if I hadn't dragged you from the river and would soon be dead if you run off. The nights around here are dangerous," the lion explained with a low growl.

Anthi was half listening while digging his teeth into the lion's paws to try and make him let go.

"Yeah, keep me for fresh food, more like! LET GO!" he tried to growl but turned into a whimper.

This lion was used to pain, only wincing slightly. He placed the weight of his other paw on top of Anthi's back to flatten him down onto the ground to stop his protests.

"I would squash the life out of you right now if I wanted to eat you. Besides, I've killed a cub for a lot less than food," he growled and stared at him soullessly. He lowered his head to Anthi's eye level, who stared at him back but now more settled and slight fear in his eyes. "However, as much as my empty stomach protests, I would not kill a cub for food... yet, unless you anger me more. Now are you going to be obedient for the rest of the night?" he demanded. Anthi nodded quickly in agreement. The lion then released his grasp. In turn, Anthi felt faintly at ease from his words.

"'The rest of the night,' are you... helping me?" he questioned. The lion scoffed and growled in reply.

"Of course not! I am merely sparing you! Cubs eat half their weight in food. You will be just another whining mouth to feed in the morning, let alone struggling for food myself. You are staying with me until the night is over, then you are on your own. Whether nature kills you after that or not, my conscience is clear, I at least saved your life once."

Anthi raised his brow at the lion's weird definition of 'saving' someone. Knowing now this lion isn't a danger, his typical overconfidence grew back.

"Thanks, I guess," he said, confused. "Well, thanks for saving my life and stuff, but don't worry, I can take care of myself!" he said proudly, puffing out his chest with his eyes closed and head held high. The lion raised his brow, and for the first time in as long as he could remember, he cracked a faint smile at the cub's confidence. He soon wiped the smile away, not wanting to be seen with it. Anthi opened his eyes and looked back at the lion.

"Well, since we are together for tonight, erm, lion. My name is..."

"NO!" the lion snarled, interrupting. "We are not friends, we are not buddies, I don't do names!" he growled. Anthi stood back a few steps, startled by the lion's sudden outburst, and put a little more into his place. "Names are for lions who have a belonging, to address one another. If you live alone, then names are pointless. We are together just for one night then you find your mum on your own. My debt is paid," he paused, glaring at the club. "Now come!" he instructed, raising his deep, rasped voice. "We have to cross the river the long way around, then my den is not far."

Anthi decided to play it safe to obey the lion's demands and follow him. After all, if he *was* going to be his dinner, the lion would have already killed him. A dead unprotesting meal is easier to carry. Anthi noticed just now as the lion walked past, how thin and malnourished his body was with his ribs rolling under his skin. Anthi could imagine how a lion this thin *would* resort to eating anything. He was grateful that he didn't and instead was helping him, even if it was just for one night. Anthi knew that once he was on his own again, the chances of survival would drop dramatically.

This lion only cares about himself and doesn't come across as the nicest, regardless of whether he saved him. After all, he did mention that he killed a cub, or was that just a scare tactic? Something about his "debt is paid" confused Anthi too. What did that mean? Why only one night? He soon dismissed his questions. He suddenly had an idea of his own in the hope this lion could stick around longer until he found his mum.

"Say... erm... Lion?" Anthi questioned. The lion glanced back to acknowledge him. "My mum is the best hunter in these lands. She could kill an elephant!"

The lion scoffed at his remark.

"Quit your *exaggerated* lies. No lion or lioness can kill an elephant alone, maybe a whole pride if they are lucky. Where is this supposed to lead to anyway." he grumbled.

"*Aaaaanyway*," Anthi rolled his eyes. "It looks as if you have trouble finding a good meal. If you protect me while I'm trying to find mum, I'm *sure* she will reward you with our next dinner," Anthi pitched to him, slightly nervous. The lion paused and turned to face Anthi.

"Look at me, Cub," he growled. "Do you think I am a lion that can protect?" he grumbled with a less harsh tone. Anthi cracked a faint smile.

"*True*, but you look all scary and stuff. Besides, having you by me is better than nothing at all, *and* you'll get all the meat your belly requires when we find my mum." Anthi's confidence grew with a faint smile.

"'When'? Don't you mean 'if'?" he raised a brow.

"Mum is clever and has a good nose. As long as I'm safe, she will find me. We haven't been separated long."

The lion stared at the cub for a moment, reading his expression and body language. The confidence in his mother finding him was undoubtedly there. But *would* this lioness go and hunt for him as a way of thanks? She could easily just walk off with the cub, and he would be too weak to retaliate. However, for the first time in ages, a full belly for just walking next to a cub sounded a good, all too tempting deal for him. It was worth the risk of wasting his time.

"Very well, Cub, but on the condition that if my 'scary appearance' doesn't work and there is any sign of a fight"-the lion moved his head closer to Anthi- "Any at all. I'm gone!" he stated firmly. "Also, stop calling me 'Lion'. I don't deserve that title. I'm nothing to anyone," he snarled.

"Deal! Well, you keep calling me 'Cub', what am I supposed to call you?" Anthi pondered for a moment in thought with his paw brushing his muzzle. "*Well*, you look like a rogue-y type lio... thing, so I'm gonna call you Rogue!" he smirked.

Now apparently called Rogue, the lion let Anthi off with his witty comment this once. He commended his bravery for it, almost admitting that he kind of liked his sarcasm and confidence. He disguised his amusement with an eye roll and a sigh.

"Whatever... let's go! My den is not far from here, but the river is too wide and dangerous to cross. I'm in no fit state to do it" Rogue turned his head. "However, the river dips down into a valley further downstream, and a fallen tree lays across the two cliff sides. We'll cross there," he explained. Anthi then nodded in agreement. Rogue started to lead the way, with Anthi following, but it wasn't long until he fell behind.

"Can you carry me as you did before? I'm cold, weak, I almost drowned! Plus, I'll slow you down!" Anthi whined intentionally. Rogue turned his head and lowered his brow.

"Don't push it, Cub! that wasn't in our agreement. If you fall behind, you're left behind. It will be your own doing, so my conscience will remain clear. Now walk!" he demanded, then turned his head back forward.

Anthi mocked his words with mime, flapping his muzzle. He then proceeded to quicken his pace and catch up.

This wasn't *the* perfect solution for Anthi's problem, but the only logical and safest choice he had right now. Somehow, he had to trust this Rogue.

7. Night Of Change

For a while, the journey stayed silent. Anthi kept his concentration on keeping his pace up with Rogue, his gaze locked on his bad shape. Anthi was surprised that Rogue had even lasted this long in his state. He watched as his legs dragged along the ground. His ribcage looked to dance under his thin layer of skin, swaying side to side with his natural stride. With virtually no fat, he could see what muscle remained clearly, as it contracted and twitched under his pelt. Anthi felt slightly guilty and concerned for him.

Compared to himself, he had plenty of weight surrounding his small, healthy yet slightly chubby body with an always satisfied stomach, thanks to his mum. It was like they were at opposite ends of the food chain.

Anthi's thoughts shifted back to his mum. He had no doubt she was ok, in his eyes she was indestructible. However, he still worried about her, and she must be worried about him too. He knew he should be following the rules she had laid if they ever got separated; stay still, hidden, and listen for her roar signal. Yet here he was, trailing further away with a rogue lion at that! He knew that it was for the best he had some sort of protection and a safe place to sleep, rather than staying all night near a river where all sorts of predators would be using. However, he still couldn't let go of the thought of going against her advice.

He had weighed up his options with this current situation and thought this was the most logical thing. Though Rogue's den seemed like a distance away, it was because they had to detour the long way around to avoid the wide river. When they arrive, it seemed they would only be a small distance away from where they started but on the opposite side. They could then look and listen out for his mum in the morning.

He nodded to himself confidently, and he couldn't wait to wrap his paws around her, an excited expression already gaining on his muzzle.

Anthi suddenly remembered what his very same paws had done to her. He hadn't had time to think about it in all that had gone on, but now he could. His excited expression soon dropped, and his pace lessened. A guilty tear escaped his eye and blended in with his already wet fur. His throat tightened, and he let out a compressed sniff, trying not to bring attention to himself. Rogue sensed his slower pace, the sound of his paws squishing through the mud had gotten delayed and quieter as he dragged behind.

“I won't repeat, Cub, keep up!” he groaned.

"I'm sorry... I just... I'm scared that I... anyway... I'll keep up," he murmured under his breath as he shook his head, trying to rid his increasing number of tears.

Rogue glanced back and set his eyes upon him. After almost drowning, being separated from his mum, and dealing with Rogue himself (which he admitted he wasn't the easiest lion to acquaint with), this cub had powered on with a confident and cheeky demeanour.

However, something was bothering the little cub, breaking him a little. The helpless look of this little ball of fluff started to ignite something inside of Rogue. Something deep down began to ache a little, and he couldn't understand what exactly he was feeling. He turned around to take another step forward but froze mid-step and closed his eyes. Rogue took a long sigh, annoyed at his feelings, and glanced back again at him.

"Speak, Cub. What's the matter with you?" he said with a slightly softer tone. Anthi, looking down at the ground, slowly lifted his head, wiping a tear with his paw.

"I don't... want to see Mum," he mumbled, breaking into a small sob.

"Well, this makes our agreement short-lived," he scoffed. Anthi's sob became more consistent, slowly turning into a subtle cry. He slumped down on the ground, ignoring the mud now sticking to his body. He then covered his paws over his face to hide his crying, making his face even muddier.

Rogue rolled his eyes but was still drawn to the upset cub. He let out another sigh though this time a little more heartfelt. He paced towards the cub and sat down next to him. He just sat there staring at him for a short moment, not knowing what to do or how to act, his eyes flicking back and forth from him. He lifted his paw slowly and hovered it over him, hesitating for a moment, not knowing how to deal with such a thing. After a short moment, he slowly lowered his paw and rested it gently on Anthi's head. He wasn't used to making such gentle gestures for such a long time, that he almost forgot how to.

"Erm..." Rogue hesitated, clearing his throat. "Any reason as to why?" he asked, almost sounding concerned.

Anthi lifted his head with the gentle weight of Rogue's paw on top of it and looked up at him. Also, with a slightly surprised expression from Rogue's concern.

"I was holding on... holding on so hard"-he sniffed- "When a log hit us, I tried to hold on so much that I dug my claws into Mum as I was being pushed off her. My claws then ripped through her skin."-he lowered his head- "She roared in pain, and it sounded angry like she hated me for it. I have never... ever heard her sound so..." Anthi paused for a moment, taking a trembling breath. "Why would she want to see me again; she won't love me after what I did to her." He then just flopped his head into the mud.

Rogue just stayed silent for a moment. All that was on his mind was just the need to continue walking back to his den. He didn't have time for this. Yet he didn't want his impatience to get the better of him and couldn't shake the fact that he and this cub shared a comparable situation.

He decided to share his experience, anything to try and get this cub moving again. He lowered his eyes to Anthi's level.

"Listen to me carefully..." he demanded firmly yet with a sense of calm. Anthi lifted his head and made eye contact. "A mother or father can and will endure any pain or suffering, if it means protecting the ones most dear to them, they will sacrifice anything..." Rogue turned his head away and looked up at the night sky, the drizzle hitting his face with his eyes closed. "Trust me... I know." Anthi's subtle crying paused, looking up at Rogue with a confused expression across his eyes.

"What do you mean by-"

"It doesn't matter," Rogue interrupted. "A mother loves her cub regardless. If anything, she *would* have been angry if you *hadn't* tried to hold on the way you did. A few claw wounds is a small price to pay instead of..." he said solemnly but hesitated mid-sentence. Anthi nodded in acknowledgement regardless but then raised a brow.

"I was trying to ask though, what do you mean by a father? What's one of them?" Anthi asked, curious and confused. Rogue dropped his head towards Anthi with a matching confused expression, mirroring Anthi's raised brow.

"*Doesn't this cub know what a father is?*" he thought. This now was going to start opening a whole load of questions that Rogue didn't have time for and just wanted to get back home.

"Let's continue these questions in the morning. We will have plenty of time for all this then," he instructed while circling to the back of him.

"Thanks... I guess she does still love me?" Anthi questioned. He half expected Rogue for a reassuring answer. Instead, there was silence.

Anthi lowered his head, letting out a disheartened sigh. Then all of a sudden, he felt the pressure of teeth gripping the nape of his neck and his weight being lifted from the ground. Rogue had picked him up and continued walking. Anthi was now taken by surprise a little by Rogue's sudden change of heart.

"She better! I have her cub here, which promised me a meal for their reunion, and I'm still starving!" he said through his teeth with dry, subtle humour. "Plus, you're a heavy little thing. What did your mum last feed you? A whole zebra?" he sarcastically whined.

Anthi's eyes started to dry, and he could not help but let out a slight giggle.

"Thanks!" Anthi returned the sarcasm, but with a hint of gratitude for cheering him up.

They again began to travel through the night, but now it felt they were ever so slightly closer.

Anthi bobbed up and down, watching the

night landscape roll by. He thought he would try and do Rogue a favour by keeping quiet for a while. They were cutting across a long wide bend in the river to which the crossing was at the end. When they had finally reached it, they crossed over the log. It seemed to of been here for a while. Vines hung below it and laid across along with other wild vegetation. Rogue's paw almost got stuck in a vine loop and stumbled.

"Be careful, Rogue! Looks like these vines could be a death trap!" Anthi blurted out, to which Rogue replied quietly with a huff and an amused eye roll.

They then continued to walk back upstream on the opposite side around the bend. They then veered away from the section of the river where they would have crossed initially. They entered a stretch of long grass for a while before hiking over a steep hill. At the summit, Anthi gazed over the natural beauty lit up by the patches of moonlight still leaking from between the clouds. In the distance was another long steep incline that stretched across with a large Baobab tree standing prominently on top to the east side.

"Not long now, cub," Rogue said with a sigh of relief through his nose, which made the oddest of sounds. Anthi questioned this in his mind. The deep battle wound on his nose must have run a lot deeper than he was led to believe. It didn't look very nice to start with.

The land flattened out with a rocky

formation nearby after reaching the next incline and making their way up to the top. After such a long walk, Rogue was glad to finally arrive. They approached the rocks and entered through a small opening that led to a hollow cave inside, but not before traversing a network of old branches lying outside, unavoidably making crunching and snapping noises.

"This is... awesome! Mum and I have never had a solid place we call 'home' like this," he said in awe as his voice echoed around the emptiness. Rogue lowered his head and placed Anthi on the ground.

"Well, what do you normally live in?" Rogue asked raising a brow.

"Anything my mum can find for the night, she says we have to keep moving to get to our 'dream home', but I don't know when we will finally get there," he said with his voice lowering.

"Well, she sounds like a lioness with a persistent willingness to keep you safe. She must think the world of you," he replied in a softer tone that even surprised himself. What was happening to him? A cub comes along, and he gets all mushy! Rogue flicked his head to the side to shake off such thoughts. Anthi already noticed.

"Thanks..." Anthi shyly smiled. Rogue nodded grudgingly, then motioned with his head towards a corner of the cave.

"You will sleep there, and don't - touch - anything, OK?" he instructed with his stern tone returning.

Anthi nodded in acknowledgement, took a long yawn, slumped down onto the hard ground, and curled into a loose ball in the corner. Rogue lay down a few paces away on the opposite side and closed his eyes.

The cave fell silent, and Anthi felt an eerie atmosphere throughout. The cave gave off a vibe that a lot of history was within these walls, various claw marks on the sides and ground gave the impression of multiple struggles. A couple of lumps of rocks lay near the sides, again with claw marks but made by smaller paws like a toy or plaything for cubs. They hadn't been used for a while, as a light dusting of dirt had settled on them. Most confusingly, a nice set of large old leaves and dried grass were piled in another part of the cave and looked to have made a perfect bed. However, this looked to have suffered the same fate as the play rocks. The bed was covered in dirt, seemingly not having been used for a long time. Even Rogue would not sleep near, or in it. There was history in this place that made Anthi curious, though he felt asking questions based on Rogue's life story wasn't right at this time. However, Anthi thought of a few things on his mind less personal and couldn't resist speaking up.

"Rogue?"

"Please, let this be important. We need our sleep for the morning," Rogue grumbled with his eyes half-open.

"Well, just curious, but..."

Rogue sighed.

"Doesn't matter, continue." he groaned, giving in.

"You must have a good sense of smell being alone all this time. Could you track my mum by using my scent? We could kinda smell the same. Oh, and also, why are there sticks outside?"

Rogue huffed through his nose out of the tiresome questions, making the odd sound again.

"I'll answer, and then we sleep." Rogue lifted his head with his eyes half-open. "Our agreement was for me to 'look scary' for protection and *wait* until your mum finds you..." Rogue paused, opened his eyes fully and looked at Anthi. "I have no sense of smell. This injury you see on my nose runs deep and has cut off my senses, the air just about passes through, and that's it."

Rogue's stomach suddenly let off a harsh growl. He groaned at his unintentional sound display. "I cannot smell any lion, lioness, prey or the slightest scrap of meat. So you can figure out why I look how I do."

For the first time, a display of sadness appeared on his face. He curled up tightly and closed his eyes, hiding his emotion. "My ears are now the strongest alarm for any unwanted visitors while asleep. The sticks make a sound from anything wanting to come in... now can we sleep?" Rogue murmured with a sleepy huff.

Anthi tilted his head and gazed upon Rogue,

who quickly drifted off to sleep. A lack of food, therefore no energy, was most likely the cause. For the first time, Anthi could now properly gaze at him without the consequence of him staring grudgingly back. This lion looked like he had been through a lot in his life. His scars, war-torn fur, deformed nose, non-vibrant coloured pelt, and skeletal body showed that. Looking at how helplessly he lived, Anthi started feeling sorry for the lion. Although he had rough edges in his personality and hospitality, Anthi could see a genuine soul inside, though it just seemed like it was 'broken'.

Anthi was always taught by Sukari that a small gesture of kindness or trust goes a long way to repair something broken. He had nothing to lose at this point except a sharp growl or a snap if Rogue awoke and disagreed. Anthi slowly rose to his paws and trod softly over to him. He stopped one step away, hesitating for a moment in case Rogue suddenly burst out in disagreement, but his long deep breaths huffing out were a sign he was fast asleep. Anthi took the final step, lay down next to Rogue's front paws, rested his head on top of one of them and quickly closed his eyes.

Rogue felt something. Always being on edge, this quickly woke him up. He half-opened his eye to see in almost shock, the cub resting peacefully on him. He let out an ever so slight tremoring growl from his throat in this awkward situation and went to move his paw. He only had pushed it a tiny amount before pausing. He couldn't help but stay frozen, gazing at this furball for a while. Anthi looked so peaceful and content on his paw, now acting pillow. The cub's tiny breaths soon developed a rhythm, showing that he had drifted off to sleep. After today's events, it wasn't surprising that he fell asleep so quickly. A sense of trust and responsibility flowed through Rogue. Tonight, he felt like it was up to him for this cub's well-being and protection, a long-lost sense he hadn't experienced in a long time.

A flow of emotions started to flood his body, overwhelming him, and he couldn't block them out. As he continued to stare at this cub, a tear formed in his eye, blurring his vision. He blinked it away to regain focus, his attention then diverted to how muddy the cub's face and neck were from earlier. He scanned his eyes up and down his body like he felt something was telling him to do something.

The mud would dry during the remainder of the night, which would cause discomfort in the morning. Rogue, without thinking, instinctively started licking the cub gently, bathing him. Anthi stirred a little in his sleep but did not wake. Rogue's tongue gently brushed over Anthi's ears and cheek without questioning himself. To him, it just felt like a natural thing to do at this very moment. He continued licking for a short while until Anthi looked decent, ensuring he hadn't missed any spots.

He was just giving him the final lick from this bath when his exhale blended with a short soft rumble from his throat. It could have almost been mistaken as a sign of affection. Rogue suddenly froze in confusion with his tongue hanging from his muzzle, and his eyes widened in shock. He quickly snapped out of whatever mental mindset he was in.

What exactly just happened? What was he even thinking or doing? He quickly composed himself, slid his head away onto his other paw and promptly closed his eyes, hoping he hadn't woken the cub up. That would be embarrassing! He was tired and needed rest. In his mind, he just put it down to that.

All of tonight's events were a lot of change for Rogue's regular routine. He too felt, just for that one short moment, he changed in himself.

8. The Tree Of Life

The clouds broke apart just before dawn. Sunrise soon came, and the lands were greeted by a surprisingly clear sky. The sun's edge peeked over the horizon for the first in many days, and a new beam of morning sunlight embraced the land. The light lay upon the closed eyes of Sukari, making her stir in her half-asleep state. She hadn't adequately slept last night, only nodding off now and then. She was too worried about her missing son. Now that the sunlight was on her side, she took no time sliding out from under a hollowed-out rotten log not too far from the river. A once-living thing that was now no more can still serve a purpose, keeping Sukari dry during the night.

In the back of her mind regretting that she hadn't continued searching during the night, she had to reassure herself that it was the right thing she had done. Searching in the dark would have only attracted nocturnal scavengers, and if Anthi was led to her roar but not in her sight, she wouldn't have been able to protect him. Now at least this way, she had a better view.

If Anthi followed what she had taught him, he would be waiting for her call in the nearest and safest place. She began letting off her three-roar call while scanning the area with her ears held up high. She waited a moment in between her signals to listen out for any reply or focus on any sign of movement. She repeated this routine several times while walking downstream. The only movement she saw was small prey, scared away by her display. Her mouth watered, and her stomach whined, but she had to ignore it. This was no time for food! She took long, deep inhales through her nose to sample the air but couldn't catch any scent that resembled or gave a clue of Anthi's whereabouts. The rains had dampened any chance of scent trails unless very freshly made. Her confidence in finding Anthi started to dwindle, yet she continued her routine.

After a while of pacing, Sukari paused, her thoughts soon getting the better of her. If she still had her group in a situation like this, they could have split up, and without a doubt, would have had a better chance of finding him. She wondered how the group were now doing, now used to her absence and getting on with their lives. Sukari's heart yearned to see them again, even if she had just passed by to say 'hello'. Anthi, after all, was now at an age where he could be safely re-introduced back into the group as a mother lioness and cub would generally do. As much as the group meant to her and had a special place in her heart, it wasn't the same after Sheek's death. Without him – father and dominant male- she didn't feel Anthi was safe with a group of wanderers, something her instincts told her from the beginning, and anything could still happen. Tefnut was the exception as she was family. However, Tefnut was half leopard and a solitary natural animal. How long would she have stuck around until her nature's calling? Maybe now, without Sukari, she too could have left the group.

Sukari's emotions from her past and current situations began to surface. The last time she felt this isolated was when she was exiled as an adolescent. Now with no Sheek, no Anthi and no friends... she never felt so alone. She slammed her paw into the soft ground and sliced her claws through the mud.

"NO!" she growled. She would not let this get the better of her! She let out her unique call again, her eyes filling up and blurring the landscape. She flinched her head to shake them off and then paced powerfully downstream. She would not give up. She had to continue. She figured she needed to get to higher ground so her roar could be carried further through the air. A familiar hill lay to the northeast of her.

A warm glow started to fill the cave where Anthi and Rogue lay. Anthi had not moved from his spot, on top of Rogue's paw. Rogue was the first to open his eyes, doing so slowly as to adjust to the surprising sunlight during this wet season. A slight sigh of relief came from him. At least for a short while, the morning sun would be more pleasant than the last several days of continuous rain. It will also make finding Anthi's mum easier due to better visibility. Rogue lifted his head and slid his paw away from under Anthi, which in turn made him stir in his sleep and wake up. A long squeaky yawn stretched across his muzzle. He looked over to the entrance staring at the welcome sunlight coming through. He then turned, looking up at Rogue.

"Good morning, a nice sunny one at that," he said, excitingly yet sleepy. Rogue looked down towards Anthi and motioned a single nod.

"Well, it makes things easier," he agreed. "But you will realise one day, Cub, nothing excites you as you get older; you will have seen it all before." He mumbled. Rogue raised to his paws, took a long stretch, and yawned. His rear legs were slightly trembling, and his front legs were almost buckling. He was getting weaker by the day. Anthi looked up at him, slightly concerned about his deteriorating health.

"When we find Mum, I'm gonna make sure you get more than we agreed, you need it," he reassured.

"Don't take pity on me! I had enough of that last night!" Rogue snapped, but his expression soon softened after realising he startled Anthi "...it's not worth it," he lowered his voice. Rogue walked past Anthi to break eye contact, heading towards the entrance. "Brave move though... and thanks." He muttered, almost heartfelt.

Rogue stood by the entrance and looked out to the new day, letting the sun warm what thin fur he had. Suddenly, Rogue's ears stood on end, and his body froze. He heard a weak roaring call coming from afar, the exact unique pattern he heard last evening. “No, no, no, not now... why now?” Rogue growled. Anthi jumped to his paws and ran towards the entrance, wanting to run past Rogue, but he was soon stopped by a tug of his tail.

“Not so fast Cub. Something is out there. Stay put!” Rogue instructed firmly.

“Is that... roaring?” Anthi questioned, perking his little ears up and listening in on it too. They both stood silent with their matching ears standing on end. The unique roar sounded again, seeming closer. A slight gasp escaped Anthi's muzzle. “Could that be...”

“A challenging lioness!” Rogue interrupted, “I heard her last night. She doesn't sound friendly. It's certainly a challenge!” Rogue pulled Anthi closer to him. “We are moving... NOW!” he demanded.

Anthi protested, trying to break free from Rogue's paw.

“No, you don't understand; it sounds like my...” Anthi was suddenly interrupted by an enormous thundering yet raspy roar from Rogue. It was still powerful enough to feel the ground vibrate. This was a roar of challenge back towards the lioness. Rogue was surprisingly protecting him!

Anthi suddenly was lifted quickly by his neck before he could repeat what he was trying to say.

However, in Rogue's hesitation, he hadn't grabbed Anthi properly and was not biting by his nape but instead his neck itself, slightly squeezing his windpipe.

"Rooooogue... it's muuuuum!" Anthi tried to yell but only came out as a hoarse whisper. Rogue didn't hear it and darted out of the cave at full speed, running towards the Baobab tree. It was the highest point nearby and so the most prominent observation point. There he could hopefully see the lioness's location and run away in the opposite direction. "You're huuurting me!" Anthi again tried to yell out, but Rogue's grip was still stopping his voice from being heard. Anthi tried to wriggle free as hard as he could. If he didn't do anything soon, Rogue would disappear from this place and separate both Anthi and his Mum even further.

They approached the tree, and Rogue turned his head, making them both see the sun-blinded silhouette of a lioness near the bottom of the hill a short distance away. Rogue then headed in the opposite direction. Anthi continued his struggle, and eventually, dislodged a little from Rogue's grasp. He took a deep long gasping breath and let out the most vigorous roar he could emit, which came out as an extremely high-pitched cry. The sound rang in Rogue's ears and made him wince, screeching to a halt.

"WHAT'S YOUR PROBLEM!" Rogue yelled through his teeth, unknowingly loosening his grip a little on Anthi's throat.

"MUUUUUM!" Anthi yelled out, breathing heavily before coughing to clear his throat, "That was her roar signal. IT'S HER!!"

"You better be right, or we are both in a very tricky spot!"

Rogue turned his head around and quickly paced back to the Baobab tree. All this sudden running wasn't good for him at all. He felt his chest tighten and his breathing shallow. He had to rest very soon, and he now hoped that this lioness *was* the cub's mother. He peeked over the hill's summit, looking down and this time squinting, focusing more on the lioness, which was now sprinting up the hill, teeth and claws bared. Rogue froze in absolute disbelief.

"LET GO OF MY SON!" Sukari roared while advancing. Rogue's jaw immediately dropped in shock, letting go of Anthi simultaneously, landing with a slight thud.

"Sukari?" he sputtered and gazed into her approaching and fearless eyes.

Sukari gasped and ground to a halt. She now had a small moment to properly gaze upon this feral lion that had her cub (almost) held captive. Her jaw dropped, and her head started shaking, taking a few nervous steps back. She did not recognise this lion and wondered how he knew her name.

She stared through his thin mane, half-covering his helpless and sorrowed eyes; to the face that lived underneath.

"No... Impossible..." she panted, trying to

catch her breath as Rogue took a slow step towards her.

"Sukari?... You're here? You're... alive?"

While half angrily raising a brow, Sukari took another step back.

"What do you mean by *I'm* alive? You must have me confused with another lioness who shares that name, you're not-"

"MUM!" Anthi gleefully yelled and interrupted them, not paying attention to what Sukari had said and happily pranced over to her, brushing his body around her leg. "Mum, this is Rogue... well, that's what I named him. He wouldn't give me his name, so I made one up. I like it. It suits him I feel. I mean look at him!" Anthi blabbered on excitingly. "He pulled me from the river, I almost drowned, but he saved me, and then we made a deal for him to protect and help me try to find you and stuff if you give him food in return. How clever am I? I think I'm clever because then we both get something we want...!" He continued blabbering.

Anthi though soon paused and grew a confused expression, as neither of them was moving or saying anything. All the while he was talking, gave Sukari the time to focus on Rogue. Each passing moment made it harder for her to believe it wasn't '*him*'. Sukari quickly glanced down at Anthi, her muzzle trembling and tears dripping onto him to his discomfort, making him flick his head. She then looked back up at 'Rogue'. She hesitantly took a couple of small steps forward. It felt as if she may be walking towards a ghost of her past, her muzzle almost touching his, scared it may pass through. She lifted her nose and took a couple of short, concentrated sniffs while gazing into the returning and tear-filled eyes of Rogue. Her eyes widened after her nose gave the definite and final answer.

"Anthi... this is Sheek, your father..." she managed to squeak through her now tightened throat.

"My... father?" Anthi replied, not taking in the whole meaning. After all, Anthi had grown up alone with just a mum and never even heard of a father.

Sheek's eyes shot wide open. He took a step back in disbelief as he heard for the first time this cub's name... 'Anthi'. His questionable behaviour while in the cub's company is now answered. He had been looking after this cub the past night, and it was his son all this time. Sheek thought he was killed before he was born, along with Sukari; it was in his knowledge that she didn't escape.

Sheek now gazed upon Anthi with a new set of eyes, that of a father. *He* is a father. The tears began to flow away from his eyes and down his cheek.

The stunned silence continued, both Sheek and Sukari trying to understand what was happening. A breeze brushed past them both. Sheek's thin and matted mane blew to the side, fully revealing his face and muzzle. The injuries he had received from Legacy were now viewable. Although healed, they left scars in the exact places where Sukari had remembered them. His deeply damaged nose was a new addition, she wondered for a moment what could have happened to receive such a thing, though it immediately self-explained why Sheek couldn't recognise the scent of his offspring. Sukari took a few silent steps to the side to fully assess his state. Tears once again ran down her cheeks, and her heart started to break. She noticed how thin and malnourished he was, with his bones sticking out to the likes she had never seen before on a lion. Anthi mentioned a deal for Sheek to receive food for helping him. She completely understood why. Many more new scars from bites and swipes of other confrontations were visible. His pelt was also thin and dull without a healthy shine. His breathing seemed shallow and unhealthy. He was in a terrible state. Sukari's brows softened, and her mouth hung, slowly shaking her head.

Sheek 's eyes tracked Sukari's movements as she assessed him. A shameful and embarrassed expression for how he looked flowed across his face, he wasn't proud of what became of him, but he was yet to fully explain the reasons as to why and how. He cleared his throat, gazing at them both standing before him, his trembling muzzle widened to a faint smile. He then focused his gaze on Sukari.

"You always liked the name Anthi..." he recited.

Sheek and Sukari suddenly burst into an embrace, both wrapping each other's paws around each other and squeezing each other tight, their muzzles rubbing side to side. Just the single slightest touch of warmth they now had shared felt like a thousand missed opportunities, now repaid.

"Hey! Where's room for me?" Anthi announced excitedly. He climbed up Sukari's back, over her head and slid down her face, wedging himself between them. Sheek and Sukari just laughed at his actions, Anthi giggling in response.

This single moment felt like a repeat of history. The Baobab tree sat where Sheek and Sukari had first got reunited a long time ago. They had started their lives together anew and onwards from this place. Now the same reunion had happened again after they thought each other had died. However, they were here together again, with another life, that of a cub they had created together.

This happening could not have been any more fitting for the situation the three of them were in. A Baobab tree in African culture has always been known as...

"The Tree Of Life."

9. Broken

Half a year ago, the time when Sheek lay motionless on the cold dewed grass of the evening, stained by his blood and his father's.

He had given Sukari and the group enough time to escape, by injuring Legacy enough to force him to retreat. Sheek had made the ultimate sacrifice, using his own life. Though his life wasn't taken tonight, Sheek was to live through something more painful than death.

Sukari and the group saw and felt Sheek take his 'final' breath. Once he stopped breathing, they knew nothing could be done. It was even more heartbreaking that they quickly had to disappear fast and leave his body behind. This place was still not safe, and Legacy's backup could turn up at any time. They would have to mourn their loss later and leave his body for nature to claim. They all sprinted through the long grass and down a descending hill from view. Sheek's body soon lay alone and abandoned, the only company being the stars and the gentle breeze in the night sky.

He hadn't taken a breath for a short while, though his heart still hanging onto a thread of life, it was soon to break. Beating so weak and slow, it was almost non-existent. He soon entered a half-unconscious state after. Now starving of oxygen, his eyelids flickered and his eyes rolled back while his chest pulsated, begging for air. He soon began to spasm violently, and his legs, head and tail jolted profusely. His muzzle was wide open but no air could enter his lungs, only drool trickled out. His end seemed inevitable.

Suddenly, a pushing sensation and a crack came from within his chest. What caused it? The spasm? His body's final attempt at survival?

Whatever it was, it worked. A long, shallow, struggling breath finally squeezed into his lungs. A painful groan followed as he fought to breathe again. He strained another long, shallow inhale, trembling as it entered his lungs, followed by a blood-soaked cough. The other half of his consciousness slowly returned until he was fully aware of his surroundings.

As he repeated this, each breath became slightly more profound and manageable. He mainly used his mouth to gasp for air, but a lingering scent of dung crossed his nose, but this was the least he had to worry about. Sheek's eyes faintly opened, with his vision hazed. He swore he saw a blurred silhouette of a lion in the darkness, maybe Aramile, blend into the grass. He tried to call out to alert him that he was alive, but not even a whisper could escape his throat, he could barely manage to breathe as it was. His eyelids grew heavy, and his vision faded. His consciousness was short-lived, and he felt himself drift away again. He let out a faint whimper, expecting to not wake up again.

A day passed... his eyes flickered, soon widening in shock that he woke up again! His breathing was shallow but constant, his body ached all over. He attempted to move his front legs just in preparation to try to stand up. The moment he moved them, he was drained of all energy and blacked out again, groaning in the process.

Another day passed... he came around again, and a feeling of faint strength flickered inside. He knew he couldn't keep lying here. He was a magnet for scavengers. If he were spotted, his already rare chance of survival would drop even more. They would take no time in ripping him apart alive for a fresh meal, knowing that he couldn't fight back. His legs still in the position where he left them last time, he moved them further in front of himself and twisted his rear legs, ready to push himself up. His breathing started to tighten, and his strength began to deteriorate. Regardless, he gave himself a strong push as hard as possible; he got halfway but then collapsed back to the ground with a slight thud. A long creaking sound came from his throat as he exhaled a sigh. He groaned in disappointment and drifted off into the darkness again without caring he could be attacked at any moment.

Another day passed... he was awoken by a

terrible sharp stabbing pain from his stomach and a raspy, drawn-out hiss. A buzzard had found him! Survival instinct kicked in, and he tried to flap his paw at the bird to scare it away, but it was only vaguely startled and immediately came back to peck again at his pelt, causing nasty wounds. He tried to roar to show some defensive aggression but just came out as a pathetic whine. This, in turn, announced he was weak and helpless, which only gained the buzzard's confidence. In turn, this attracted more to the ground that was circling from above.

He knew his strength was minimal and had to use it wisely. With the correct timing, an idea in his mind may work. He gritted his teeth and waited patiently as more buzzards flew down and started pecking into his stomach, rump, and thighs. He winced heavily from the many beaks now nipping into his skin. He would perish more painfully than he could ever have imagined if this didn't work. He continued to lay as still as possible as he needed the attention. He purposely let off another whine to increase their attraction and confidence. His plan then seemed to work. A buzzard bravely landed by his front leg, thinking he wasn't a threat any more. He immediately lurched his paw forward with claws bared and sunk them into the spine of the buzzard, then lunged his jaw deep into its neck with a satisfying pop and crack. The others fled in fear. Sheek lay there panting heavily, the unhealthy creaking noise still coming from his throat. His energy quickly drained, and he faded away again, with his claws and jaw wrapped around his potential lifesaving kill.

Another day passed... Sheek awoke, still with the kill in his possession. He felt a trend of getting stronger each time he awoke. This time he could move a little without feeling drained immediately, and his breathing had become about manageable. However, four days without food and water in his condition posed another problem, so he took no time to consume the buzzard. Birds don't have that much meat for a full-grown lion to have a satisfying meal, but it was his only lifesaving opportunity. He left almost nothing behind, apart from the buzzard's solid beak. Generally, if a lion catches a bird, it plucks the feathers with its teeth for a more pleasant meal. Sheek, however, didn't have enough time or energy to do so. His stomach would complain about this later, but it was a worthy sacrifice to make. With nothing left behind also meant less chance of attracting other scavengers. He also felt slightly lucky yet confused; for these past four days, he had been immobile yet hadn't seen or heard any other predators or scavengers. He tried not to ponder on this and started thinking about the next step in his recovery, water. Moisture from the meat would give him a little hydration for now, but he knew he needed to find a decent water source soon, which meant him getting up.

For the first time in the last few days, he closed his eyes to get some rest on his own accord.

He knew sleeping could be risky, but it was the best way to recover. He could still attract wandering scavengers but hoped his luck would hold out for one more day. It was the only choice and chance he had to survive.

Another day passed... The extra rest and small meal gave him a boost. His strength had returned a little more potent, which meant he could finally manage to push himself up. Though his legs were trembling and slightly unstable, he was at ease. Thankful another night had passed with no incident; he was now more hopeful about surviving. He dragged his paws across the ground and limped in the direction of a river he knew himself and the group had passed before he led them to Legacy. His panting started to increase quickly, and the creaking from his throat returned, but he managed. His paws began to drag heavier the longer he walked. The river eventually came into view, but his body drained once again. Added uncomfortable pains from his stomach added to his struggle; he knew he would have regretted eating the feathers!

He finally arrived at the riverbank, immediately slumping down, taking no time in lapping up water. The feeling of the cool fresh liquid slipping down his throat felt like a cure already. He stayed awhile, wanting to drain the entire river or wait until his belly was full, whichever came first. Naturally, it was the latter. He soon slipped into the river, giving himself a soak to clean his wounds from the buzzards earlier. A sharp stinging sensation indicated that the water was doing its job. It also invigorated his body, rushing around his aching muscles and refreshing his mind. Sheek now had a genuine glimmer of hope for survival and a more significant opportunity to track down Sukari and the group. A tear trickled from his eye at just the thought of seeing them again. He faintly chuckled to himself, imagining their faces of seeing him alive. Tears began to form from the thought that he may now see the day when his cub, Anthi, would be introduced to the group.

He had no hesitation knowing that would be the name. Sukari always went on about having a family, and Anthi was the name she always mentioned, the name suited if the cub would either be male or female to avoid embarrassment.

Sheek now needed to stay hidden around the area for a little while to gain more strength and stamina until he attempted to track down the group. He knew the general direction Sukari was to take. He wanted to get up and go right now, but he knew he had to be patient and see if his body could improve further.

Another two *days passed...* Sheek now felt considerably better. He was still not fully recovered, but he could at least stroll without feeling weak or his chest giving him trouble. He had to at least try and get back to the group, though his mind started to hesitate for a moment. What group would want a lion that cannot defend or protect? A lion that may not ever fully recover? Would he just be a liability to them all? He shook these thoughts away for now and decided to make a start. It's not healthy for the mind to keep thinking about what may happen. Just take in what will happen when it happens. If he could see his cub just one time, he would be at peace.

He was now standing back by the river, having a decent drink before leaving. He did not know when the next water source would become available, so he didn't want to leave it to chance. He then made tracks back towards where he lay while injured and followed the same direction as Sukari.

Sheek's paws dragged. Walking felt like he was running, but his stamina remained constant. This was good enough for him. He panted heavily to get as much air into his lungs as possible. He had only got as far as the long grass approaching the hill descent when suddenly he felt a strange presence in the air. He could only see the yellowing grass with a dung scent in the air. He heard the grass rustle when he took another long-focused sniff.

He couldn't react in time. A lion suddenly leapt out, flanking Sheek from the side. The lion swiped with extended claws, causing three extremely deep gashes across Sheek's nose, causing a severe injury. Sheek's whole top muzzle was immediately flooded with blood. He let out a roar in agony which turned into a hoarse gasp. He dropped to the floor in shock and pain, wrapping his paws over his muzzle, instinctively trying to stop the bleeding. His shoulders immediately felt claws digging in, pinning him to the ground as he let out another painful roar. A slimy and menacing voice spoke...

"If you move a single muscle, speak, or do anything else but listen and nod to acknowledge what I'm about to say, your group is dead!" the lion demanded.

Sheek was in no state to attack this lion, he knew he would fail. This threat could not be taken lightly. He slowly nodded with his face half-buried into the ground with his paws still wrapped around his muzzle.

"I have been watching you, Sheek, with great interest and admiration, may I also add that your will to survive is inspiring. So let's see how well you fair." He grinned.

"Legacy is badly injured thanks to you, but also surviving just like you. However, he still had friends close by, which you have not. I have the pleasure of telling you that when Legacy was returning home, barely holding onto life, I was nearby. He sent me to track your little group while he recovered. Can you figure out what my orders were?" he teased.

The lion paused and grinned purposely for effect, proud of his achievement. "I took great pleasure in killing Sukari as she dragged behind. With a powerful slice through her throat, she was dead before she hit the ground and before your little group noticed," he said sickeningly proudly.

Sheek distraughtly roared out, wanting to lift

his head but was soon overpowered by the lion's paw, slamming him back into the dirt.

"What did I just tell you? You pathetic fool! Another stupid outburst like that, and mark my words, your surviving group will have the same fate as her!" The lion growled. He lowered his head to Sheek's level, who quietly sobbed, numbed with uncontrollable grief.

"She is dead, which also means your cub inside her too, your pathetic attempt at continuing your tainted bloodline is now gone." he soullessly chuckled. "And ooh, you are going to like this... what you choose to do now can save the lives of the rest of your little group." He hovered his mouth over closer to Sheek's ear.

"A message from Legacy, if you are alive, you have just saved the rest of your group's life... for now. He wants you to suffer a long and pitiful remainder of your life after you betrayed him. A quick death in Legacy's mind is the easy way out. He wants you to suffer, all while knowing that your betrayal towards him ended the life of Sukari and your unborn cub" - he edged even closer, his mouth almost touching Sheek's ears- "with the words repeating in your mind, 'it's all your fault.'" He whispered slimily.

Sheek gritted his teeth with tears pouring down his eyes, blending into his already blood-soaked muzzle. Suddenly a swipe of a paw met with the side of his face, knocking him powerfully over to his side as he let out a defeated whimper.

"Now, look at me!" The lion demanded. Sheek

weakly raised his head. He knew he needed to be obedient towards this lion, already losing Sukari and his future cub; he couldn't risk the group's lives too. He blinked to clear his vision from tears and could only see the menacing eyes of this lion, right up close to him. "We both know your strength will never be the same again after your fight. You know that, and so does Legacy. A lion's strength and smell make them the king of predators across the whole land. Now with my 'little modification' combined with your lack of strength, you will live your life at the bottom of the food chain. No friends, no partner, no family, just you, alone. If you ever grow a conscience to try to find them... we will find out one way or another, and it *will* be a slaughter."

The lion took a couple of steps back and stared plainly at Sheek, by this time Sheek's eyes were closed in a torrent of emotion and weakness.

"You are a pathetic excuse for a lion Sheek. Now you will live a pathetic life for the sake of keeping theirs. When you finally die alone, Legacy will see that your punishment has been served, and your group will be spared." he sneered.

Sheek flopped his head back onto the ground, getting dizzy from his wound.

"Enjoy your new so-called... 'life'," the lion scoffed, then soon darted off into the long grass, leaving Sheek where he lay, speechless and tormented. His only company now is the unbearable guilt of his actions and the strong vision in his mind of Sukari lying dead, with their cub inside never having the chance to experience life. This second chance at life that Sheek now had, no longer served a purpose.

Another three days passed... Sheek had been wandering around the area with now no aim, no feeling of a goal in his life, and no future. He became at a total loss. His muzzle was still caked in dry blood from his wound. He didn't care about cleaning it just as much as he didn't care about anything else. He hadn't eaten; he didn't have any appetite, as he constantly felt sick from guilt.

Consequently, his stomach had already shrunk and had grown extremely weak once again. He didn't care, as his quickened death was self-intentional. He felt that dying would be a blessing, and he had nothing to lose. It also meant his remaining friends and half-sister would live, and they wouldn't miss him anyway because they already thought he was dead, being none the wiser.

Another week passed... Sheek was still aimlessly wandering around but had travelled a little further from the area he used to be in, his legs constantly trembling, and he was panting heavily. He felt his time was nearing its end, at last. A large rock nearby cast a welcoming shadow for his final resting place. He dragged his paws and struggled over, soon collapsing against its side, and lay in wait for his body to shut down. He was broken... Legacy had won.

"*Legacy has won... Legacy has won... Legacy has won.*" the thought repeated in his mind.

Sheek dug his claws into the ground in anger and defeat, letting out one last deep growl. Suddenly, an African wild dog sprung from a hole underneath the rock. It growled in challenge to him. In one last ounce of strength, he roared and took a swipe. It then thankfully fled. Sheek's last dying breath would not be by an animal that dwarfs him in comparison. His ears then perked up from a sound of distress coming from under the rock. Out of curiosity, Sheek dragged himself along the ground and peered inside. Two little pups sat there against the inside wall, looking terrified.

He gazed at the two briefly, almost feeling sorry for them. Suddenly, the pupils in Sheek's eyes narrowed, his own view of morality inside of him started to dim, and his inner instinct to survive started to set alight. He would *not* let Legacy win, and he will *not* die intentionally out of his self-pity and guilt. He would instead forever live with it and fight to survive. It would be tough, gruelling, and life-altering living with his poor health, but at least he would have a shred of dignity left.

His eyes that glared at the two pups were no longer that of Sheek, but of a lion with no name, no identity, and no friends or family. He would now just be a lion whose sole purpose was to simply live, only letting death take him by true natural causes and not by his own doing.

He lunged towards the two pups in the burrow and quickly killed them for his nutritional needs. He left the den empty and abandoned, fresh blood dripping from his muzzle. It used to belong to a thriving family, now wiped out in the blink of an eye. This situation reflected of his own. Maybe another animal will use the burrow to create or protect lives one day. It was an ironic circle.

Another month passed... Since leaving the burrow, Sheek had wandered back past where he 'died' and had continued walking. His lower jaw started to hang a little, and he constantly breathed through his mouth as his nose became increasingly redundant. His body had gotten thinner, looking slim but still borderline healthy. He couldn't eat that much. Any sort of hunting by running after prey was practically impossible.

He once was lucky when he took down an injured antelope but became terribly drained afterwards. The fresh meat attracted a pack of hyenas, and he couldn't protect his kill, soon getting surrounded and attacked. In a better situation, he would have the protection and intimidation of other group members. However, being an alone wanderer, he had to flee with an empty stomach, bearing multiple bite wounds and no dignity.

With no sense of smell and a lack of reliable strength, he solely started to rely on scavenging scraps and small prey alone. Some pieces were questionable how they got there or how lucky he was to get to them before another animal did. Also, they seemed fresher than typical scraps with no signs of being chewed. He didn't want to or be bothered to think much about it, food is food after all, and he was just grateful for his finds.

That lion was right. Sheek was now at the bottom of the food chain. His empty eyes gazed upon the endless lands with a belly that continuously complained every day. He never felt full or properly fed with what small chunks of meat, if any, he managed to find. Sometimes it could be several days until he came across any.

Another two *months passed...* Sheek's lower jaw now entirely hung down, breathing heavily. His body looked concerning, his ribs had started to show through his pelt, and his stomach had retracted. He knew he wasn't in decent shape but didn't seem too fazed. He could still breathe, and that was good enough for him.

Ascending over a hill, his eyes widened in disbelief. He gazed upon a Baobab tree standing on the next distant hill. He knew what he had just stumbled upon, and it was that of his old life.

This was his old home... his old group's home. The place where he watched cubs he had taken in and vowed to protect, watching them grow up. The place where he watched good friends live and die. He and Sukari first reunited and started a fresh new life together here. As he gazed upon it, he thought it would be upsetting, and memories may flood back, but he oddly felt... nothing. No emotion, no tears, no remorse. He just stared at it with his empty eyes. Emptiness cannot be hurt or felt.

He approached the top of the hill and stood by the tree, gazing out over the surrounding lands, yet still, no emotion invaded his stone heart. He then proceeded to walk towards the large cave set further back. Without hesitation, he walked through the opening and looked around inside, surprised that nothing else had settled in. Even the small rocks Safila and her friends played with as cubs were still there, with the claw marks present.

A bed made out of large leaves and dry grass was still in one of the corners, decaying but still present. He and Sukari had made it together when Sukari was in heat. It was not just for sleeping in, it was in preparation for their planned family extension. A place where she could keep their cubs safe and warm after she returned from a successful pregnancy, birth, and nesting period away from the group.

It was like a part of his old life had been frozen in time. It was like how he left it, back in a time when things were much more carefree and happier.

The evening was ending, and now the start of the night. It was time for him to get some sleep. He approached the old bed but froze, simply staring at it. Soon he turned around and settled in the corner of the cave instead. Something in the back of his mind couldn't bring him to sleep where he used to with Sukari. He curled up against the cold walls of the rock face and soon drifted off.

His sleep was soon short-lived by the sound of scurrying and rustling, more precisely, inside the old bed. After adjusting to the dark, his eyes suddenly caught more movement, and he heard another rustle. Sheek let out a deep growl and a snarl. He tried to smell what it may be, momentarily forgetting that his nose was useless.

"Whoever you are, show yourself!"

Suddenly, a little head of a cub popped up from under the leaves, her muzzle trembling.

"I'm sorry... I... I got separated from my pride. I needed to find a safe place for the night, can... can I..." she trembled.

"LEAVE! GET OUT OF THAT BED!" Sheek snarled.

"But... but it's," the cub started to break into a sob, though her tears didn't faze him.

"I don't care! Spending a night outside will toughen you up, NOW LEAVE!" He roared.

The cub sprung out of his bed terrified, sprinting out the entrance as Sheek pursued, keeping his eyes locked on her. His teeth remained snarled with a heavy pant and growl vibrating through his throat with each breath. He stopped a couple of paces outside of the cave, hearing her little paw steps fade away as she ran into the night, followed by a call of a buzzard that most likely had been startled. He turned around and took no time in settling down again inside. He lay in his corner and closed his eyes, not before taking one last glance at the bed. He shuffled around to get comfortable, his lack of body fat and developing bony frame made it a little more difficult. He soon set his mind on sleeping once more, with no concern or worry for the little female cub. He was instead relieved that he was alone and had his solitude. He didn't want anything undesirable coming in again. When he and Sukari were cubs, he remembered making their little dens. Being imaginative, they liked to create 'traps' as a way to 'defend' their den, one of which was to place sticks outside in a way they would make noise if their 'enemies' came near. It was an idea that may have some use for his current situation. He would keep this in mind.

The morning soon came. Sheek awoke and soon made his way towards the river that he remembered wasn't too far from here. He stopped by the Baobab tree and looked over to the opposite hill that the river lay behind. However, he had spotted a lone Hyena feeding on something on the summit of that hill. One hyena alone was easy to scare away, so Sheek could then steal whatever that hyena was eating.

He quickly made his way down the hill and headed towards the next one. As he got closer, the hyena spotted him below. Sheek gave a false charge towards the hyena with a deep growl, bluffing that he was strong and would fight for its kill. Since the hyena was by itself, it soon scurried off, dropping its kill behind.

Sheek, breathing heavily from his poor stamina, licked his muzzle. Breakfast was served! He trekked up the hill to where the abandoned prey lay. He reached the top but was now entirely out of breath. He gazed upon the prey before suddenly freezing his advance and taking a couple of steps backwards. He was staring at the half-eaten carcass of the young female cub from last night.

He just continued to stare at the lifeless body. He had seen a lot of death and almost experienced it himself. Many members of his group have perished over the years. To him now, death was just another inconvenience. Sheek did, after all, send this cub away, literally sending her to her fate. Though also in his mind, it was her fault for getting lost in the first place. It had nothing to do with him. It was just cruel nature playing its part once again.

"May your soul find the stars, little one. I will repay your life by helping another, once and once only. I am in debt to you." he said plainly and solemnly. Sheek then stepped over the body like an inconvenient stone was in his path and continued towards the river for his morning drink. The cub's body had been retaken when he returned, most likely by the same hyena. Not a single tear was shed.

Later in the day, not too far from the cave, he crossed paths with a couple of lionesses, one of them looking quite upset and both also without a dominant male. They noticed his state and sympathised with him, which led them to offer their hospitality. While he briefly debated it in his mind (he was now used to his solitude after all), the upset lioness mentioned she had lost her daughter. She asked if he had seen or heard anything (seeing his nose, they knew not to ask if he had smelt anything) as they had sensed a few spots of her scent in the area. Sheek froze. His empty, soulless eyes looked into her own, full of worry and love for her cub. He replied with a quick but polite 'sorry' and a shake of his head. He simply thanked them for their offer but declined, turned his back on them, and walked away. This time, however, a single tear escaped his eye. This tear was not just about a pang of developing guilt over the cub. He knew that if his timing was correct, this would have been when Sukari should have welcomed their cub into the world. Sheek and this lioness both shared a connection, the loss of their cub.

*Another three months passed...*The wet season had started, and Sheek had stuck around the cave. It was not an emotional attachment, just purely a logical one. It was a decent solid shelter, a nearby water source, and a great vantage point by the Baobab tree. The chances of finding another place like this would practically be non-existent in his living range of travel.

Sheek's body had deteriorated into a terrible state. His ribs, spine, joints, and muscles now stuck out potently from his skin. You could see his whole ribcage moving around under his thinly stretched skin and pelt. His belly was sucked in as far as it seemed unnaturally possible. His natural colour didn't glow without sufficient nutrition, coming across as bland and dull. His mane was now frayed, thin, matted and knotted and lacked any volume. He hadn't groomed it as he had no interest in self-care.

Being alone, there was no point in keeping up his appearance as he just didn't feel it was necessary. The Sheek he used to look like was practically unrecognisable.

During these three months, a thought in his mind repeated and consumed him. He did not have the audacity and common decency to give that lioness closure and inform her that he found a dead female cub nearby. He didn't even have to mention he was the cause of it. Neither did he have any reason to send her to her death, she wasn't a threat to him in the first place. He imagined how things could have been, he could have looked after that cub, and they would have found her mum. Saving that cub's life could have been the start of redemption. Regardless of how empty and soulless he felt, this thought started to devour and rip him apart piece by piece.

It was clear more than anything now, he was no longer a lion, just a faceless and cruel... thing. A lowlife without a shred of decency. His actions constantly kill the innocent, his friends, his family, and his soul. With his life fading, it was getting too much. Everyone has their breaking point...

Sheek, trapped in a shroud of depression of his own doing, suddenly snapped. He cried out multiple roars, pacing rapidly back and forth in the cave; his head twitched violently while panting heavily. He started to frantically maul the cave walls, feeling his claws break and chip away as they channelled deep crevices all over the rock face. His mind felt clouded and blocked from all emotion, with only negativity remaining. He let out a long whimpering growl as he thrashed his head repeatedly against the wall. This caused him to go short of breath once again as his chest tightened. He took long slow breaths to control his temper and calm himself down. The pupils in his eyes shrunk and his jaw hung pathetically, leaking frothing drool. Finally, a single tear ran down his cheek, which he quickly flicked off. This is who he was now and will be for the rest of the time he felt he had left... broken.

The night passed... Sheek set out once again, his instinct calling for a daily patrol for food. His mind was in the same state but felt that a bit of pressure had lifted from him after his meltdown. It was now like he truly accepted who he was. The only achievement he held onto was he kept going, kept breathing, stayed alive and vowed never to take his own life for the satisfaction of others, namely Legacy.

He had crossed the river that had swollen a little throughout the day and searched through the thick trees and surrounding areas for any small or abandoned half-eaten prey. Then as the night started to draw near, he began to make his way back home. This was when he heard the unique call of a lioness far in the distance. This was when he continued further down back to the river, spotting an animal floating on the surface.

10. Food Over Thought

Back to the present day, Sheek and Sukari were still in their embrace; coming to terms with this would be a lot to take in and process.

From Sukari's view, Sheek died protecting her and the group. From Sheek's view, Sukari had been murdered as revenge because of it. Both their lives had been completely ripped up by these events. They had both been through many dark and testing times from a completely altered way of life. Although a light now shone for a future they both always wanted, adjusting to this new way of life could prove to be a little less smooth than they thought.

Anthi had crawled his way over to the top of Sheek's head, who in return showed an expression of discomfort and awkwardness. He thought he was destined to die alone all this time without ever seeing a family of his own. Instead, his very own son was clambering all over him while in the embrace of

Sukari. It started to feel overwhelming. Anthi continued to trot on top of Sheek's head in excitement, knowing he had a male lion with which he could interact.

"This is gonna be great! You can teach me everything! Like how to fight, rule and roar!" he said enthusiastically. He grabbed Sheek's ear with the tips of his teeth and tugged it, trying to get his attention away from his mum. "Promise, promise, huh, huh, Sheeeek?"

Sheek uncontrollably let out a slight disapproving growl, flicking his head and forcing Anthi to slide down his side.

"Anthi!" he said raising his voice in irritation while glaring down at him. Anthi stared back at Sheek with the most prominent eyes, confused at his sudden reaction. Sheek soon softened his demeanour and sighed. "Please, just give me time, it's a lot for me to..." He then looked back up at Sukari, whose smile had flattened with slight concern from his actions. "It's a lot to take in. Shall we go back to the cave?" Sukari and Anthi nodded in agreement. She brushed her head alongside Sheek's shoulder for comfort before turning around. They then walked side by side towards the cave while Anthi pranced ahead.

"You should see Rou... I mean Sheek's cave mum, it's so cool! It's an awesome sheltery place with plenty of room, even for all of us three. It even has a bed, though I was told I can't touch it and..." Anthi's excited blabbering faded into the distance as he walked ahead with a spring in his step.

"He doesn't know that I used to live here too, huh?" Sukari asked rhetorically with an amused chuckle.

"Technically, he *had* lived here. If him floating around the size of an ant in your belly counts!" He tried to chuckle, but a lump of emotion quickly blocked his throat. He was at war with his feelings, one moment being irritated with Anthi, then the next being emotional. Sukari promptly comforted him.

"We both didn't know at the time..." she tried to reassure him before giving a soft brush on his cheek with her muzzle.

The two then fell silent for a moment, not knowing what else to say, there was so much that each other wanted to ask, but both could not even begin where to start. Instead, they both just stared at their son bobbing up and down in the distance with carefree vibes. He sniffed random rocks and plants on the ground before his attention then turned towards a butterfly, flapping his paws with a playful growl, trying to catch it as it fluttered around him. "But just look at what *we* created," she said proudly with a flick of her tail curling around his own. Sheek regained a faint smile with a subtle agreeing 'hum'.

They both stared at their little creation, happily keeping himself amused as they walked. A gentle breeze brushed over them, closing their eyes momentarily and embracing the cool air massage over their pelts. Sheek's mane blew entirely away from his face, fully showing the extent of damage to his nose while a wheeze trembled in his throat. Sukari tilted her head towards him and opened her eyes, seeing up close the scope of the damage for the first time. She cleared her throat with her eyes swelling up, unable to control her concerns and curiosity from spilling out.

"How... did that injury happen? Have you been living in our group's cave all this time? How did you survive? I watched you fall lifeless in my paws, I..." Sukari started to blurt out but soon got interrupted by a lick from Sheek.

"I promise Sukari, all will be explained, but it's no conversation for your... our son to hear. I'll talk about it at nightfall when he is asleep," he reassured. Sukari nodded in acknowledgement, then returned a lick on Sheek's muzzle before brushing her head underneath it.

"Ewww." the distant voice of Anthi sounded out. "You lick juicy meat like zebra or antelope, not each other. Are you that hungry!" he teased. Sheek and Sukari chuckled, gazing, and then smiling at each other.

"I know someone who might be," she said softly towards Sheek. "You and Anthi head back to the cave. I owe you a meal, according to Anthi earlier anyway," she raised a brow and smiled.

"You OK hunting alone?" Sheek asked, concerned.

"How do you think I've managed all this time?

I've got used to hunting alone." -she reassured and brushed her muzzle across his- "I'll be fine, besides, you need to rest until we get your strength back up. You go and catch up with your son."

Sheek Returned the nuzzle, and they both split away. He headed towards the cave where Anthi had already hopped inside while Sukari cut into a long grassy area nearby.

Sheek entered the cave, his legs starting to tremble again while his breathing shallowed. The real shock of the situation began to sink in. He flopped onto the ground and then slightly curled up. "*How do you think I've managed all this time? I've got used to hunting alone.*" He knew she didn't mean it in a mean way. However, these words repeated in Sheek's mind with a wave of guilt flowing through him. Knowing all too well that Sukari was driven to survive alone with Anthi *because of him.*

Many chains of events have led to this point up to today. Many of Sheek's *and* Legacy's actions were the cause and effect of Sukari's, Anthi's and his own life. His mind became clouded and overwhelmed by what he could have done differently and the alternate possible outcomes.

-What if he never followed Legacy's orders from the start? Legacy would have killed or hunted Sheek down, Sukari would have never seen him again, and Anthi never would've existed.

-What if he didn't change his mind at the last moment when handing Sukari and the group over? He would be a healthy, full-bodied lion along with

Sukari. Though they wouldn't see each other a lot as Sheek would continue in his duties of collecting more wanderers, Sukari would stay in Legacy's pride and be a breeding vessel for his lions. After Anthi was born and killed, that was.

-What if he didn't hand Sukari and the group over at all? They would all continue to be a group of friends and misfits, Sheek as the dominant leader and Sukari being second in line, both happy and healthy. Sukari would see their son come into the world, knowing he would grow up with the protection of herself, Sheek and the group after she returned from nesting. However, they all would eventually be hunted down by a now furious Legacy, using every power and fear at his disposal to dispose of them.

These three scenarios splintered into several sub-scenarios in his mind, plaguing it with what could of and what would have been in each. Before long, he came back to the scenario that *had* happened. In this one, Sheek was sick, in a pitiful mental and physical state, with life-changing injuries. He was also skin and bone on death's edge. Sukari was now with no group or friends for security. She is just managing to be a mother to their cub and surviving alone all this time. She's now also burdened as a carer, food provider and protector for Sheek too. In all, he felt like a failure.

"Where's mum?" Anthi questioned,

Sheek suddenly flinched out from his thoughts and turned his attention towards him.

"She has gone hunting... alone. Seems like she is quick to keep to our deal," he mumbled.

"Oh, that's great! I'm starving! Can't wait to sink my teeth in. I've started to eat meat just like Mum. Now we can all eat as a family!" he said excitedly with his ears perked up with a swish in his tail. Momentarily looking away from Sheek and towards the cave entrance.

Sheek's eyes suddenly narrowed, and his stomach groaned. His muzzle wrinkled slightly, exposing his canines. He quickly shook his head to snap out of whatever mindset suddenly came over him.

"Yeah... erm, me too!" he said plainly, though trying to add a little enthusiasm.

Anthi got a vibe since the reunion that these recent events had taken an emotional toll on Sheek, who seemed moody and irritated. Anthi was accustomed to Sheek being like this anyway, and he was still the same when Anthi first met him last night. However, Anthi assumed things would be slightly different now that they both knew they were related, and he felt a little disheartened.

He thought it best not to bother him too much, telling himself that once Sheek had eaten, rested, and got some energy back, they could start to get more acquainted. He laid down quietly, not too close by the side of Sheek, who had now closed his eyes, and he did the same.

After some time, Sheek was stirred from his light sleep by the sound of Sukari grunting as she dragged an adolescent antelope into the cave. It was the only prey nearby. Hunting an adult is too tricky alone, but she managed to pick off the less experienced one. He jumped up out of eagerness with his legs trembling. This would be his first decent meal in half a year. Anthi sprung up too, tippy tapping his paws on the spot while licking his muzzle.

"Take it easy, Sheek, lay down." Sukari said concerned. She dragged the body over to them both and dropped it in front of him. "Now, before you ask, take whatever you need, and I'll eat last. If it's all gone, I can manage for now. The most important thing at the moment is you."

Sheek gazed at the kill, and his pupils shrunk, not even paying attention to or looking at Sukari. His hearing blocked out her words as his eyes just stared at the meal in awe. Without saying a word, he lunged his teeth straight into it. The taste of fresh meat danced in his mouth and sent him into a feeding frenzy, soon ripping the flesh apart frantically.

Sukari watched half in amusement but couldn't help sympathising with Sheek's desperation. Anthi looked at his mum with his usual big eyes when food dropped. It hadn't been long since Anthi had transitioned onto solid food, yet he knew his manners to let the adult (in all cases up until now, this was just his mum) eat first until given the sign he could start. Sukari waited a short while for Sheek to have the first several mouthfuls before motioning her head towards Anthi, permitting him to start.

Anthi leapt towards the Antelope, claws bared, digging into a soft squishy part his growing teeth would allow. It was still a fresh experience for him to be eating meat and always done so excitingly. Out of the corner of Sheek's eye, he saw Anthi gnawing away at 'his' food. His heartbeat started to hasten, and he couldn't help but let out a few growls under his breath. Anthi dismissed and ignored this as a regular eating routine and sounds that were usually made. His mum made similar sounds, but he was inexperienced to realise that there was a difference.

Sheek's heartbeat started to race, his eyes narrowed significantly and locked onto Anthi with a deep growl now escaping his throat. Anthi again dismissed this, not understanding this as a warning. He took another bite, ripping out a chunk of flesh with a happy chirp in his throat.

It happened so fast; before Sukari could process the warning, Sheek's mind suddenly snapped. He let out a spine-shivering snarling roar and lunged towards Anthi, his teeth sinking into the side of Anthi's cheek. Anthi let out a terrified yelp and tried to pull away.

Sukari gasped in disbelief at what had just happened! Her motherly instincts immediately took over her mind. Regardless of her love towards Sheek, nothing taints her protection towards her son. She let out a fierce roar before giving Sheek a brutal swipe with her paw across the side of his head, purposely going for the mane not to cause a potentially fatal blow. It would be a lot more severe attack if she had to do it a second time!

Sheek flicked his head away from Anthi and towards Sukari, snarling at her with soulless eyes. However, this didn't faze her, and she returned the stare.

"WHAT DO YOU THINK YOU ARE DOING!" she roared.

Sheek didn't reply. He just continued his glare back at her, his pupils just two small empty dots and his muzzle dripping with blood, either from the meat or from Anthi, she didn't know. She didn't want to.

Anthi raced around the carcass and wrapped himself around Sukari's hind leg with a whimper. Sukari kept her threatening glare, never breaking eye contact and never showing any form of submission. Sheek's body is weak but still well-equipped to deal damage. However, a mother's will is impossible to deter, and she would do anything to protect her cub. She could feel Anthi wriggle underneath her as he let out sounds of distress. This, in turn, just fuelled her anger towards Sheek.

The tense standoff lasted a few moments, which felt like several. Sheek's breathing slowly started to shallow back to normal as his eyes gradually widened again. He was the first to break eye contact with Sukari, giving her an indication of his submission. However, Sheek had also broken eye contact because of looking down at Anthi, who was terrified and shaking. He, in turn, looked back at Sheek from the corner of his sad glistening eyes with one of his paws still wrapped tightly around Sukari's hind leg. The expression of betrayal after being hurt by his very own father was unmistakable on Anthi. Sheek's eyes started to swell as it was like looking into a mirror of his past; he took a tender step towards them both.

“I'm sorry... I... don't know what came over...” he tried to explain.

“Get back! Stay away!” Sukari growled deeply, her nostrils flared and her ears flattened. She sprung into a tense crouched position while shielding Anthi, ready to pounce if needed. Her pelt stood on end, her whole body fluffing up to look as big as possible while adrenalin rushed through her body. “I don't know what you've been through or what's going on in that mind of yours, but *don't - you - dare - ever* - harm MY SON!” She thundered.

Sheek blinked, expelling the tears that had built up around his eyes. “*My son*” echoed in his mind, like he now had no relation to Anthi any more. After her strong words, he couldn’t find any to say himself. He took a couple of steps back and walked towards the cave's exit with his head hung low and tail dragging along the ground.

He stopped at the exit and glanced back behind him to the two of them, seeing Sukari calmly tend to the bite, gently licking the small wound clear of blood and making sure it was clean. She shifted her head away from the wound and towards the top of his head, giving him some needed comfort with more licks and humming her lullaby. Anthi had closed his eyes, resting his head on her paw while his tears soaked into her fur. Sukari paused momentarily and glanced up at Sheek with a scowl of disgust, which he returned with a full expression of guilt. He then turned and left.

It had only been a short while since their reunion, and he felt he had ripped it all apart in a blink of an eye. He slunk his way over to the Baobab tree and lay down in the shade. He still was hungry and weak as he didn't eat much, but this was now the least of his worries. He felt as if he had just lost the two most important companions of his life... again.

His closest companion was now that of guilt. It consumed his mind once more. He couldn't control what he had done to Anthi, and he didn't want to ever have that situation happen again. How could he even begin to apologise and convince them it won't happen again? Though how could he even convince that himself? What if this was all now out of his control? He needed to keep a little distance from them for a while as he processed his thoughts. Even though his family was only a short distance away, he had never felt so alone in his mind.

He closed his eyes, knowing this wasn't the first time his actions had caused pain for others. He started to recite his memories as his only company, processing his life and choices from years past.

He took himself back to the time when he was under the command of Legacy.

11. 'The Group'

"I've made my father proud once again. These wanderers are finally being put to effective use!"

Sheek then set out once again, stalking the lands for more of them. The last group he handed over consisted of two male lions, two lionesses and two new parents who he said would help find their daughter. On route to Legacy, he also picked up another lion. He didn't know much about what he looked like as the lion was covered in mud and stunk terribly of dung. Because of this, he kept his distance, not paying much attention to him. He seemed a bit of an odd one.

It didn't matter to Sheek anyway. He didn't care about what fate lay for them all, as that wasn't his job. All he cared about was proving to his dad that he was a good and faithful son, dedicated to his father's cause. If he couldn't have the love and companionship of Sukari who deserted him, then at least he could get acceptance and appreciation from his dad, making him proud.

He patrolled across the vast lands, keeping

his eyes, ears, and nose constantly on full alert, ready for his next target. After a few days, his first one came into view, a little cub alone. He hadn't scented any nearby markings for a territory boundary, so this cub was a wanderer. There were two scenarios: either the parents were nearby, making a good head start in his new 'group', or the cub was lost or abandoned and somehow miraculously survived. A third scenario suddenly popped into his mind, was this the missing cub of the parents he recently handed in?

He put on his friendly face and slowly approached the unaware cub from behind. As he got closer, he could gradually hear her quiet sob and bore a familiar smell from two of the previous lions. His third scenario soon felt more the case.

"Hey, little one? Are you OK?" he said, concerned yet cheery.

The cub turned, staring at him unafraid and unstartled. It was like she had given up on all hope and knew her days were limited without the protection of her parents.

Sheek started to make small talk for comfort, she told him her name, 'Jenna'. She explained she had lost her parents. She gave him a complete description of what they looked like, and he knew then it was her parents for sure that he had handed over to Legacy.

He promised her that he would try his best to reunite her with them. In his mind, he wasn't lying *completely*. He *would* reunite her with them, just not in the way she assumed.

The little cub embraced him, wrapping her little paws around his leg tight with glistening eyes and a tear of relief. Sheek lay his paw on her head and gave it a playful fluff. A sense of responsibility and being wanted, flickered inside of him. He needed to dismiss these feelings for a more significant reason. This was the start of his next 'group'.

As they both travelled, it wasn't long before more wanderers joined. An adolescent lion 'Mino' plus an adult lion 'Aramile' and his adopted daughter 'Safila.' During these travels and part of his disguise, he 'bonded' with them all. However, as more time passed, the more this 'bond' started to feel genuine. Sheek fought a continuous pain in the back of his head, and it felt like a thorn was constantly pressing into his skull, that of guilt. This group felt different.

It came to the stage where Sheek had now led them to his 'safe haven'. It was a place 'away' from Legacy where they could all live their lives in peace. Jenna and Safila were getting a little bigger, Mino's mane was starting to form, and Aramile was now a true past-mature adult.

Then came the time when everything changed. Having a lazy day under the shade of the Baobab tree, he debated in his mind the right time to tell the group that he had 'spotted' Legacy and initiate the final phase of his plan.

Suddenly a breeze passed over the summit of

the hill. The scent that was carried, hit him like a rock had just been thrown at his face. He peered over the hill's summit. To his complete shock and amazement, his eyes laid upon Sukari. She stood at the bottom, looking back at him with the same shocked response. She was with his uncle, Pulsar, who he hadn't seen since he was a cub.

They hadn't seen each other for years since she had run away. He was overwhelmed with joy but this soon conflicted with emotions of upset and anger. He had one question, why did she do it?

After their heartfelt reunion and exchanging their accounts of what happened, it soon became known that Sukari hadn't run away from him intentionally. She was ordered to be killed by her father, made by none other than Legacy. Sukari's father luckily decided to let her live but to run far away and never look back. He even ran with her for a bit for a final goodbye. After this information, Sheek realised that he had been lied to and manipulated by Legacy, and soon it all made sense.

As Sheek and Sukari grew up, their friendship turned into a kindling love, their instincts soon igniting it into a full flame. They knew their lives would soon fully become entwined, unfortunately so did Legacy. He knew this would interfere with what he had planned for Sheek, Sukari would only get in the way.

The night she had vanished, Sheek was told by Legacy that he spotted her with a wanderer and even took him to Sukari's pride's territory. When

Legacy stated his presence with a roar, Sheek saw the black silhouette of Sukari. This was noticeable by her incredibly unique fringe, and she was running off into the night with a male lion. He couldn’t figure out who the male lion was as all-male lion silhouettes look similar, but by this point, he was too upset and confused to even care. Sheek, now in a deep state of upset, shock, depression, and heartbreak, turned to his father for his only comfort. His frail mind could directly be easily moulded and influenced to his father's will and do his bidding. Sheek quickly developed bitter hate for these ‘wanderers,’ as one of them had taken Sukari’s heart from his own. Legacy’s plan that night had fitted into place perfectly.

Sheek and Sukari were now together again though. Now realising Legacy's scheme all along, he wanted nothing to do with his plans. He had been deceived all along. He wanted to stay right here, with the group and his den. He wanted to start living a fresh new life with Sukari again while keeping a *now* truthful promise to the others to keep them safe and protected. Because of this, he felt it respectful to come clean with the entire group that Legacy is his father. He didn't tell them what his intentions used to be. He wanted to put that past far behind him. The only time he ever wanted to see Legacy again was when either one of them would die.

The following night, while taking a private walk, Pulsar explained to Sheek that he left Legacy's pride as he disagreed with his ideals as well. He was trying to track down an old friend who had an annoyingly great ability to keep himself hidden in plain sight. He was one of the best-skilled fighters Pulsar knew to start a rebellion against Legacy.

Sheek too, confided in Pulsar, telling him of his original task that Legacy had set him and how he had abandoned it. Pulsar had to break the unwelcome truth that he needed to continue his mission. Legacy needed to believe he was still winning and in power over him. Sheek being gone for so long will only anger and make Legacy suspicious of betrayal, which would have disastrous consequences. Pulsar insisted on the greater good; Sheek had to hand them in as his original plan. That way, they would at least have a chance at staying alive. They then would hopefully be freed if Pulsar's plan worked.

Sheek, blinded by his love of the group and the slight uncertainty of Pulsar's plan, disagreed with this. He suggested he just lead the group and run further away to safety. Their strong contrasting opinions on each matter soon turned into an argument. Pulsar stormed off, unknown at the time, never seeing Sheek or the group again.

Time passed over the group, and they all continued to get closer, though disheartened by Pulsar's leaving. Sheek still had ignored his advice and watched proudly as Jenna grew up to adolescence. The upset of her missing parents had faded, and she learned to have a new adoptive 'mum and dad'. Sheek and Sukari had, over time, turned into her unofficial parents. Watching Jenna and Safila grow up, play, and interact with each other. When either one of them didn't want to play, they kept themselves occupied by their favourite rock in the cave. They pawed and clawed it like a ball. It was plain adorable! All these cub antics and cuteness lit a flame that one day, Sheek and Sukari would want to be parents of their very own cubs.

Sheek knew he had gone against his father's orders and Pulsar's advice, he knew what would happen if Legacy tracked them down, but he had always pushed this to the back of his mind and locked it away. He just wanted to live a life of his own with Sukari and give these wanderers a taste of a comfortable life, giving himself redemption for the others that he had betrayed. Though deep down, he knew it may not last forever.

As the group lived their lives, they soon came across more lions. Desmani, with his baby brother Anmani and a wondering orphan Kisima, entered their lives. Also, to Sheek and Sukari's amazement, an old friend had found them too, Tefnut!

They both had great admiration for her. She was, in straightforward terms, not a natural animal. She was a hybrid species of lion and leopard. While growing up, Sheek learned that Legacy attempted to create a strong and pure-powered lion with a leopard's speed and agility. She had inherited the speed and agility, just not the strength.

Legacy was patient in letting her grow up in

the neighbouring pride where Sukari resided. Sheek would visit Sukari and Tefnut regularly, and they all had become best friends. Legacy waited until Tefnut's adolescent age to see if anything changed as she grew. The only thing that did was her instincts of being solitary and her own boss. What use is that to Legacy? He needed a strong warrior with both species' advantages - to work as a team within the pride and follow orders. To him, she was a failed experiment. Tefnut soon found peace in her solitude while occasionally secretly saying 'hi' to her friends from time to time. When she found Sheek and Sukari missing from their prides, she set out to find them to see if they were OK.

The three of them felt like it was the good old times once again being together, so Tefnut decided to stick around for a bit, until her nature's calling again, of course.

Meanwhile, Desmani and Mino started to form a strong bond. They shared similar traits in their personalities and got on well. Their bond grew into a brotherhood, always looking out for one another, training and sparring with each other for experience in attack and self-defence. This was the golden age of the whole group. Regardless of the ever-looming fear of Legacy constantly feeling nearer, it made the group feel closer and almost felt like a lion pride. However, with every golden age, darkness eventually rears its head.

Desmani and Mino had vanished, leaving the

group behind. Sheek set out on a long patrol to try and find them, concerned for their wellbeing. After a couple of days of tracking the lands, Sheek found their corpses, slashed several times with Legacy soon appearing from the grass, lying in wait.

Legacy explained how these two overconfident lions thought they could defeat him two against one. They told Legacy that it was a favour for Sheek, Sukari and the group for the better life they were given because of them. They wanted Legacy gone for good, so things would stay how they were. Legacy made quick work of killing them both, leaving them to rot while waiting patiently for Sheek to track down and find them.

He gave Sheek an ultimatum, return and bring back the group Sheek had made. He promised to not harm any of them if they agreed to be part of his pride. Mainly out of respect, other male lions would not touch Sukari if Sheek kept to his duties. Legacy would 'forgive' Sheek for being blind and stupid and class this as a little mistake he would never dare try again. They would then start again afresh.

Of course, if Sheek turned down this offer, everyone would be eventually hunted and slaughtered anyway. Legacy just preferred the easier way. Sheek knew he didn't have a choice. Legacy's presence reminded him there was no escaping his duties, and he had to go back, finishing what he was instructed to do from the start. It was the only way for no more lives to be taken away.

Sheek suddenly opened his eyes and came out of his thoughts. He still lay under the Baobab tree, glancing over towards the cave where Sukari and Anthi lay. Hearing a slight echo of a whimper escape from the entrance.

Seemingly no matter how hard he tried for a good life; it always turned its back on him.

12. A Cub's Wisdom

Back in the cave, Sukari cradled Anthi while licking his bite mark. When the blood had cleared, she could get a better look at the wound, and it seemed not to be that deep and should heal fine in time. Now the tension had settled down with Sheek out the way; the aftershock of the whole situation shuddered through her. She could not help but let out a little whimper and a tear. It had only been a short while since Sheek and herself were reunited, and harm had reared its head already. It felt like a consistent curse that always loomed over her life and anyone involved.

In a moment of thought, she tried to piece together what happened and why.

Sheek was starving, on death's edge, and he was desperate. So, interfering with his meal could have made him uneasy, but that was why she let him take the first few bites before allowing Anthi to eat. However, since he had not adequately bonded with Anthi yet, did something deep inside him see Anthi eating, threatening to his meal? It seemed Sheek had been through a lot, maybe too much for his mind to manage? After all, everyone has their breaking point, and the kind-natured personality he usually possessed could have altered or even perished.

However, a light slap or even a warning snap would have been somewhat of an acceptable action for Sheek to take. But for him to bite was too concerning. Had the Sheek she remembered gone?

A tear ran down her cheek during her thoughts. Anthi had also started to calm down, he felt her tear hit his ear, which he flicked away. He then looked up at her.

"Mum, if these father things are lions that are mean and bite their cubs, then I don't want one," he said plainly. Sukari looked down at him and then squeezed him tight.

"Anthi..." she spoke softly, pressing her head against his. "I'm sure he's just confused, we'll give him some space, and then I'll go and talk to him," she reassured, although not being too sure herself. Sheek may be alive, but could his spirit be saved? "Fathers are meant to be like me, but the male kind. They, like me, will play with you, bathe you, help you hunt and teach you to fight. They also love their cubs unconditionally and will do anything to protect them."

Anthi raised his brow.

"Sheek doesn't seem to be like any of those things though," he said, confused. Another tear dropped down Sukari's cheek and gave him another squeeze.

"I know Anthi... I know. I'm sorry I noticed too late. I was blinded by how I used to remember him," she said, disheartened, then continued to lick Anthi's tuft of hair for comfort.

Anthi lowered his head while Sukari did so, which diverted his attention to the wounds on her neck. These were the claw marks that Anthi gave her by accident yesterday. His heart sank with guilt, regardless of what Sheek explained to him last night.

"Mum, I'm sorry about your neck, I didn't mean to... it was an accident, the log pushed me and-" he croaked.

"Anthi Anthi..." she hushed and placed her paw over his head. "Don't worry about it. Yes, I may have roared, but everyone does when they feel pain. It's just a natural reaction. I'm not angry at you for it. You were trying to hold on," she reassured.

"But you're my mum, and I should've never hurt you."

"It was your natural reaction to hold on and survive, even if it meant harming the one you love. I would've been upset if you didn't try to hold on. So please, don't worry about it, OK?" She reassured gently but firmly.

Anthi's faint smile returned by his mum's words. Sheek practically said the same thing last night, this showed that Sheek and Sukari shared their wisdom as a couple. Anthi stood up on his hind legs and placed his paws gently near Sukari's neck to stabilise him. He then gave her wounds little licks, mirroring what Sukari had done to his own. Sukari's throat began to rumble, and Anthi let off little chirps in return. A completely warm wide smile spread across her muzzle, proud to have such a thoughtful and caring son. Once again, their bond shone brightly.

"Anyway *you*, seems like *someone* is growing up, huh? You've started to bathe yourself, by the looks of things. You're exceptionally clean for a lost cub in the rainy season. I'd expect you to be covered in mud?" she teased.

"*Hilarious* Mum, I get it. I'm filthy, though I think I have a good excuse, huh?" Anthi Chuckled in response, to which Sukari then raised a brow, confused.

"No really, Anthi, your face and sides are clean. They were clean when I found you with Sheek this morning."

Anthi noticed the genuine confusion on her face, returning the confused expression by raising his brow too. He turned his head to the side of his body, now only noticing his pelt was indeed mud-free and his usual colour.

"Well, that's weird because I definitely remember being covered in mud before I slept last night, though I did sleep next to Sheek. Then I had a weird dream of... being licked-" Anthi paused. "Oohhhh," he said as his eyes lit up.

"Anthi... are you saying that-" Sukari pondered.

"Uhuh!" he interrupts her with an added grin.

Anthi jumped out of Sukari's embrace and padded over to the antelope, tearing off a large chunk of meat from it before walking towards the cave's exit.

"Anthi, what are you doing?" Concerned, she leapt up and blocked his path. She briskly pawed the meat away from Anthi's mouth.

"You said one thing a father does is bathe his son. Sheek must have bathed me last night! All that other good stuff of a father is in there somewhere, just trying to get out. I'm sure of it!" Anthi assured confidently.

"I understand *that*. It's overly sweet of him to do so and sweet of you to think that about him, but he *did bite you*, remember? We cannot trust him straight away after what he's done."

"But Mum, as you said, I hurt *you* by accident by trying to survive. Sheek was starving, and he *could* have hurt me by accident in the same way, by trying to survive!"

Sukari tried to respond, but she couldn't. Her words just blocked in her throat. Anthi, however, said such wise words, especially for his age. Sukari smiled faintly and looked at him with a sense of awe.

"Anthi... you may be right, and I'm proud of you for that. Still, be careful, though. I'll be watching from a distance. The moment you feel threatened, turn away and let me handle it, OK?"

Anthi nodded and grinned, picking the meat back up into his mouth. He then padded out of the cave with a slightly amusing waddle in his step from the meat's weight. Sukari followed with a gained smile before stopping after a few paces outside, closely watching Anthi happily waddling towards the baobab tree in the near distance.

Anthi slowed his pace down as he approached Sheek, who was lying down facing away from him. Sheek's ears perked up as Anthi slowly edged closer. He turned his head around slowly and gazed at Anthi, who had the meat hanging from his mouth. He immediately noticed the wound he had caused on his cheek, and his eyes displayed immediate guilt.

“Please, Anthi, please don't come any closer with that. I cannot guarantee that what I have done may not happen again, and I've made too many wrong decisions to know any more.”

Anthi smiled and rolled his eyes before taking a few more paces forward. Sheek retreated his head out of hesitancy. Anthi then dropped the meat so he could speak clearly.

“Thanks for saving me from the river. Thanks for carrying me when I was weak. Thanks for looking after me, and thanks for helping me find my mum.” he said friendly yet sincere. Sheek turned his head slightly away and huffed, interrupting Anthi's words.

“But we both know that was just influenced by food. I didn't even know who you were until this morning. It *means nothing!*” he said ending with a snarl, and still not wanting to keep eye contact.

“Oh, thanks for the bath last night...” Anthi

smirked. Sheek suddenly turned his head towards him. His eyes widened with a hint of embarrassment while Anthi let out a small chuckle. "I don't think it was *all* about food, Sheek. Deep down, I think you did what felt right in your heart without you knowing." Anthi then plopped down, giving Sheek a confident yet heartfelt gaze. "You were being thoughtful and caring and stuff, though still maybe a little rough around the edges, heh!" Anthi chuckled as he bum-shuffled a little closer. "Then me laying by your side, that must have set something off inside you. That 'father' instinct thing came out, and just like my mum does, you bathed me."

Anthi cautiously picked up the meat again, motioning downwards with his eyes for Sheek to take it.

The sight of the meat in Anthi's mouth triggered Sheek's inner instincts once more. The pupils in his eyes shrank, his brow hardened, his muzzle twitched, and a low tremor of a growl vibrated in his throat. Anthi instantly became nervous, taking half a step back, ready to drop it and run, fearing the previous event would repeat itself. He looked into his threatening eyes, trying to see past them and into the lost soul that may still lay inside. Against his mum's advice, he took a chance. He squinted his eyes shut, pushed his muzzle out further towards Sheek, and took a deep breath. "My instinct... thingy, tells me that I... I trust you," he said through his clenched teeth.

Anthi's whiskers felt the air being pushed from a grunted exhale coming from Sheek as he hovered his head closer. His heart started to race as another tremor came from Sheek's throat with a strong huff of air, making the hairs on Anthi's face stand on end and his whiskers flick back. With the long croaking growl changing pitch, he could 'hear' Sheek's jaws opening wide. In a split moment, his jaws could lunge forward and around Anthi's head like last time. Anthi shivered from the fresh memory of that happening and the emotional and physical pain of his father's teeth sinking into his cheek. Instead, he felt something different happen. He felt the tension of the meat being tugged from his teeth. He opened his mouth slightly and let it be taken, surprisingly gently. The growls then soon subsided.

He squinted his eyes open to see Sheek's own eyes right in front of him, but his pupils were now back to normal with an expression of compassion with the meat now dangling from his muzzle. Sheek retreated his head and took a step back, and he quickly flicked the meat into his mouth. After a couple of quick chews and a swallow, it was gone. It was only half the size of Anthi, a small helping of food for a fully grown Adult. However, the gesture of trust meant so much more to him.

"I guess we can learn together how to make you better, huh?" Anthi said curiously, tilting his head and a flick from his ear.

Sheek's brows softened, and his eyes started to shine. He slumped and sat back down, releasing the tension stored in his body.

"Ever since I knew I was going to be a father, I vowed to myself I would do anything to keep you and your mum safe, and I couldn't even do that." he croaked and lowered his head. Anthi then took a step towards him.

"But Mum *is safe*. I don't know what happened to you when I was growing up, but whatever you did do, it kept mum alive, and *I am alive*. That bite from earlier was an accident, and we all have accidents, like when I told you about me hurting mum. Plus, you were just cranky from not eating properly for so long, I'm sure, ha!"

Sheek looked back up with a raised brow and couldn't help but crack a smile at Anthi's little remark with a lightened huff. However, with his self-esteem still unstable, he soon let out a slight sigh.

"I just want to be the father I always imagined myself to be. I want to-"

"Sheek!" Anthi interrupted, softly lowering his head and scrunching his nose. His eyes widened and started to glisten. "I know you will be because I... I wanna be your son."

Sheek's eyes immediately started to fill up, tears quickly escaping and rolling down his cheek. He sat up, shifting his weight onto his rump before reaching out.

Anthi leapt between Sheek's open paws, wrapping his paws around Sheek's chest as far as his little legs would allow, embracing him tightly.

His ears pressed against Sheek's chest; they absorbed the sound of his racing heartbeat. As fast as it was, it was still soothing. Their embrace continued for a short while, letting silence speak for both of their now loss of words.

Sheek then loosened his embrace slightly to expose Anthi's head and gave the tuft of his hair a big, long lick.

"I missed a bit of cleaning," -he then lapped his tongue over one of Anthi's ears- "and another" - he then licked his other ear- "And another." he chuckled.

"Faaaaather stop iiiit!" Anthi laughed. "Great, my father all along deep down is all mushy 'n' stuff... pfft. That bite was nothing *really*, now I know why," he said sarcastically, then wriggled free from Sheek's loosened embrace. He then leapt up to the side of his head, grabbing his ear with his muzzle. "I'll show you how to do it right!" He chuckled and started pulling it. Sheek then let out a playful growl.

"Ahhhh, the paaaaain, the aaagony!" he wailed playfully, leaning then flopping onto his back. This forced Anthi to let go and land on the ground. Sheek quickly grabbed him by the nape of his neck and dragged him over his stomach.

"Nonono no" Anthi giggled.

Sheek then pressed his paws over him.

"Aha, but now the lion has captured the cub, and is unable to break free!" he continued playing along but purposely kept his grip loosened. Anthi laughing, wriggled himself free again, then jumped onto the upper part of Sheek's chest, pressing his paws on him.

"Now the cub has pinned the almighty lion! Haha!"

They both laughed and chuckled together as they continued their play fight, jumping over each other and trying to grab each other's neck. Soon they started to run around the Baobab tree, each changing their direction, trying to trick each other. The play fight ended with Anthi latching onto Sheek's tail which, in turn, he pretended to stumble and fall on the ground. Anthi then climbed onto Sheek's back and pounced onto the top of his head, hovering his head over the top so he could see Sheek's face. "Looks like I found another lost piece of my father, huh?" Anthi said, upbeat, regaining his breath from the play fight. "Though saying 'father' now takes like... twice as long as 'Sheek,' plus it sounds a bit booooring." he teased with a grin.

Sheek looked up at Anthi and smiled warmly. Gently reaching up with his paw and placing it over Anthi's head, fluffing up his tuft of hair.

"Well then, how about calling me 'Dad'."

Sukari observed from a distance as Anthi and Sheek spoke to each other. Her legs were tensed, ready to sprint if the situation turned sour, especially seeing Anthi Bravely (almost stupidly) reach out to Sheek with the meat in his mouth. However, as soon as Anthi and Sheek shared an embrace, her heart immediately melted. She then watched in awe as the two continued to play fight with one another. Tears ran down her cheek while sniffing a gentle sob of happiness and contentment. She realised how much she underestimated Anthi. Though the personality of a cub, he had the heart of a deeply thoughtful and wise lion for his age. She knew him growing up hadn't been easy. He had so far lived a very sheltered cubhood. There were no other cubs his age to play and learn social skills with, and no older male role model to look up to. She tried as much as she could filling in these roles, but as a team of only two trying to survive in these lands, Anthi still had to learn to grow up very quickly. Maybe now there was hope? Perhaps now, Anthi and Sheek could help each other and regain what was lost inside each of them.

Sukari loosened her tense stature, slumping down on the welcoming cool, dry yet fresh grass. Soaking up the warmth from the surprising gift of a sunny day in the middle of this wet season, felt like a blessing. She absorbed the calm and happy atmosphere as she watched her partner and their son goof around. Today was about the three of them and their new beginnings as a family, once broken but now reborn. She felt her search was almost complete. Though one last major concern lingered in her mind, for this one day it didn't exist. Today was about the three of them, being as one.

13. The Calm Before The Storm

The sun slowly travelled its course across the sky, during which Sukari had been basking in the generous warmth it gave. She now lay atop the large rocks above their cave, laying on her back with her legs stretched out. Inside the cave lay Sheek and Anthi, both chewing away at the kill from earlier, now eating side by side. Sheek had ripped a large chunk off for Anthi, which he happily nibbled away on, while Sheek focused on the main bulk of the carcass. In time, the antelope slowly disappeared with only the bones remaining and polished clean.

By this time, Anthi had already finished his share and leaning on Sheek's side, resting his eyes and full tummy after such a meal. Sheek had intentionally left a final chunk for Sukari, not regarding what she said earlier. He still wanted to leave at least a snack for her. His now distended stomach displayed a satisfied large meal. He rolled over onto his back to take the pressure off his belly, causing Anthi to slide onto the ground. Anthi, now disrupted, opened his eyes to be met by the skeleton of the once Antelope.

"*Woah!*" he chuckled, "I can't wait until I'm all grown up and can eat so much!" he teased.

Sheek let out a lightened huff at Anthi's remark and started to lick his paws clean of blood, doing so with a smug and proud look on his face. He had every right to be, being a lion in his condition. Anthi turned to Sheek and poked his stomach lightly, teasing him. "But not as greedy as you, ha!" he mocked. Sheek turned and raised his brow with a smile.

"Oh *really*," he replied in the same tone, letting out a soft, playful growl. "Well, *maybe* this *greedy* lion is still hungry, huh? *Maybe* I didn't eat you last night to save you fresh for today." he continued as he licked his muzzle with a playful smirk. His eyes widened, and he gazed at Anthi, who grinned unconfidently and stepped back.

"No, Dad, no!" he giggled nervously. Sheek lunged his head forward as Anthi tried to dodge him. He then wrapped his paws around him, nibbling his ears and the nape of his neck. Anthi's giggle now turned full belly laughter, begging his dad to stop while trying to wriggle free from his playful grasp. "Noooo!" he laughed as Sheek continued nibbling, making lively 'nomming' sounds.

Their playful scuffle was soon interrupted by Sukari, who had walked in. She cleared her throat to get their attention with a raised brow, but not without a warm, amused smile.

"Gee, you males are all the same, food-food-food," she said while rolling her eyes.

"Well, *this* male has at least saved you some." Sheek motioned to the chunk of meat laying nearby, separated from the Skeleton and ready to eat with ease. Sukari's expression then softened.

"...are you sure?"

"Of course, he's sure. I mean, look at him!" Anthi butted in, poking Sheek's stomach again. Sukari turned her attention to it, showing an expression of amusement yet sincere relief that Sheek had eaten well. She then glanced back at Anthi.

"Now-now Anthi, leave your poor Dad alone, go and torment something outside," she chuckled and motioned him to move on, pushing his rump with her muzzle.

"Hehe, OK OK Mum, sorry!" he replied with a cheeky giggle before padding outside.

Sukari Lay down by the meat and looked at Sheek, who in turn smiled and nodded, signalling for her to eat it. She wasn't going to lie to herself that she was glad there was some meat left, though her priority was still him. If there would've been nothing left, another hunt for a small prey wouldn't have been much trouble. She dug into the meat with her wide-open jaws and began to chew away at it. Her head lowered towards the ground, but just in the corner of her vision, she could see Sheek looking at her with a cute faint smile on his muzzle.

It was a genuine one of peace and contentment.

Her unanswered questions about Sheek's survival and injuries still plagued her mind as she ate. She didn't want to bug him again about them. They could potentially wait until tonight when Anthi was asleep. However, after all the excitement and drama of today, she wouldn't be too sure if she didn't fall asleep before Anthi! She couldn't wait until the night after. She needed answers to put her mind at peace. She picked up the courage to ask while she ate in silence. Then when it came to the last bite, she swallowed hard and looked up at him.

"I'm sorry to ask again, but while Anthi is occupied..." Sukari glanced over to the cave entrance, seeing Anthi outside and out of earshot, entertaining himself by pouncing and clawing an old branch. She couldn't help but crack a faint smile, though it soon flattened as she turned back around. "But what happened? It's eating away inside me. I can't wait until tonight to..." she started to croak before Sheek interrupted with a soothing hush. He motioned her to come over. She stood up and walked around the Skeleton of the antelope. It sunk in further how hungry he had been. She snuggled up beside him, feeling the warmth and comfort of his body like she remembered. However, being able to feel his ribs press into her felt strange. She then lay her head on Sheek's paws.

"My memory was a bit hazy during those times, but I'll explain everything I possibly can," he softly spoke while giving her a gentle head rub with his muzzle. "Well, until Anthi gets bored and decides to torment me again," he huffed light-heartedly. Sukari chuckled in reply.

Sheek began telling Sukari his timeline of events to the best of his memory. He started from when he first re-opened his eyes and took his first desperate lifesaving breath, to his continued struggle of improving a little more day by day. Then he went on to say that after a week passed, he'd gotten to the point of feeling hopeful for his future, optimistic that he could soon start to track her and the group down. Then all this improvement got wiped out in the blink of an eye, by a loyal follower of Legacy, the one who savagely attacked him.

"He told me that he killed you, Sukari... so also killing Anthi. This was not before brutally attacking me, giving me this nose injury, and I'm now unable to smell anything. He said he wanted me to suffer alone and hungry with the guilt of your 'death' because of the actions of my own," his voice trembled.

Sukari felt a tear drop onto her. Sheek continued his story, mentioning he was ready for his life to end. However, a chance moment gave him one last push to survive by raiding an African wild dog's burrow, eating the pups for food. In Sukari's mind, this echoed the situation of her having to eat a newborn zebra to keep her and Anthi alive.

Her ear perked up, remembering her first night leaving the group, finding an abandoned burrow she used as shelter. Could this have been the same burrow that Sheek raided, causing it to be left empty? She knew there were several, if not hundreds of burrows in these lands, so she decided not to complicate things and keep quiet. However, deep in her heart, she felt it was the same burrow. It was like Sheek helped them both without either knowing.

Time passed as Sukari listened to Sheek's events while exchanging affectionate licks, her eyes glistening with tears. Sheek struggled to keep himself composed throughout. This included when he wouldn't let a lost cub stay in his cave for the night, and then found it dead the following morning.

"When I found the lifeless cub, I felt... no emotional pain. All I felt was a debt to save a life. Time passed, and I came across that fluff ball in the river," Sheek smiled faintly and motioned to Anthi outside. "I promised to shelter him for one night like I would have done with that other cub. Furthermore, he persuaded me to help him find you with the deal of food," Sheek ended with a chuckle.

"Regardless of you being starving, that sounds like an offer my Sheek wouldn't reject! Ha!" she scoffed.

"Oi!" he protested, giving her a firm playful nudge.

His expression soon lowered. "But I can't help but think, if it weren't for that cub's death, could my actions for helping Anthi not of existed? Or would I still have helped him? If I didn't, it could've been the death of my own son, and we may never have met, and if we did meet and we both figured out Anthi's fate, I would never... ever... been able to forgive myself!" He then sighed deeply and lowered his head and away from Sukari. "Sorry, I'm just thinking out loud." Sukari then lifted her head, giving him a reassuring lick on the cheek.

"You didn't know that this cub was Anthi, as far as you knew, Anthi didn't exist. All that matters are the events that did happen that got us to where we are. There is no point in thinking about what could have happened because it didn't. Some choices in life are just an illusion of the inevitable." she started to say, breaking up, realising her own words. Sheek let out a soft sigh in agreement.

"I guess."

Sukari rolled onto her back. She then wrapped her paws around Sheek's neck, pulling his head back towards her before giving him the tightest embrace she could offer.

"No one... no one should ever have to endure the life and decisions you have been through. I'm just sorry for leaving..." She couldn't continue and started to cry softly; the sound muffled by Sheek's mane. Sheek held her tighter and nuzzled her, knowing what she was about to say.

"Don't you dare say you are sorry for not coming back for me. You had nothing to be sorry for. As far as you knew, I was dead. Just like me not knowing Anthi existed, what happened, happened. All that matters is right here, right now, all these events got us to where we are... together again."

Sukari leaned her head out and gazed into Sheek's eyes with her tear-filled own.

"I missed you..." she sniffed. Sheek returned an affectionate gaze.

"I missed you too..."

They both quickly buried their heads into one another, their inevitable sobbing that followed being muffled by each other's fur. They both had carried so much compressed emotion the moment they found each other again, it was just a matter of time until it was released.

After a short while, they calmed down and their breathing settled. They proceeded to enjoy the near silence while in their embrace, the only sounds were short tender huffs from their throats 'speaking' of their affection for one another.

After a while, Sukari completely broke the silence with her own story.

"It's strange... you encounter a lion that wants to kill me and let you suffer. While I encountered a lion that saved me." she pondered. Sheek raised a brow in reply.

"What do you mean? What happened?"

Sukari shifted her head onto Sheek's paw, and he lowered her head down onto the ground. She then began to tell him her story that happened a couple of months after Sheek's 'death'. The group had kept on moving from place to place to try and avoid any of Legacy's scouts.

"I was now becoming overwhelmed with the weight of my pregnancy, both physically and mentally. I could feel our little furball was due at any time, and my energy was running low. While we were walking, I started to fall behind without the group noticing. I didn't try to get their attention as I thought I was just becoming a liability and a burden. I didn't want to annoy them. We were all getting tired that night. Soon enough, they disappeared over a hill while I still dragged behind, and then that's when something unexpected happened."

Sukari then explained that suddenly, out of nowhere, she heard a growl in the darkness near her side. A lion then leapt out straight towards her in a split second, she didn't have time to react, but she didn't need to. Instead, this lion flew straight overhead and landed his jaws and claws on another lion that had stalked her upwind. The stalking lion was killed instantly and silently. She was shocked and amazed at this lion's combat and ability to attack and kill with such ease, and it questionably echoed the capabilities of Legacy. His combat skills were certainly far superior compared to his appearance, he was covered in a wide variety of mud and filth, along with the most off-putting of smells.

After that, her memory got a bit hazy due to the shock of the event. She could remember that the lion that saved her knew her by name. However, she had never seen him before. He said she was lucky that he was at the right place at the right time as he had many duties to fulfil. One of which was a promise he made to Pulsar, an old friend. Pulsar had finally managed to find him just before his life ended tragically due to sustaining a snake bite on his travels. He accepted Pulsar's dying wish to try and watch over her and Sheek as much as his schedule would allow. He couldn't be around all the time due to 'complicated matters', but he would endeavour to try his best.

He told her to use a unique call consisting of three roars of different lengths and tones. This he demonstrated to her, so she knew them. He assured her that *if* he were in the area, he would come to her aid if possible but only call him under extreme circumstances. In her mind, she felt like she had a shadowed protector. He soon disappeared after, knowing his roar may have caught the group's attention.

Sukari kept her 'guardian' a secret from the others. She didn't want to freak them out with an unknown lion claiming to be a protector. She felt he was genuine; the group wasn't there when he saved her, so she was concerned they wouldn't understand. A few days later, she gave birth to Anthi, knowing that she would have been severely injured or even dead if it weren't for that lion that night. Sheek's 'death' would all have been in vain.

Sheek lay silent for a moment in thought after Sukari's story. She had a protector, a lion that made a promise to Pulsar to watch over her, Anthi and Sheek. Meanwhile, Sheek had a lion ordered by Legacy to kill Sukari and let him suffer. The timing, however, didn't make sense, as Sukari was still alive and saved just before giving birth to Anthi, long after Sheek was told she was already 'killed.'

Something behind their backs was going on that Sheek just couldn't make sense of. He didn't like the uncertainty. However, knowing it was unhealthy to let it get the better of him, he just had to take it as it was; she had a protector for all three of them while he had a torturer and a vowed killer for them.

"Well, whoever it was, I owe him my thanks and to tell him he has some tough competition if he tries to make a move on you," he teased, lightening the mood and booping Sukari's nose with his own. Sukari rolled her eyes with a smile.

"Well I won't lie, he did give off a certain vibe, not one of him being interested in me, but I felt a sense of calm and comfort." She said half puzzled, before scrunching her nose. "However, no way I was attracted to him. Besides, he looked all scruffy and in a right old state, kinda like you!" she teased as she stood up and circled him with a mischievous grin.

"Oh *really*? It's all coming out now!" he replied sarcastically. He rolled on his side and stretched out, letting his recent meal settle better. Sukari took this vulnerable posture as a welcome invitation, and she promptly turned around and leapt over, pinning him by his shoulders. They both then shared an affectionate stare.

"Unless I fix you up..." she mewed and brushed his cheek with her own.

She lowered her head over Sheek's knotted and matted fringe. She began to wet the hairs of his mane with her naturally rough tongue, so it was also effective in combing it. Sheek closed his eyes with a warm smile radiating from his muzzle. The feeling of this intimacy was long missed, and he mentally felt like his soul was gradually being pieced back together. Sukari knew that a gesture of kindness goes a long way to repairing something broken. She lifted one of her paws from his shoulder. Unsheathing her claws slightly, she ran them through his mane, giving it a more substantial comb to eliminate the more challenging knots. Sheek felt his mane getting pulled and tugged. His brows flickered from her good intentions' slightly uncomfortable yet wholesome feeling. A couple of grunts vibrated through his throat from the more painful knots that ripped through her claws. Sukari then moved her head around the sides of Sheek's mane, licking it and continuing to use her claws. Sheek took this opportunity to give her ear a few playful nibbles while cradling her head with his paw. They both exchanged subtle chuckles and affectionate soft growls. This was a special moment they had yearned and dreamt about ever since being separated. Believing they would never have been able to do this again, it instead had become a reality.

Sukari continued her grooming routine, making her way all around his mane, while Sheek continued using every open opportunity to return a loving lick or nuzzle. They had not spoken to each other the whole time. They let their actions be their words with the tranquil natural sounds from outside as their melodic symphony. The odd growl or squeaky roar from Anthi keeping himself entertained outside added an extra sense of contentment and calm as a family.

Sukari had now come back to where she started at his fringe, giving it one last big lick before brushing her head against his. She released her pin, sat up and admired her extensive grooming work. Sheek rolled back onto his belly and gave his mane a good shake to let his hair settle back into place.

"Yeah, thinking about it, I'll have you," she smiled and tilted her head. Sheek sat up next to her and gave her a tender nuzzle with a chuckle.

"Why thank you..."

Sheek went in for another lick on Sukari. Just as his tongue touched her cheek with her eyes closed and a sweet smile, he froze from hearing another voice...

"Muuum, Daaad, I'm booored now," Anthi whined, padding back into the cave, catching Sheek and Sukari in the moment. "Oh, sorry, mushy stuff... I'll come back," he said sheepishly and went to turn away, his tail close to his rear legs.

"It's OK Anthi, come in." Sheek chuckled.

Without hesitation, Anthi turned back around and sprung towards the two with a bound of energy.

"Wow, Dad, your mane looks awesome!" he said in awe.

"Well, thank your mum for that," he said warmly and turned to her with a caring glance.

Anthi padded around Sheek, looking up at him and his clean smooth mane with the spiked tufts that made it stand out. Anthi then looked up at his own fringe with a smile.

"Now I know where I got it from, haha!" he grinned. His attention then turned to Sheek's still matted tuft of hair at the end of his tail. "Mum, you missed something!" Anthi then pounced onto Sheek's tail, using his little claws to comb his dad's knotted hair. It didn't take too long for him to finish. Sheek then flicked his tail from side to side, giving it chase to Anthi, who had found this very amusing and saved him from boredom. He chased it back and forth with a happy chirp and growl in his throat. With Anthi's attention diverted, Sheek looked back towards Sukari, smiling with his head tilted.

"Now where was I… oh yes…" he whispered, giving Sukari the lick he intended from a moment ago. Sukari brushed her head underneath Sheek's muzzle, letting out a soft affectionate growl. Meanwhile, the sounds of mischievous growls were coming from their cub's tail-chasing antics behind them.

"Love you."

"Love you too."

In the far distance, a faint deep rumble travelled across the afternoon sky, soon diverting their attention. The three took a few steps outside the cave, Sheek's tail proudly being carried in

Anthi's mouth after 'catching his kill'. Anthi's short attention span meant he soon dropped it when he heard another rumble of thunder. He quickly sat by his mum for a little comfort, and she wrapped her tail around him. Sheek used his 'now freed' tail and flicked it around Sukari's own. They then all sat side by side, observing the powerful yet beautiful force of nature in the distance.

This warm sunny day had brought a much-needed break for them, making it a calm, cosy and relaxing atmosphere from the wet season. However, this combination of hot and wet weather meant it would get a substantial retaliation.

A storm was coming...

Unknown to the three, in more ways than they thought.

14. Allies & Betrayal

Later, the day drew to a close, and the night descended, along with one of the worst thunderstorms that these lands have had to endure. The sky lit up regularly with bolts of lightning, pummelling the landscape. The thunder that followed vibrated and crackled through the air. The downpour of rain caused new streams, rivers, and lakes to form and spread across the land.

The entrance to the cave now hosts a cascade of water. However, this made it feel cosy and secluded for the family of three inside. They were all curled up together, using the old bed of grass and leaves that Sukari and Sheek had made. Now with the added addition of Anthi, the bed was finally being used for its intended purpose. The bed effectively trapped heat from their bodies making for a snug and warm sleep regardless of the storm outside. The storm didn't scare Anthi like it used to. He instead found it quite exciting to listen and gaze upon, which posed a problem, he couldn't sleep! Mum and Dad were deep in their slumber. They had seen and heard it all before, so they could tune their ears out of it. But Anthi couldn't, he was still a cub and events like this fed his curiosity and excitement.

Giving up trying to sleep, he gently wriggled out between his parents, trying not to wake them. He didn't want to be trapped in this cave all day tomorrow with groggy parents that hadn't fully recharged. He stepped carefully and silently towards the cave entrance, stopping just before the waterfall. A slight shiver travelled through his spine as the cooler air wrapped around him. He hoped that if he gazed and stared long enough at nature's own epic light and sound display, he would get tired of it. So, he sat down, with his tail swaying side to side along the ground, watching this mighty show. Sometimes he flinched when the lightning came a little too close for comfort, and other times his jaw dropped in amazement as strings of lights danced on the horizon with a more soothing melodic rumble afterwards.

A less charming melodic rumble suddenly came from inside the cave, his dad's snoring! Anthi turned his head and looked at Sheek in amusement, he hadn't heard snoring before, and it almost made him giggle. He placed his paw over his mouth to keep himself quiet just in case. After a couple more snores from Sheek followed by a half-asleep headbutt from Sukari, he repositioned his head, and the snoring stopped. "*Yeah, you show him Mum!*" He thought to himself in amusement.

He then turned back around to the view. Suddenly it lit up with a flash of lightning and a snap from the branches left outside, the sound overpowered by a crack of thunder. Immediately a black silhouette of an enormous lion flashed before his eyes from behind the cascading water. Anthi dropped his jaw in terror. Before he could make any sort of loud noise to alarm his parents, his muzzle was wrapped around with a huge paw and a set of jaws sunk into the nape of his neck. His attempt to roar only came out as a muffled hum, which was also overpowered by the thunder's continued rumbling. He was pulled out through the water in the blink of an eye and vanished. Sheek and Sukari were undisturbed, still cuddled up to each other, asleep in each other's embrace.

A short while passed. The two were still fast asleep and none the wiser of the worst scenario a parent could ever bear for their young.

Suddenly another snap came from a branch outside. A lion burst through the waterfall and into the cave with a strong leap. He was out of breath and panting heavily.

Sukari and Sheek jolted out from their sleep and formed a defensive stance in front of the bed, with both sets of claws bared with menacing snarls. Sukari was about to turn to grab Anthi before being interrupted by the lion calling her name.

"Sukari..." he spoke firmly before hesitating. "Sh... Sheek!"

His body then was illuminated by another flash of distant lightning. Sheek recognised his eyes straight away, burned into his memory from that harrowing day.

"You... YOU!!" Sheek roared and leapt towards him instantly. The other lion had already unsheathed his claws, ready to defend himself. However, Sheek was immediately tackled mid-pounce by the whole weight of Sukari's body, pinning and flattening him to the ground. This took him by complete shock. "SUKARI? WHAT'S YOUR PROBLEM? THIS IS THE LION THAT WRECKED MY LIFE... WANTED ME TO SUFFER! THE VERY LION THAT SAID HE KILLED YOU!" He bellowed while jolting and clawing the ground, trying to break free from Sukari's pin.

Sukari, although now extremely confused, looked back up at the lion just to make sure she wasn't mistaken, and she wasn't. She gave the lion a reassuring nod.

"SHEEK!" She growled, pressing her paws deeper into his shoulders to reassure her actions. "THIS... *this* is the lion that saved my life!"

Sheek's eyes widened in disbelief at Sukari's words. He refused to believe them, and it didn't make sense. How *could* they make sense?

"That's impossible! How could *he* let me rot while promising to keep you safe," he contested, still clawing the ground, trying to break free. Sukari soon shared the same bewilderment.

"SHEEK!" The lion thundered. "We don't have time for this. I will explain everything later, just please... is everyone here? Are you all safe?"

"Safe?... SAFE?! You have some nerve!" Sheek

wheezed in denial, the weight of Sukari now straining his breathing.

Ignoring his remark, the lion quickly scanned his eyes around the cave, his face soon dropping in defeat, and his heart sank.

"Where is... your cub?"

Sukari turned her head, soon letting out a broken gasp.

"Anthi" she called... met with silence. "ANTHI!!"

Sukari leapt up from Sheek and frantically looked in all the nooks and crannies of the cave, including the bed, to make sure he hadn't buried himself underneath. "HE'S GONE!"

Sukari's release on Sheek gave him his opportunity. He took a deep breath and then leapt up, pinning the lion to the ground before extending his claws, and pressing them against the lion's throat. The lion didn't retaliate or even flinch, and it's like he allowed Sheek to do it.

"What have you done with our son!" Sheek demanded, growling and panting heavily from the adrenalin coursing through his veins.

"Sheek! I came here to warn Sukari and yourself of Legacy's movements. This wasn't how my plan was meant to be. I ran as fast as possible to get here, but I wasn't fast enough." The lion said calmly yet elevated. "Sheek, right now, you need to trust me. If not for yourself, then for your cub. Legacy has taken him, and I don't think anything good will happen. If I came here to harm any of you,

I could have snuck in a lot quieter while you still slept, just like Legacy did!" Sheek looked deeply into the eyes of this lion, weighing him up. He did claim a valid point.

"If this is all a trick... I swear... I swear!" Sheek attempted to say dominantly, but his voice started to break up, with his eyes beginning to fill, all while pressing his claws harder against the lion's throat, on the brink of piercing through his skin.

"Sheek, the more we talk, the less chance he stays alive. I promise I will explain, but I need to keep my promise, which means saving him!" the lion said firmly, getting impatient.

"Sheek?" Sukari mewed from behind him. He turned his head and stared into her breaking soul, her ears flat, and her eyes glistening. "If you don't trust him, then please... *please* trust me. This *lion* saved my life, and I trust him with it. If Legacy has our son, we need any help we can get... we have no one else..." Sukari begged, placing her paw on Sheek's shoulder. "*We-need-him..*" her voice trembled.

Sheek turned and stared deep into the lion's eyes. He glanced back at Sukari, whose soul was quickly crumbling apart. Turning back to the lion with a low growl rumbling in his throat in warning, Sheek retreated his pin and took a step back, releasing his grip.

Sheek offered out his paw as a notion of a deal and trust. The lion grabbed it and heaved himself up.

"Thank you... a wise move," he said solemnly before quickly turning around and sprinting towards the cave entrance. "Now, we must go. I know the heading Legacy will take."

Sheek and Sukari both looked at each other. Sukari showed concern for Sheek's still deteriorated stamina and strength. He only had one decent meal and no way near strong enough to confront any lions, let alone Legacy. Sukari saw the fire in his eyes and the determination to go, and there was no point in telling him otherwise. He already sensed her concern and nodded a reply.

"Let's go," she stated confidently, speaking for them both.

The lion leapt out into the torrent of rain from the storm, and Sheek and Sukari closely followed. All three ran to the Baobab tree, where the lion stopped momentarily. He let out his three-roar signal, powering out over the opposite side of the plains between two thunderclaps that lit up the sky. A brief moment later, a muffled reply of the same pattern came in the far distance.

"Who's that?" Sukari questioned.

The lion gave a confident smile.

"Backup..."

Sheek and Sukari nodded. Their own confidence in getting Anthi back now rose slightly. This lion knew what he was doing.

All three sprinted down the hill in the direction of the river. As they ran, the rain pounded their bodies like pebbles, their pelt already soaked through, their eyes squinting trying to shield them from the harsh torrent of water, their paws sinking then flicking mud into the air as they ran.

They eventually entered the area of long grass that towered above themselves, cutting through at full speed. Sheek fell behind by a few paces as his muscles ached and breathing shallowed. As they sprinted, the lion raised his voice powerfully over the sound of the pummelling rain and crashing of the grass.

"Remember, Legacy took your cub and left you two alone. This could be bargaining or an ambush. He loves playing mind games. Keep your cool, play along, and don't retaliate, it makes a greater chance to keep you and your cub alive. My promise remains to keep you all alive and safe. However, we have to wait for the right moment..."

"What '*right moment*'?" Sukari questioned.

The lion let out an almost trembling sigh.

"We will know..."

Sukari and Sheek became confused with the lion's cryptic instructions and replies, but they had to shrug it off and keep following. What other option was there?

They eventually burst through the end of the long grass and into the open. The river came into sight, greatly swollen and raging due to the storm, the worst they had seen it. The lion already knew there would only be one place Legacy could cross this, so he changed his course and started to run alongside upstream. They followed the river around its natural bend. The banks rose as the river sank into a valley. In the distance, the giant tree log that stretched across the two steep banks lay ahead.

At the beginning of the log stood silhouettes of lions and lionesses. The large lion was about to cross, with a cub hanging from his muzzle. There was a bittersweet sense of relief between the three. They had caught up with Legacy and Anthi, and they knew that the next upcoming series of events would test their mind and body in the most brutal ways imaginable. The sheer presence of Legacy already started to make their spines shiver in a mix of fear for their lives, yet also anger for trying to steal Anthi's.

The lion called out to Legacy to get his attention as they all approached closer. Legacy stopped in his tracks and turned to face them; his followers locked eyes with them with devilish grins. They all turned back from the log and began stalking towards them.

"Do as they say… don't speak unless spoken to… co-operate with them… until I…" the lion whispered with another tremble, stopping mid-sentence.

Sheek and Sukari got a worrying suspicious feeling that this lion was hiding and mentally preparing for something. However, it was too late to change their actions now, and they had no choice but to trust him and go through with this 'plan.' It now was the *only* choice they had to rescue Anthi; or, worst-case scenario, one last time to see him.

They soon met with Legacy and the group, slowing down on their approach, and he came towards them. Sheek's eye's started to burn with hatred seeing his father still alive, who had a smug smirk on his face whilst carrying Anthi, who looked terrified. Anthi locked eyes with Sheek and Sukari but was scared stiff. All he could do was let out a whimper. It pained them both to see him like this. The other lions and lionesses started circling, chuckling, and taunting them by pretending to bite and take swipes with their claws. Sheek and Sukari did their best to follow the advice given and not react to it. Legacy bellowed in a deep low tone for them to lie down. They quickly obeyed.

Instantly, Sheek and Sukari were leapt upon and pinned very heavily to the ground with claws digging into their skin. Three lionesses were on her and two on Sheek. Being thin and weak, they didn't see him as a challenge. Sheek and Sukari growled deeply while their 'guardian' lion stayed silent, sitting, and untouched. He glared at them both like he was telling them to get their emotions under control.

They now realised what was happening, as this lion wasn't being pinned as they had. However, as long as Anthi was in the clutches of Legacy, they would cooperate at all costs and not risk his life. Legacy then came forward, towering over them like they were helpless bugs. He dropped Anthi onto the ground who landed with a slight thud. Legacy flipped him onto his side and pressed his paw firmly onto his rib cage, Anthi then making a strained gasp.

"Thank you for bringing them to me. I knew I could depend on you. Excellent work on Sheek's nose as ordered too." Legacy said plainly yet with a slight scoff, exchanging a faint smile towards the so-called 'guardian' lion.

Sheek and Sukari couldn't hold it in, and they snapped, maniacally clawing the ground and roaring as Legacy put Anthi in his death hold. They exchanged glares at the lion, 'Sukari's guardian', who now seemed to of tricked and betrayed them.

"SILENCE!" Legacy bellowed, his thundering voice immediately making them freeze. He scanned his eyes between the three of them.

He smirked with a snarl, exposing his extra deadly long canines. "I didn't expect you so soon, though it will make your sentence quicker and easier for me. Alas, this way seems boring," he scoffed with an underlying growl vibrating from his throat. "Though I must say I'm *very* disappointed in you," his voice loudened, before taking a deep, grunting breath. "How could you sink so low... I trusted you. You were going to be next in line as ruler of my pride. You have idiotically thrown that all away for Sukari and your so-called *love* for a group. You betrayed my pride and me. You know your penalty!"

Sheek lifted his head, gritting his teeth.

"Just do it, father... I know what I've done and am fully responsible for my actions... I should've died already," Sheek shouted out with strained pants in between to catch his breath. His eyes filled with hatred and locked onto his father's own, through his soaked mane sticking over his face. "Kill me however you want, suffocate me, slice me, break me apart... again." Sheek realised his own words in half defeat already. He lowered his head and sighed. "Please show a shred of dignity and let Sukari and Anthi go. Their lives should not be taken because of my own actions." his voice trembled.

Legacy raised his brow, almost smirking, keeping himself from chuckling.

"I wasn't talking to *you*, Sheek, you fool! I was talking to him..." Legacy then motioned his head towards the lion sitting next to them. He was immediately pinned down by three other lions, and Sheek and Sukari's jaws both hung in confusion.

"*This 'him'* has a name!" The lion bellowed. "My name is Kikome, friend of Pulsar, sworn protector of Sheek, Sukari and all they hold dear," he said proudly.

"Ha! To think you were my most trusted lion. You had the perfect skills to be my successor, and you could easily have continued my rule of fear." Legacy scoffed. "I was blinded by your talents, and I should have known... never to trust a wanderer!"

Legacy looked back at Sheek and Sukari, who both seemed very confused. "Ah, let me clear things up for you both," he grinned while lowering his head to Kikome's level. "You see, Kikome here was ordered to kill you Sukari, and your group. Then he was to make sure Sheek stayed alive and suffered for his betrayal, ironically to become the one thing I hate, a wanderer," he uttered in disgust and spat out some rain that had settled in his mouth.

Sheek and Sukari both looked at Kikome, whose head hung down towards the ground. "Kikome, before you die. Redeem yourself while you can, please tell us all your intentions. I'm sure we are all curious," Legacy said smugly.

Kikome took a brief sigh before then explaining his intentions. He knew he couldn't just kill Legacy with his claws or jaws. Like every other lion, he didn't bear ones long enough to penetrate his extra thick mane 'armour' covering his neck and chest. Even if he attempted to, Legacy would be all over him before he could even make a scratch.

Kikome knew only time would have to be the killer. Legacy eventually would succumb to old age and would need a successor. Kikome saw this as the perfect opportunity. He got close to him to gain his trust and loyalty over the years. He impressed Legacy with his almost supernatural skills in fighting to show he was a worthy successor over Sheek in keeping the fear alive. All Kikome had to do now was keep up his disguise and wait. When Legacy passed, he would end all that he built. He knew most of Legacy's followers were only so because they feared him and his loyal ones. Taking that away would break the chain, bringing freedom and peace to them all and the lands. The remaining lions loyal to the cause wouldn't be too much of a problem given Kikome's fighting abilities. It was a perfect plan which meant minimal fatalities - the innocent forced-followers of the fear would stay alive while the loyal would perish.

However, something not planned got thrown into his path. Sukari and Sheek he had sworn to protect, yet also he was ordered to kill Sukari and torture Sheek until death. He couldn't and wouldn't.

Kikome turned his head to Sukari.

"That night I saved you, I was meant to kill you, but instead I killed the lion who was aiding me. I said I couldn't help you all the time because I was living two lives - one as your protector, the other as Legacy's successor, which included tending to Sheek's punishment."

Kikome then turned his head to Sheek with a wave of guilt spreading over his face. "Sheek, if you can, believe me, I regret every moment," he said apologetically, lowering his head. "I *had* to keep my disguise as a loyal. I said I killed Sukari so you wouldn't track her. I sliced your nose not only to keep to my orders but also so you were unable to smell her scent if it got carried in the wind. Anthi took care of Sukari's inability to do the same to you."

Sukari Nodded in realisation, the scent of Anthi had always been remarkably familiar to that of Sheek's. If she *had* come across Sheek's scent in the air, she would have just assumed it was Anthi. Why would she even think it could be Sheek? To her, he was dead.

Kikome flattened his head on the ground, "I had to reduce any chance of you both meeting each other, as it would complicate my plans and expose me and put all of us in danger. Alas, it happened tonight."

Legacy then gave a low chuckle.

"Yes yes, I must commend you for such efforts to uphold your 'double life'. Your scheme may have still worked if it wasn't for one thing you didn't plan. *My Compassion*," He grinned as Sheek and Sukari bared confused faces, '*Legacy... compassion?*'

Legacy sat down, acting calm and savouring the moment. Anthi still lay tightly under his paw, letting out whimpers and squeaks as he struggled to get his breath under Legacy's weight.

"I *do* have *some* morals, you know, and I'm an excellent counter of death..." -Legacy flicked his head over to address Kikome- "Sorry, your plan would've taken your lifespan to 'complete' and be dead before me. I physically feel half the age I am. A gift I've kept very close to my chest. Though it would've been nice to have an expendable successor as a backup." -he grinned smugly before turning back to Sheek- "Aaaanyway, I calculated that Sheek would be in his final days of living through his punishment."

Legacy took a confident step towards him. "Thanks to my scouts... beside Kikome, I knew where he now lived."

Legacy let off a self-proud subtle chuckle and grin. He laid down at Sheek's eye level and glared directly into them. "I planned to visit him alone to state his punishment was served, and I would offer to end his misery and suffering quickly... but to my disappointment, I see him..."

He then flicked his head to Sukari and rage filled his eyes. "*With you, Sukari!* Who is alive and with your cub? After being told by Kikome that he killed you!" he bellowed.

Legacy raised his head and shifted his eyes to Kikome. "I knew then he was a traitor and held loyalties elsewhere. What now confuses me is that Kikome *knew this too* when he brought you both here, making this cub-napping less fun... for me."

Legacy stood back up with an angered huff. "I don't know what game Kikome is playing, but I'm done playing it! So here is my new plan, a fresh start."

He pressed down harder on Anthi, who in turn let out a painful gasp and wheeze, the pupils of his eyes shrunk as he felt his life slowly being squeezed out of him. Meanwhile, Sukari and Sheek raged and begged him to stop. "I kill Anthi here, this tainted offspring of his treacherous father, who will also die along with Kikome. But Sukari..." Legacy then paused with delight. "Dear Sukari..."

He stared into her eyes with a warm grin. "Since I ordered your execution at a younger age, you have survived all this time, especially later on with a cub to tend to. I see fire and determination inside of you, thus any cubs you produce may do too. I promise your eternal protection, respect by all members of my pride, and an abundance of food and companionship. You will never have to struggle to survive ever again. In return, all I ask is your complete obedience and silence. With Anthi's death, instinct will make you go back into heat. You won't be able to fight nature's law of providing cubs... my cubs... my future heirs!"

"NEVER *will I*-"

"With your inner fire and determination!" Legacy bellowed "...and my gifted abilities... *our cubs* will be *unstoppable*!"

Sukari and Sheek roared in retaliation and disgust. Both were now trying as hard as possible to break free, clawing at the soft mud but still overpowered by the other lionesses. All while Legacy continued to grin. "Your refusal will end your life, as you will be no use to me. Either way, these three need to die, so excuse me while I carry this out. I'll give you plenty of time to mourn, then you can decide your fate."

"No... NOOO!" Sukari cried out.

"Sukari... I'm sorry..." Kikome yelled over to her. "I was too late to warn you of him, to avoid any of this..."

Kikome sank his claws deep into the soft ground, pawing and kneading it to get a firm grip. "However! I promised to protect you and your loved ones... and that still stands..."

Turning towards Legacy, a confident smile grew across Kikome's face. Legacy, in turn, retracted his head a little, looking uneasy. "Because Legacy, as you said, you should've never trusted a wanderer... and besides, all wanderers help each other out!"

Kikome then pushed up as hard as he could. His legs trembled from the pure pull of his muscles bulging under his skin. The lions were now mildly confused about how three of them were unmatched against his pure strength.

Kikome slowly rose, giving enough room for his chest to expand sufficiently, while the three lions clambered and hung over him, trying to pull him back down, like trying to pin down an elephant. Kikome's body rattled and vibrated as he pushed himself up further, along with a long, straining yell! "and one thing always remains..."

His pupils narrowed, his brow confidently raised, bellowing a growl before taking a deep breath. "I'm always... one - step - ahead!"

Kikome then roared...

He roared a second time...

Then for the third time...

In a never seen moment, everyone witnessed Legacy's eyes had widened... in fear!

"NO! THIS ENDS NOW!" Legacy thundered.

He lunged forward towards Kikome, sinking his long canines deep into his neck. At the same time, Legacy intentionally pressed down hard with all his weight onto Anthi's chest, followed by a harrowing pop, crack and crunch from his ribs. Anthi gasped in such pure agony that his voice escaped him as his life too escaped from his wide-open eyes.

"ANTHI, KIKOME!" Sukari and Sheek cried

out in horror as they watched hopelessly two lives be taken from them at once.

Legacy then retreated his jaw with a demonic chuckle. Kikome fell back to the ground with the weight of the lions on top of him, the fur surrounding his neck quickly soaked in his own blood.

Legacy then immediately latched his jaws around Anthi. He wailed in terror but only came out as a weak squeak as all his breath had been stolen. Legacy shook him vigorously from side to side like he was mauling a scrap of meat. He then swung his head as powerfully as he could before opening his jaw, launching Anthi incredibly high into the air, above the raging river in the valley below. Sheek and Sukari froze in horror with their paws stretched out across the mud, seeing their son freefall before descending to his demise. Time seemed to slow as they took in every second to gaze upon their helpless son and his last few moments before he would disappear forever, below the valley edge.

Suddenly, the long grass behind them rustled. A figure of what looked like a smaller lioness swooped past them all. Everyone, including Legacy, turned their heads in confusion towards its direction of travel. They watched as in a blur, this unknown 'lioness' jumped onto the log over the river. She immediately leapt off diagonally high into the air, twisting her body and catching Anthi in her muzzle with a confident growl. Her body continued to twist back upright, paws spread out ready, before landing on the other side of the river with a grunt and forward roll. She immediately stood up strong and proud, staring back over to the other side towards them. A flash of lightning in the sky lit up the animal in all her unique colours and physique, with Anthi safely in her mouth.

Sheek and Sukari gasped in shock yet awe.

"TEF!" Sukari yelled with a wave of pure relief spread all over her. "GO, GET ANTHI SAFE... RUN!" she cried out.

Tefnut, her best friend and Sheek's half-sister had just saved their son, a whisker away from what would have been his certain demise.

Tefnut knew she had to do what Sukari instructed and nodded in acknowledgement. They had only seen each other for a split moment and had to part ways again to get Anthi safe. She darted off into the forest nearby with him. Tefnut wanted to help Sukari and the others with the impending battle, but she need not worry about this.

Unlike her half-leopard solitary nature, she had not come alone...

15. Pride Over Power

"After her! Make sure that cub is finished!" Legacy demanded, motioning towards the log that was several paces away.

One lioness leapt from Kikome to pursue Tefnut. Suddenly, as the lioness was about to jump onto the log, a larger older lion sprung out from the long grass, shoving her off the valley edge and falling below.

"*Aramile*?" Both Sheek and Sukari whispered in disbelief.

"FORGET KIKOME. HE'S FINISHED! GET THAT LION OUT THE WAY AND GO AFTER THAT CUB!" Legacy thundered.

Two remaining lions leapt off Kikome, who now lay limp on the ground. Another lioness sprung off Sukari and joined the pursuit. Aramile stood firm in their way, blocking the path to the log.

However, he soon was overwhelmed by the three who piled onto him. He tried his best to keep them at bay, grabbing and pulling them back if they tried to make a pass. Unfortunately, the two lions managed to overpower him after a short scuffle and passed while he kept a lioness in his grasp.

Legacy's attention was diverted, ensuring the two lions continued across unchallenged. He took a couple of steps forward, ready to follow if needed.

It all happened in a split moment. Sukari watched in awe as Anmani and Kisima (now looking a little bigger since she last saw them) leapt together and pulled one of the lionesses off Sheek. At the same time, Sheek sees Mlinzi and Mkuki leap out, pounding the two other lionesses off Sukari, setting her free. She glanced over at them as they fought the lionesses, they were toughened wanderers, and they could take care of themselves. However, Anmani and Kisima were still only adolescents. Even two of them against an adult still risked being an uneven battle. Sheek, still pinned by one lioness, motioned his head at Sukari and pointed towards the two. She knew what he meant. They needed help more than he did.

Legacy, flicking his head around from hearing all the commotion, leapt towards her before she had time to fully stand. He gave her a massive swipe with the back of his paw, sending her sliding across the ground and stopping right next to Sheek. She was then immediately pinned on her side, directly facing him. Legacy pressed one paw down hard into the side of her chest while the other was on her neck. She immediately began gasping for air.

"Look into her eyes, see what you have done!" Legacy raged. "*All this* could have been averted if you had just stuck to your original purpose!" He growled. He gradually twisted and pushed his paws deeper, leaning more of his body weight onto her with a gleaming snarl, savouring the moment. Sukari, gasping in agony, gazed at Sheek with her eyes full of fear, waiting for that deadly crunch.

Sheek weakly clawed the soft mud, trying to free himself, but the lioness was too heavy and bearing a solid pin, too much for his weakened state to break free from. All he could do was watch in distraught, seeing Sukari suffer and her demise seeming inevitable.

Soon, life was all but gone in her eyes. She then strained her paw slightly into the air as a dim flash of distant lightning lit up the sky.

"Too late for submissions, Sukari. Kikome chose your path!" Legacy chuckled maniacally.

Oddly Sheek then huffed with a smirk, with a laugh almost escaping. Legacy looked across and glared at Sheek, slightly confused. "Something amusing about her last moments?" he grunted.

"Five members of my group have counter-attacked yours. Seems like Kikome had many scenarios figured out." Sheek paused and flicked his eyes to Legacy. "A few moments were all we needed... she isn't submitting... you told me to look into her eyes, and I can see..."

"What are you rambling about?" Legacy interrupted, raising a brow.

"Currently there is no wind, yet the grass is swaying behind me. There are five members of my group here, but I remember there always being Six..." Sheek smirked.

"One... step... ahead," Kikome called out, grunting with exhausted breaths.

From the tall grass behind Sheek where Sukari was pointing, Safila sprinted out with a slight limp, tackling Sheek's final capturer, thus releasing him. Sheek then quickly lunged towards Legacy, tackling him away from Sukari with what strength remained in him. They rolled a couple of times before Sheek briskly and efficiently was pinned by Legacy.

Sukari burst into life, taking a desperate gasp of air before coughing and clearing her throat. Her vision blurred and delayed as she wearily turned her head from side to side. Her ears absorbed the muffled sounds of battle, along with her thumping heartbeat and deepened breathing. Friends of her past all engaged in combat with the opposition. Risking their lives for the lives of herself, Sheek and Anthi. For this one moment - she didn't feel like they were a group of misfits, rejects and wanderers. They were a pride, protecting their own.

Still weak and trying to gain her strength, she glanced over at Sheek, who now lay a few paces away, pinned by the neck and being repeatedly battered by Legacy. He wasn't using claws. It's like he wanted to cause Sheek as much pain as possible with the least damage like he was enjoying it, savouring Sheek's defeat. A mighty blow followed with every swing from Legacy, rippling through his body. Sheek soon lay limp on the ground, though this didn't make Legacy stop. It just made it easier for him. He simply loosened his grip on Sheek's neck and continued his torment, beating him repeatedly. Sheek's body and face were inflicted with such blunt trauma that he just started to feel numb. His cheeks and eyes began to swell, becoming unrecognisable.

Sukari strained to get up before collapsing again. What if she had been more alert tonight? She always used to be when sleeping, for the sake of protecting Anthi. Maybe she would've stayed more alert without the comfort of Sheek? What if she had never even crossed that river two nights before? She and Anthi would've never been separated and thus never found Sheek, and all this confrontation with Legacy would never have happened. Would that of been a *better path*?

The battle of the prides continued around her as her thoughts consumed her mind. She then had to remind herself of what she said to Sheek yesterday.

"Some choices in life are just an illusion of the inevitable."

Her vision and senses suddenly cleared. She snapped out of her self-guilt, and her soul lit ablaze into a state of fury. Her eyes flashed into an emotionless gaze - her teeth bared - her jaw hung - her claws extended – her heart raced. This was *her life*, and she knew everything happened for a reason. For Sukari's search to end and for her new life to begin, she knew what all this led to. This was the night Legacy would die... by her paws.

Adrenalin rushed through her body; a deep rumble vibrated through her throat, turning into an almighty roar! She forced herself up with a newfound strength that had ignited inside her. She leapt at full speed towards Legacy, who now had his claws extended, ready to give Sheek his final deathly blow. Legacy's ears flicked to the sound from her, and he was thrown backwards before he could react to Sukari's powerful charge. They both rolled across the deluge of mud before Sukari embraced a dominant pin. She glanced up, noticing Kikome had struggled up and staggered towards her, although still injured.

"All promises can't be kept tonight, Kikome. So just keep one." Sukari insisted, yelling over to him.

Kikome couldn't argue, and he knew what she meant. He nodded in acknowledgement, then started to pick up his pace the best he could and left.

For that short moment, her attention was diverted. Sukari felt Legacy's paw break free, pounding across her face and sending her sliding. However, she was unfazed, immediately lunging back at Legacy before he could stand. She tried to sink her teeth into his neck; unfortunately, his thick mane stopped any significant harm. He wrapped his paws around her using this open opportunity, twisting his body and rolling her over so now he had a dominant pin.

He now, in turn, went for her neck. However, she instinctively blocked his attack with her paw. Sukari winced yet embraced the pain of Legacy's long teeth sinking through her skin and flesh; she knew her paw just saved her life.

She now needed to do something, anything to get him off her. There was only one current opportunity she could think of. She pushed and strained her head forward with a grunt, before latching on hard, sinking her teeth into one of Legacy's ears. Legacy opened his jaw, roaring out in pain while retreating his head, He felt and heard his ear stretching and tearing away from his head. In turn, she sank her teeth deeper before hearing the tearing skin 'snap'. She wouldn't lie to herself; the sound was satisfying. Legacy, now in a short daze, meant his pin had weakened. Sukari rolled over and leapt up to regain her stance, with his ear dangling from her bloodied and exposed teeth, before spitting it out. Landing on the mud with a rewarding splat.

Legacy took a few steps back as fire now started to ravage in his eyes from what she'd just done. He proceeded to stalk towards her with deep, grunting breaths as she defensively started to back up, thinking of her next move.

"Your self-defence skills are commendable Sukari. However, why keep enduring more injuries, pain, and suffering? Just simply submit. I'm giving you one last chance, and we both can live the life I intend for you. You will be a valuable asset, and I will treat you like one."

Sukari continued to back up as Legacy pursued. Her eyes still locked onto him, showing no pain or emotion. She continued to pant heavily, her breath filtering through her bared teeth. From the corner of her vision, she could see Sheek lying motionless. His scars and malnourished body reminded her that he had everything taken away in his life, yet he had kept alive through it all and survived. Legacy then spoke her mind.

"No claws or jaws have ever penetrated my neck enough to kill me, and nothing ever will. Have you ever wondered why anyone stupid enough in my pride hasn't tried to betray me? Just look at what became of Kikome, he doesn't have long left to live." He growled with a smirk, his eyes glaring deep into Sukari's own, breaking into her soul. "Just give up, Sukari..."

She had now inadvertently backed up against the log. Her brows softened as she felt trapped. She could see more clearly how extraordinarily thick and woven Legacy's mane is. She remembered that night when Sheek delivered a clean swipe into his neck and the vast amount of damage he inflicted, yet Legacy still survived. What chance did Sukari have with her own smaller weapons that nature gave her? What fighting skills does Sukari have compared to Kikome, a highly trained warrior who knew he couldn't defeat him with combat?

Her confidence started to shallow, and her claws began to retract. She knew she would ultimately come off a lot worse from his counterattacks. Maybe it *was* time to give up. She started a submissive gesture, letting Legacy's fear wrap around her body, and consume her.

"That's it, my dear, keep yourself alive. It's in your instinct to stay alive, even if it means only yourself."

She then paused, with his last few words echoing in her mind. If Sukari took the offer and stayed alive, all her friends and family would still eventually be captured and enslaved or perished. She would feel she had betrayed them, and her life would not be worth living. Sheek almost had betrayed them all in the past, and he was willing to sacrifice his life to change that. It was now Sukari's turn to sacrifice her own life, for the benefit of killing Legacy.

Knowing that she couldn't do so with claws or teeth, she had to think outside that. She glanced along the log stretching over the valley, seeing a final chance. The risk was extremely high, but she had nothing else to lose. She leapt onto the log, her rear leg narrowly missing a swipe from Legacy as her back was turned. She sprung forward and stopped in the middle, directly over the racing torrent of water far below. Legacy growled and rolled his eyes in disapproval. He then followed her.

"Bad move, my dear." Legacy watched in slight amusement as she lay down on the log facing him, with her front legs dangling from each side. This was an extremely vulnerable position. Blinded by her 'stupidity', Legacy grinned and chuckled. "I guess this is the way you want to go then. This is shameful and boring," he mocked, stalking closer towards her. "I thought you would know better than this, Sukari. I'm not stupid about your intentions. You do know that if I fall, you are coming with me. I'll take a chance at my survival," he smirked confidently, Sukari nodded in reply.

Unknown to him, Sukari wrapped her paw around a vine dangling from underneath, out of his field of view. She hoped it was strong enough to keep one from falling.

Time froze in her mind. She was prepared for the risk and knew the consequences. Legacy was correct; her strength alone could not push him off the log. She had to use all her body weight to overpower him, which meant they together would fall below. This is where the vine would come into use.

Legacy started to get irritated that throughout their fight, no matter what he said to her, she wasn't giving him the satisfaction of replying with typical heroic speeches or words of wisdom. She had stayed silent all this time with a cold and quiet demeanour.

"Please, Sukari, say any last words before I crush or drown them out of you, your choice!" Legacy growled deeply, now annoyed, and Sukari just replied with a subtle growl and a snarl. She took a deep breath and closed her eyes, feeling the rain roll down her face for potentially the last time. It gave her a calming effect, preparing her for what was coming. A subtle cold smile grew across her muzzle.

Legacy snapped and had enough. Just two paces away, he pounced on her. In a flash, her eyes opened, and Legacy's head was met by a powerful headbutt from herself. His vision darkened and blurred while feeling an embrace; it felt like Sukari wrapped herself around his shoulders and neck for grip, ready to push him. He blindly crossed his arms and grabbed her with the first thing his paws touched, one wrapped around the side of her head, the other on her shoulder. Legacy's vision regained slightly enough to see Sukari's dead stare.

Her eyes raged alight.

Her ears pressed flat against her head.

Her nostrils flared.

She let out a deep pounding huff.

"NEVER... piss off a mother. She will sacrifice anything... ANYTHING for the safety of her cub!" she bellowed with a deep furious growl that thundered through his body.

Legacy's eyes widened as he felt her body press against his neck and shoulders with a powerful push using all her weight. He held tight onto her as they tipped over the edge of the log. At that moment, his vision fully regained before realising that just her paws were only on his shoulders. However, he could still feel something tight around his neck. He then saw a blurred line of green pass across his line of sight just as a flash of lightning illuminated it. It was the vine! Nature had given her another, and final weapon.

Now tipped over from the point of no return, time seemed to slow down in their last moments. Sukari pushed her rear legs as hard as possible, forcing them downward with extra momentum, bellowing roars as they fell.

They both plummeted towards the river. Legacy's fall was then suddenly cut short with a sharp jolt of the vine as it locked to a sudden stop, instantly binding around him. A loud pop and crack followed, but it wasn't that of the vine; it was that of Legacy's neck. A blood-curdling gasp ripped from his throat as his life was torn from his body. Though he had one last parting gift for Sukari.

The sudden stop jolted Sukari through his grasp. One set of his claws sliced through her shoulder, and the other set sliced up her cheek, piercing through her eye as she fell through his hold. She roared in agony as one side of her vision instantly turned red. She instinctively wrapped her front legs tight, clinging onto Legacy's rear legs at the last moment instead of falling, digging her claws in for extra grip. He strained to lift his front paw to cut the vine, but it fell limp halfway.

She hung there grunting heavily with each breath from the searing pain in her eye. She swung abnormally calm from side to side. She could feel the warm blood now soak into her fur before being diluted by the continuing rain pounding down. She heard faint final desperate gasps for breath from

Legacy, which soon subsided and fell silent. Sukari knew from hunting prey that any damage to the neck quickly makes the target lose control of their limbs. Unfortunately, it was not quick enough with what injury she had just sustained.

Anxiety started to flood her body, her breaths deepened, her heart began to race, and she let out a whimpering growl. She had just cheated death; however, she had paid a terrible price.

She wasn't going to lie to herself; being responsible for Legacy's death came with a sense of guilt that it *had* to come to this. For the greater good though, herself and the pride came before him and his ruthless fear over these lands.

Sheek lying near the bank further downriver watched in horror at the events that had unfolded, his jaw hung, and his outcry was silenced by shock. He struggled to get up, only to fail. He then tried to roar, growl, shout; anything to get anyone's attention, but it just came out as a hoarse breath. He scanned the area noticing his group was still occupied with fighting the other lionesses. From their perspective further inland, Sukari and Legacy were now out of view. If anything couldn't get any worse, he saw a lioness by chance had spotted what had happened and slunk away from the confrontations. She was heading towards the log where Sukari and Legacy hung! He tried harder to get up again, but his legs gave way. He resorted to clawing across the soft mud, but it slipped through with no grip, he tried to get Sukari's attention to the impending danger by shouting, but his voice just came out again as a hoarse whisper. His efforts were all in vain and he felt helpless.

Sukari couldn't stay here. She couldn't see anything or anyone to alert, and she was too far below the cliff edge for her roar to be carried. She turned her head and glanced around at her surroundings with one working eye. To her shock, she saw the lioness that Aramile had pushed off earlier. She was perched on a part of the cliff face that stuck out, trapped. The lioness oddly enough looked at her curiously with no hostility, she could quickly have leapt onto the vine above Sukari and cut her away, but she didn't.

Before Sukari could question her own morale to save her or not, she had to try and save herself first. She slowly climbed up Legacy's lifeless body with all her remaining strength, using her claws for grip, ignoring her injured paw throbbing with pain. She finally managed to pull herself past his head as her body began to ache all over. She tried her best to climb up the vine but kept slipping down, her injured paw was unable to grip such a narrow thing compared to a lion's body. The vine started to creak loudly, showing signs it would give way under all the strain.

She looked up with the rain hitting her squinted eye, blurring her vision on one side while still seeing red through the other. Her paw continued to throb, and her body continued to ache. Searing pain shot through her shoulder, and she felt as if she was breaking apart. The vine made a loud crack and jolted a little; she now mentally prepared herself for the inevitable event and gazed at the thundery sky for her final moment.

She suddenly saw a large lioness silhouette appear, leaning over on the log above her. She could not recognise her as either friend or foe. She stretched out her paw. Sukari expected the worse that this lioness was going to cut the vine.

Instead, the lioness turned and spread her paw unsheathed, offering it willingly to her. Sukari was confused, but at this moment she had no choice. She stretched out her paw and grabbed it tightly. She then felt her weight being hoisted up as the lioness grunted and growled. Sukari was halfway up when the lioness suddenly lost her fore grip on the log and slipped, though she immediately used her rear legs as an anchor. They now were both holding onto each other and their lives. The lioness let off a thundering roar that travelled throughout the battlefield, just high enough for her roar to be carried. It caught the attention of Sukari's group and Legacy's pride. They paused in their conflicts and looked over, noticing one member from each side of the opposition was in danger, yet one was helping the other. Both sides stared at each other like their thoughts were connected for the same purpose - temporary unity to save their own. They all ran towards the log and a couple of members from each opposition leapt onto it, quickly helping their allies up. Sukari and her unexpected saviour were now both saved.

Aramile soon spotted the trapped lioness he thought he had pushed into the river. She looked distressed, and her eyes were full of resentment and fear. He lay down with another lioness supporting him, stretching out his paw. The trapped lioness stretched out her own, their paws connected, and she was then hoisted up.

Sukari took a long look at her friends that she left behind all that time ago, some now looking a little older than before. She thought she never would have seen them again, they all now stood before her during and after this whole conflict, and it felt surreal.

Both Sukari's and Legacy's pride stood in verbal silence. The only sounds were their panting to catch their breath. They were all tired, all bearing scratches, cuts, and injuries from the battle. Throughout this conflict, they inflicted damage on one another, yet they showed compassion and morale towards each other in their time of need. They all now felt at an impasse. However, Legacy's lionesses still had every reason to avenge their leader's death, so Sukari stepped forward.

"Legacy is gone, and so are his ideals, influence, and fear over this land. As a mother, I needed to do what had to be done," she said with a raised voice. Her muzzle started to tremble as the rain continued to roll down her face. "There is no need for more bloodshed, fighting and pointless slaughter. It's obvious your morale matches ours."-

she took a deep shuddering breath-. "My son is out there… I have no idea the severity of his injuries that Legacy has caused him. He could even be…" She paused. She didn't even want to say it. Instead, tears formed around her eyes.

The lionesses stayed silent and plain-faced, not knowing what to do or what to say, thinking about how each other would react if one spoke up. After all, they felt it wasn't their place; they had just been aiding Legacy. That is until the lioness that saved her earlier… stepped forward.

"I was a mother once… until Legacy captured me and killed my cub, forcing me to his cause," the lioness paused, lowering her head. "I know from personal experience the pain you would have endured if Legacy had his way. I obeyed him and his demands towards you in fear… but now, I'm free, thanks to you and your pride." The lioness bowed to her. "No more."

Sukari grew a faint smile and bowed in return. Her ears flicked as more lionesses spoke up.

"I was a mother too."

"Me too"

"I was surrendered as a 'gift', when I left, my pride tried to retaliate and was slaughtered."

"I was taken. I have never seen my parents again,"

"When my cub was born, she was taken from me for 'training'. I've never seen her again."

The rest of the lionesses joined in with their accounts, becoming a blend of mixed conversation.

They each bowed towards her now with appreciation. Sukari's tears continued but for a different reason. What she thought were true followers of Legacy were instead his prisoners, obeying orders, expendable bodies for this battle. This is what she would have become all that time back when she was pregnant. This is what she would have become tonight if she surrendered, a prisoner in fear.

She returned the bows one by one when suddenly a lioness from the back of the group came forward with Sheek placed on her back.

"When I was a wanderer, this lion was the one who tricked me and submitted my life to Legacy. Ironic now that *his life* is on my back, I could have hurled him into that river after what he did to me..." she said plainly and paused for a moment, then gave Sukari a deep bow. "That wouldn't have solved the problem. Legacy was the problem. It looks like you and Sheek have been through great measures and sacrifices to defeat that problem, so you both have earnt my respect."

Sukari sprung forward to look at him, his eyes were half-open under the swelling, as his face had been pulverised and battered, along with the rest of his body. He was lucky to still be breathing.

"Sheek, are you OK? How bad are you hurt?" she whispered, concerned.

He rolled his eyes up, glancing at her blankly. Seeing large blood-soaked lacerations run down the side of her face, which had also pierced through her eye. He knew she would be blind in that eye for the rest of her life. His son's injuries were also severe, he didn't and *couldn't* hold much hope for him. The crunching sound and Anthi's expression were burned into his memory. This and everything else happened while he was too weak to contribute anything towards stopping it. It made his heart sink further than ever before. He felt useless, a dead weight, a liability, and an empty shell.

"She should've thrown me in that river..." Sheek mumbled. He looked away with his blank expression and flopped his head down, not saying another word. Sukari, concerned, wanted to question him again. However, her saviour lioness then spoke, diverting her attention.

"What about your cub and your weird lion-ish-looking friend? They are still being chased by Legacy's dominant males. They are different to us; they are willingly dedicated to his cause. What can you... we do?" she questioned, concerned.

Sukari tried to feed herself as much self-confidence as she could. She had to be hopeful for what she did know and not dwell on what she did not. A faint confident expression grew, and she took a deep breath, puffing out her chest.

"We will go to our home. That's where she'll go. On my life, I trust Tefnut with Anthi, ever since his first night in this world." She glanced over towards the forest, where she had last seen them. "Those lions may be strong and ruthless, but Tefnut has the gift of the Leopards... speed and agility."

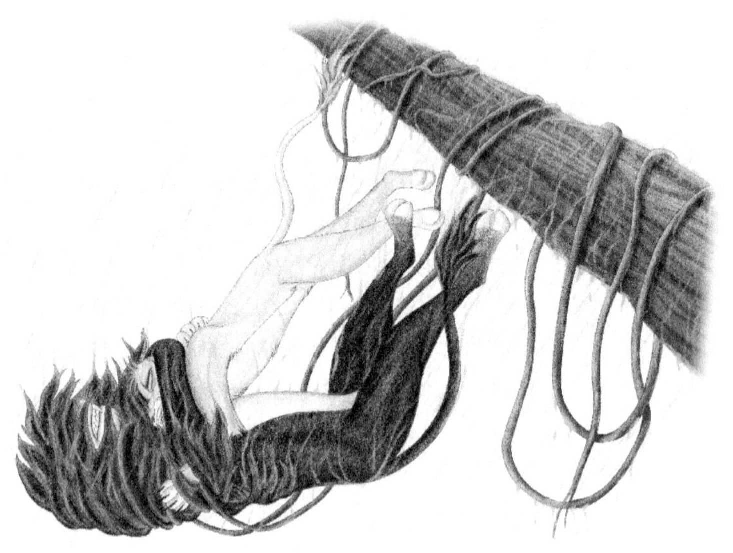

16. RUN!

Tefnut sprinted a few paces into the forest, hearing the heart-breaking sounds of Anthi's gasps, growls and wheezing coming from his crushed chest. A fire raged in her eyes; how could Legacy inflict such brutal torture on an innocent cub? She quickly mentally slapped herself back to reality. After all, this was Legacy she questioned about!

She started to slow down. During the rescue, she had no choice but to grab him the way she did, but now she had a quick opportunity to readjust her grip so as not to cause him any unnecessary harm. She soon stopped and gently placed him on the ground, noticing his neck was bleeding from Legacy's maul. Her eyes started to glisten. The last time she saw Anthi, he had only just entered this world as a tiny ball of fluff. His life had barely begun. Now he lay here only a little older, barely hanging onto it. Even though it was Sukari's choice to leave, Tefnut couldn't help but feel she had failed in her promise.

Anthi collapsed on his side, panting with his

persistent wheeze. He weakly turned his head to look up at her with confused and terrified eyes. He didn't know who this strange animal was. His eyes hadn't opened yet when he was a newborn, so he had never seen her before. All he knew was that he was about to die a moment ago, and she saved him.

"Who... who are you?" he strained with a tremble.

Tefnut closed her eyes and lowered her head. A tear ran down her cheek as she slowly approached him, then gave a reassuring nuzzle. He grew a faint smile as he returned the gesture, he didn't know her, but she gave off a sense of calm, a memory of warmth and comfort.

Legacy's voice echoed in the distance,

"*Go after that cub!*"

"I'm getting you safe. I'm sorry Anthi, but we need to do so quickly. Can you hold onto me?" she said gently but briskly. Anthi nodded subtly in reply. She then picked him up by his nape and gently swayed him onto her back. Anthi again growled in pain. "I'm sorry it hurts, but this will be better for both of us," she reassured.

Tefnut heard the conflict of lions in the distance, knowing then Aramile was right on cue to defend her escape. Kikome knew Legacy's tactics inside and out, and Tefnut knew she had to get away if Aramile couldn't hold them off. Each member of the group had their own assigned tasks.

She knew that carrying Anthi by the nape of his neck while running would cause him to swing around, throwing her off balance. Carrying him with her mouth around his body will only cause more pressure and harm to his chest. She had only one option left. “Crawl up to the back of my neck, and hold on,” she whispered, keeping him calm.

Anthi strained and gradually slid himself up, his wheeze making Tefnut's spine shiver. It reminded her precisely of Sheek's injuries the night he 'died'.

Her ears then flicked up when she heard rustling through the trees. The lions had already pushed through! Not only she now would have to escape them quicker but doing so before Anthi became too weak to hold on. He was losing blood and struggled to breathe properly. It was just a matter of time before he could pass out. She had to run fast like she never had before!

“Anthi... don't question me on this. Use your claws to dig in tight. It uses less strength and is more secure. Don’t worry about hurting me. It's a small price to pay to keep you safe.”

Given the situation, Anthi couldn't help but crack a faint smile after Tefnut's remark. To him, it reassured the fact she knew Sukari and Sheek well, in some way.

“THERE YOU ARE! SUBMIT THE CUB!” one of the lions bellowed.

Anthi gasped at the sudden outburst from the lion. Tefnut flicked her ears, pinpointing their direction. She adjusted her paws accordingly on the ground and then sprang forward. Anthi felt the sudden jolt of Tefnut's leap and soon dug his claws in, followed by a compressed growl from Tefnut.

"That's it! It's OK, keep holding... keep holding!" she reassured, before exploding forward with an immense burst of speed.

Anthi was pulled back and his front legs stretched out by her sheer acceleration. He immediately could hear a whistle as her head sliced through the air, which buffered around him. He turned his head to the side. His whiskers and tuft of hair on his head danced in the turbulence. The trees blurred past him, each with an extra burst of air as they both bolted past them. Anthi's ear was pressed against her body while he was holding on tight, soaking in the sound of her racing heartbeat.

Tefnut changed her heading, setting a new course towards where the trees were denser. The lions were hot on her tail and were fast, so she had to be faster. However, simply outrunning them wouldn't be enough. She had to lose them completely by slowing or stopping them; for her to have a safe escape. But furthermore, she couldn't fall victim to the dangers and slowing effects of the dense trees herself. That's where her agility would become her most vital asset - and weapon.

"I'm sorry, it's gonna get a bit rough and uncomfortable but keep talking to me," she insisted. It was her way of knowing Anthi was still conscious and keeping his mind off things.

Tefnut shot into the denser part of the forest, leaping from side to side, weaving her body around the trunks of the trees that whistled past. She could feel the air pressure brush past her face and ears as she missed them by a whisker. Anthi started to show signs of distress from being pulled side to side.

"Come on Anthi, deep breaths, talk to me," Tefnut demanded, firm yet friendly. She suddenly had to take a hard left turn, skidding on the soft ground, a mix of water and mud spraying away and hitting the trees.

"I'm scared. It hurts, hard to breathe." he strained.

Tefnut opened her mouth to reply but was suddenly met by an oncoming low branch. She leapt with all the strength in her rear legs, Anthi felt a moment of weightlessness as they glided through the air, his body lifting away from the lower part of her neck, but his claws still anchored in. They cleared the branch by a hair, then landed hard on the other side, making Anthi bump back onto her neck, growling out in pain. The lions behind her weren't confident enough to jump and resorted to crawling underneath, slowing them slightly.

"Scared is good, scared is one emotion of many that a pure heart possesses, a lion with a pure heart is a force not to be reckoned with..." Tefnut paused her talking to tackle a couple of large, uplifted roots, which she soon sprung over. 'SNAP.' One thin root she didn't see had looped around her rear paw, snagging it before breaking. She lost her stride and tripped. She slid along the ground with her legs splayed to stop her from rolling over. She soon regained her stride, though now the lions had gained on them. "*Stupid, stupid mistake,*" Tefnut thought, mentally slapping herself.

"I never got to know you, but I know your Mum and Dad. They are the strongest and bravest lions I have ever met, and they have seen and accomplished things no lion can imagine..."

A pool of water lay ahead. She closed her eyes and raced through it with great speed, a wave of water exploding around them. As for the pursuing lions, it slowed them down again, the water dragging through their dense manes and muscular physique.

"Your parents get scared too, you know, we all do, I'm scared right now. I took one look at you, and I saw your Mum and Dad, and you have what they have. Yes, you may be scared now, but being so is like a *superpower*. It makes you strong, your parents strong, myself strong, and -*you*- Anthi... you-are-strong!"

Tefnut's rear paw now started to throb, but she couldn't let it hinder her. She winced through her pain, which gave her more drive to push harder. Her heavy breaths matched her sprint, getting a rhythm and sprinting harder, grunting with each exhale. Her ears flicked when she heard another pain-induced groan from Anthi. Tefnut was an animal prone to be direct and not lie.

"You are in pain. Pain is also a power. I watched as your father was dying right in front of me, in the most agonising way imaginable, his injury the same as yours-"

"*Am I* going to die?"

"I don't know, but remember that your dad is still here. He is alive, survived the same injury, hold onto that thought, believing in something hard, gives it all the more chance to happen." She reassured.

"What if those lions kill me?" Anthi trembled.

"I believe they won't." -she paused- "I was by your mum's side when you were born. I watched as you were brought into this world. An extremely rare honour for any animal to witness. She then placed your tiny body into my paws. I vowed to her and myself that day I would protect you, whenever it was needed, wherever the distance."

It then suddenly clicked for Anthi, Tefnut's Scent. The moment he sensed it at the beginning of their encounter, it gave him a feeling of warmth and comfort. It was a deep-core memory from being cradled by her when he was just born.

Before Anthi could reply, they were interrupted by the sight of the two lions, now level on each side, their eyes locked onto him. Tefnut's paw was still hindering her speed, and the trees were spreading apart.

She noticed the lion's lack of attention to what was in front of him, and a wide tree was up ahead. She could still feel Anthi's claws deep in her skin, which was the only assurance she needed. She suddenly flicked both her front legs wide to the left, causing her to spring to the right, bashing one of the lions off his course. With his eyes still locked onto Anthi, he didn't notice the tree and crashed headfirst into it at full speed. The resulting sound of impact from his jaw and neck pierced through the air, that of a harrowing crunch. He was gone; now, only one more lion remained.

Anthi, although mesmerized by Tefnut's swift moves, all started to take its toll on him. The pain began to pound in his chest from being knocked around, constantly shifting and bouncing from one side to another. He started growling aloud, followed by distressed whimpers. Tefnut's ears flicked from his concerning sounds. She took a deep breath and heightened her tone.

"One down and one to go, Anthi, you can make it and he-will-not-kill-you!" she huffed in confidence.

Though her words were encouraging, his eyes flickered and drooped, his whole neck slowly turning red as it soaked up the blood from Legacy's bite. His claws started to retract as his consciousness faded and wanting the pain to end. Tefnut felt and noticed this; she knew she had to keep him awake. "Anthi! Stay with me. We can make it!" she reassured. Tefnut continued to pummel the ground, the trees becoming more of a blur the faster she ran. Every time the lion gained on her, she would suddenly weave in-between them, pouncing side to side, using her agility to her advantage. Though this was playing to her strength, it was also Anthi's weakness, so she only did so when critically needing to keep the lion off her tail. "Talk to me, talk about your dad. What was your most memorable moment with him? Was it when you first met?"

Anthi shook out of his semi-unconscious state at the mention of his dad. His eyes widened from Tefnut's question, and he then increased his hold on her again.

"Yea..." Anthi paused, realising something. "Actually, it wasn't... it's when he bit me," he mumbled shyly, Tefnut raising a brow to herself, confused.

"What? I don't understand."

"No, no, I mean because I didn't really see him as my dad when he bit me. But I knew his dad stuff was inside somewhere," he murmured and cleared his throat, straining another breath. "I showed him to trust. We then hugged, laughed, and played. He looked at me with this unforgettable face and called me his son." -he paused for a wheezy breath- "I guess the bad thing is more memorable because it caused a good thing afterwards?"

Tefnut let out a surprised chuckle at his remark, just when she leapt over a rock, then jumped towards the side of a tree before rebounding off it to change direction, landing gracefully and continuing to sprint.

"You surprise me Anthi. I like your way of thinking!"

Anthi then shyly smiled.

"You are full of surprises too. How are you

so... swishy?"

Tefnut's expression changed slightly solemnly.

"Self-taught. Someone like me can attract a lot of attention."

Anthi nodded in understanding before suddenly feeling a paw swipe right past his head. The lion had almost flanked them! Tefnut gasped from such a near-miss, which had infuriated her! "DON'T YOU DARE TOUCH MY NEPHEW!" She bellowed and roared.

Anthi's jaw hung with a raised brow, her nephew? Like learning what a father was, Anthi didn't know what a nephew was but implied she somehow is related to him.

Tefnut's paw wasn't getting any better. She felt herself further slowing and her stamina dropping. This chase couldn't continue on the ground, and she had to use her leopard half more to her advantage. She had to go onto the tree branches above. "Hold on, we have no choice. We have to go up."

Anthi nodded and readjusted his grip. Tefnut felt this as her prompt. She kept the pace of her sprinting as fast as possible, scanning the trees ahead and adjacent to each side. Her eyes flickered as they zoomed past each tree. She then found the perfect spot to ascend. She knew lions could climb too, but knowing a male lion, they are pretty slow and lazy. Instead, they would continue on the ground and follow until she had to come back down, though she had to worry about that part later. “Get Ready!” she warned.

Anthi squinted his eyes shut. His body then felt an immense pull downward as she leapt up high, his claws pulled on her skin from the momentum, making her wince. Just after the evasive manoeuvre, Anthi felt a nasty click and severe pain shoot through his chest.

He flashed open his eyes, looking to the side and now above ground, running along the branches of the trees.

His breathing quickly became shallow, his eyelids and head soon started to droop, along with his consciousness. His vision became blurred, the last thing he saw was Tefnut's fur on her neck now soaking in his own blood.

Less protected by the rain, Tefnut felt it bombarding her. She had to squint her eyes which meant her vision decreased too. Her claws came into use on the wet branches, though now she became concerned as she could not feel Anthi using his own!

“Anthi...”

There was no reply.

“Anthi!” She raised her voice, to which he only replied with a whining strained growl.

“No no no don't give up on me now! Stay with me! STAY... WITH... ME!”

Her heart started to race even more than it had ever been, feeling like it was vibrating rather than beating. She needed this pursuit to end now!

She had to get to safety fast for even a remote chance for Anthi to survive. She frantically looked around while leaping from branch to branch while the lion stalked her every move down below. She soon saw an opening up ahead where the trees ended and the sound of raging water. She had been fleeing in one wide semi-circle and had ended up further upriver.

She clawed herself to a stop so she could focus her vision better. She looked down below to the lion that had also stopped, gazing back at her with a confident grin. Both of them panting heavily to catch their breath.

"We can do this all day, I'm looking forward to killing you both..." the lion circled on the spot; his eyes locked on her. "You are Legacy's *freak* of nature, and that cub shares the blood of a traitor. Just give in... I'll make it quick," he sneered.

Tefnut looked in front of her, ignoring him. She instead was calculating the leaps in her mind. Her eyes gauged every stride, every jump and the speed and distance she would need to leap. Maybe she could just about make it? She then looked back down to the lion, who too realised what she was about to do. They both sprung off at the same time, heading towards the river. "You still need to come down to cross the river! If I don't kill you first, the river will!" he sneered again. Tefnut continued to ignore his threats.

"Anthi... if you can hear me..." She stammered in between deep breaths. "One last run, then we fly.

Please, please hold on... and we-can-make-it!"

She felt his claws gently dig in as she heard a whimpering groan, ending with a squeak. It may not be enough, but it would have to do. It was all or nothing now.

With that, she took the most extensive and prolonged set of leaps she could manage to get her speed up, her rear paw's pain now numbed as adrenalin rushed through her veins, muscles, and mind.

She leapt to the first branch.

She leapt to the second branch, narrowly missing a lightning bolt that split a nearby tree.

She then leapt to the final branch that was slightly overhanging the river.

The lion below now realised her intention. He ground to a halt just before the riverbank, and his jaw dropped in denial and bewilderment.

She leapt at the very last moment for a better chance. The branch bent as she pushed her rear legs as hard as possible. The remaining energy stored in her body exploded into this one final jump, or her last. She let out an almighty accompanying roar before it gave way to near silence. The feeling of weightlessness wrapped around her body like a blanket as she soared high above the river. The wind whistled past her ears with an almost sense of calm. The air felt refreshingly colder as it brushed over her face. The rain pattered on the water below, making its harmonic melody. For a split moment... she had never felt so free.

Her heart then immediately dropped as she could no longer feel Anthi's claws holding on. She then watched in horror as he flopped unconsciously over her head and in front of her eyes. She tried to catch him with her muzzle but missed. She crossed her front legs as he fell away from her, catching him just in time. She was now free-falling towards the opposite riverbank edge with no available front legs to land with.

While taking a deep breath, she embraced Anthi. She held him close to her chest with her head tucked in. She curled her body into a ball around him and closed her eyes, ready for the impact. She could hear Anthi's fainting heartbeat and a gentle warmth radiating from his body.

"We were strong..."

17. Guardian

The lion watched in resentful amazement as Tefnut soared through the air, never seeing any animal leap that far or even having the courage to do so. She landed hard with a resounding thud on the other side, just making it by a whisker. She rolled several times before slowing to a stop with her body still curled up tightly.

The lion had to get through the river and make sure they were dead, and if not, he finished the task. The water still raged and was deadly, but he knew failure wasn't an option. He placed his paws into the river's edge, letting them slowly sink into the soft mud underneath.

He then heard a rustle in the bushes behind him, followed by heavy breathing that gradually got closer. His accomplice must have somehow survived his impact with the tree from earlier.

"Ah, you survived, good! We can both cross the river and finish her off, tying up these loose ends," the lion chuckled with a sneer, looking ahead with his eyes locked on Tefnut and Anthi.

"Yes, I am alive, Kwakosa, and I am here to tie

up loose ends." Kikome Snarled. Kwakosa, in turn, hung his jaw in bewilderment. "Not them... but you!" Kikome continued. "I came across your accomplice, wrapped around a tree, so he won't be joining us. You should understand that if I am here, it means Legacy's reign is faltering, or he's even dead!"

Kwakosa snapped his jaw shut, huffed, and grinned, trying to hide his shock and regain his confidence.

"*If* Legacy is dead," he mocked, "I will be honoured to continue his reign, unlike his other so-called 'followers'," he scoffed again. "You on the other paw, are a traitor, and it's my duty and pleasure to make sure your penalty is finished" -he lowered his head and took defensive side steps- "regardless of our... connection."

"A connection that you never told Legacy about. You could have ratted me out anytime but you didn't, I still believe there is a decent part of you still inside."

"Pfft, ALL of me is decent. Everything I am and I do is for Legacy and the stability of power he has brought to the lands. I thought you were one of us. Our connection is irrelevant if we are fighting for Legacy's grand plan."

"You are -ill- Kwakosa, brainwashed by that tyrant. Can you not remember? Please try to remember." Kikome took a cautious step forward. "Many years ago, Legacy came to our pride demanding a lion to sacrifice its mind for his cause, in return he would give the pride immunity against his slaughter."

Kikome took another step closer and lowered his head, showing non-hostile intent. "I volunteered, but you insisted you go in my place, for the sake of my unborn daughter. You stepped out of the cave and kept me hidden." Kikome tilted his head up, Kwakosa took a step back, slightly startled by the memories now trying to 'poison' his mind. "I can help you just as you selflessly helped me. But as long as Legacy was alive, I couldn't." He gritted his teeth while his eyes began to glisten. "We don't have much time, I need to get back to the group. It's your choice Kwakosa. Please... let me help you."

Kwakosa pondered for a brief moment before shaking his head with a deep growl, ridding himself of such memories. He took this plead as a weakness and immediately lunged at him.

Kikome, in turn, effortlessly yet reluctantly deflected his paw and grabbed his neck. He leapt forward into the shallow beginnings of the river, pinning him under the water. After Kwakosa's quick struggle to breathe, he pulled him back up. "Don't make me do this... this is your only final warning, your one last choice. I will not and cannot risk any more!" Kikome snarled, yet with resentment. His forelegs were trembling, and his strength was quickly wasting away, caused by his neck injury.

Kwakosa ignored his words, as his mind was adamant about continuing his task.

"No Kikome, this is *my final warning*, never to get in my way!" he grinned. Feeling Kikome's weakened state, he pushed forward.

Kikome's forelegs buckled, allowing Kwakosa to bite deep into his already injured neck. He roared in agony and, with one last burst of strength, slammed Kwakosa back into the water, throwing his entire body weight onto him. It was the only option he had left. Kwakosa squirmed and struggled for several moments with his paws swiping everywhere, trying any last desperate attempt to injure Kikome enough to kill him.

Not being in much of a defensive position except for keeping him under the water, Kikome's pelt got violently ripped and torn by Kwakosa's razor-sharp claws. His skin and fur got sliced up effortlessly, with pieces being flayed away from his body with ease. He didn't even wince at the pain, his body was full of adrenalin and his mind full of resentment. He just stared down at Kwakosa's face submerged under the water.

"This was *your* choice, YOUR CHOICE, not mine!" Kikome raged with a tear running down his cheek. He knew that if he let him go now, he would be too weak to defend himself let alone try to persuade Kwakosa to change his mind. Kwakosa would kill him and then go after the rest of the group.

Kwakosa's struggle got weaker as the sound and sensation of water filled his lungs. Soon his chest pulsated, and his throat gurgled. His final remains of breath bubbled to the surface. His body then spasmed before soon lying motionless.

Kikome took a few steps back, with heavy grunting breaths. Blood seeped out from several deep lacerations over his pelt and his profoundly bitten neck. He then watched as the lifeless body was taken away by the water.

The rain continued to fall, running down Kikome's cheeks, along with another quick tear. “I did not want it to end this way... dear brother.”

Kikome would not feel guilty. He offered him a choice that he did not take. Ultimately, Kikome had to protect his own life for the sake of his brother not killing him or the others instead. It had been quickly made apparent that Kwakosa’s mind was beyond saving, it had been infected with Legacy’s ideologies for too long.

On the opposite side of the river, Tefnut slowly opened her eyes; her vision and hearing blurred and muffled as she came out of unconsciousness. She could still hear Anthi's heartbeat, which immediately put her at ease a little. She slowly uncurled herself and focused on him while giving him a few comforting licks.

Given the situation, a half-conscious groan with incoherent mumbling escaping Anthi's throat was the most welcome sound. Tefnut needed to get up and go, and she had no idea if she was still being pursued. Her body was hurting and aching with every movement she made, but most importantly, she had survived the jump whilst keeping Anthi cushioned and protected.

She winced her eyes tight shut in

anticipation. She stretched out her body, feeling the not-so-pleasant sensation of her joints and tendons cracking, which had tensed or sprained during the fall. She struggled up to her paws, failing a couple of times before managing it with an unstable tremble. She gently picked up Anthi by his nape and then looked over the river. Her vision wasn't perfect, but she could see that Kikome was standing on the other side by himself. She figured out the rest and sighed in relief, though concerned that his blurred figure mainly was soaked red.

Kikome looked out across the river. He also sighed in relief as he noticed Tefnut slowly getting up and taking hold of Anthi. He noticed her return the gaze, seeing if he looked OK too.

“GO! Get back to the cave! Get Anthi dry and warm! You are safe now. I'll be fine, and I will find another way.” he reassured with a raised voice.

Tefnut just about heard what he said, nodded and started briskly walking back in the direction of the cave. She wanted to thank him for everything he had done this far, but she knew it had to wait. He was in a bad state from what she saw, but so was Anthi. She had to prioritise and take Kikome's reassurance.

Kikome glanced downriver. He roared a signal into the darkness, stating everything was 'all clear'. He kept his ears perked up for the reply, almost nervous for what came, or if any. Thankfully after a delayed moment due to bad timing with the thunderclaps, a muffled reply in the distance by

Aramile came. 'All clear'.

Kikome sighed in relief, almost getting emotional. It was done. Sukari, Sheek and the group were safe and alive, and Legacy was gone. He looked back to Tefnut, who was walking away with a slight limp, though she seemed like she was OK and could make it back.

Tefnut continued her walk with Anthi dangling from her mouth. He was still half unconscious with a horrible sound of wheezing and creaking with each breath, but at least he still was breathing. Tears started rolling down her eyes, worried sick for Anthi's life. However, she knew that trying to tend to his injuries and condition in this open storm would be impossible and impractical. She started to pick up her pace to a fast walk, though her injured paw and various sprains made her legs drag. She wanted to get to the cave as quickly but as least damaging for Anthi.

She knew the cave well; It was Sheek's and Sukari's home, her old home, the group's old home. It was going to feel like taking a step back into the past. Tefnut had accomplished almost a miracle tonight to rescue Anthi. Now she just hoped one more miracle would happen... he would survive.

Kikome flopped onto the ground in a nearby area of clean long grass, washed by the rain. He spread and stretched out onto his side, panting heavily to regain his stamina while allowing the adrenalin to subside and his heartbeat to return to normal. He tucked his head in to keep pressure on his neck to stem the bleeding. His entire lower pelt was lacerated, skin hung loose and throbbing with pain. He felt the repeated stinging sensation from the rain seeping into his open wounds, however, this was a welcome 'pain' as he knew it would stop infection. After all, he hoped to survive this.

While recovering from this ordeal before hoping to make his way back to the cave, he looked back at his own actions that led him to this day...

Kikome was the lion covered in mud and stunk from one of Sheek's earliest 'groups'. Sheek handed him over to Legacy, thinking he was just another 'wanderer'. Kikome had spent years gaining intel about Legacy, one of which was Sheek's mission. Kikome planned this as an easier way to get on the 'inside', so he could reunite with his brother, Kwakosa. After all, a 'captured' lion has more believability than randomly appearing. He 'surrendered' to Legacy, vowing his services and loyalty to him, agreeing to his ideals. After he proved his expert skills in being a silent, effective, and obedient killer in a training exercise, Legacy could not resist his talents and soon took a lot of faith in him. All Kikome asked for in return is that his mind stayed pure, as brainwashing may contaminate his skills. Legacy reluctantly agreed, over greed for 'owning' his capabilities.

Over time, he sent him back out over the lands with scouts to 'help spread Legacy's fear'. Plus, Kikome could now keep an eye on his brainwashed brother from time to time whenever he reported back, hoping that when the time was right, he could break his mind free from the prison that Legacy had built around it.

Then something happened. On a sole patrol, he was found by his old friend Pulsar, who was on the brink of dying from a snake bite. Pulsar explained to Kikome that his nephew, Sheek, took a path that may not have good consequences. Pulsar's dying wish was for Kikome to be a guardian for Sheek and Sukari, plus whoever they hold dear if he wishes to. Kikome agreed.

The situation then turned a lot more complicated. That fateful night when Sheek was handing the group of wanderers over, which included Sukari. Sheek unpredictably turned against Legacy, causing terrible bloodshed. Legacy retreated and soon rendezvoused with Kikome, ordering him to kill Sukari, who was now found to be pregnant, and if Sheek is still alive, to make him suffer. It then made sense to Kikome at that time why Sheek turned on Legacy. He was protecting his cub which would have been killed the moment it was born, and Sukari would have endured unbearable emotional pain.

Kikome had to now try and live two lives, one as a guardian, and one as a torturer/executor... to both of them.

Unknown to the group, he had been more involved than met their eyes. Much of his protection throughout his whole endeavour will go unnoticed and uncredited:

-As Sheek recovered helplessly from his battle with Legacy, it was strange that no scavengers had taken advantage to try and eat him. Kikome had been keeping them at bay by patrolling the area day and night. Yet sparing the buzzards for Sheek's easy meal.

-As Sukari slept with her newborn Anthi on the first night she left the group, Kikome lay on top of the burrow and watched over them. On an extremely rare occasion, tears flooded down his cheek as he heard her lullaby echo from the burrow. Soon after, he quickly brushed them dry, then wiped his paw on the rock. He left just before sunrise, unknowingly leaving a tuft of his tear-dampened matted hair behind.

-As Sukari left Anthi in the tall grass while she caught a meal, Kikome watched over him from the nearby tree. He almost gave himself away when he accidentally cracked one of the branches, startling the birds.

-As Sheek and Sukari wandered around, Kikome would leave scraps of meat in their predicted paths, hoping they would find them. He watched over them both. Knowing this land like a map in his head, he would track and traverse between them, making sure they were OK.

How did every encounter not notice Kikome? It was simple. He was the best at what he brought himself up to be, a silent assassin and a great protector. He learnt not to let his scent give him away by paying attention to the wind and rolling in dung, which their noses would easily dismiss if they smelt 'his presence'. He knew how not to be seen by using his natural colour in the dry season and using the flourishing flora, fauna, and mud in the wet season to cover him up. He learnt how to effortlessly kill and harm with the greatest effect with the smallest effort.

A major turning point was when Sukari and Anthi attempted to cross the river and he knew Sheek was in the forest opposite, so they couldn't meet! He pushed a log into the river to aid them in buoyancy while also taking them further downstream, keeping them apart. It seemed like the perfect plan, but it didn’t work as expected. He instead had to rescue Sukari when she was knocked out from the log!

Grabbing her and leaving her safe by the side of the riverbank, he then went after Anthi, eventually finding him a lot further downstream, unconscious, and drifting. He swam to catch up but suddenly had to stop and dive under the water. He had spotted Sheek swimming towards Anthi too! Resurfacing at the riverbank further down, Kikome leapt onto the ground in the cover of darkness and lay prone in the long grass, watching Sheek bring Anthi to safety. He knew Sheek couldn't smell him, but deep down, he knew he wouldn't hurt him. He listened in to their 'deal' of finding Anthi's Mum. Sheek not wanting to know names was a significant relief and would give Kikome more time to plan. He knew it was inevitable now that they would all prematurely reunite.

He had to move his plans forward. This was the night he began a long-distance patrol to find their old group. Unknown at the time and lucky for him, the group had been travelling themselves and would find each other only a day's walk away.

However, he had failed two lions tonight. One lion was his brother, brainwashed by Legacy's ideals and beyond help. Although not entirely his fault, Kwakosa was the younger of the two, and Kikome always bore responsibility.

It was why Kikome told them to do precisely what they were ordered to do when they arrived here. He didn't want an all-out uncontrolled war, and he didn't want his brother to potentially get killed in the crossfire. The ambush he planned with the group was precise and meant minimal fatalities. Kikome wanted to try and give him one more chance to be cured. But like many other things that happened tonight, it didn't go to plan.

The other lion he failed was Anthi. He knew there would be risks tonight, but he didn't expect Legacy to brutally crush and throw him. Legacy was only meant to be distracted by the others while Tefnut grabbed Anthi and ran. Luckily, she improvised.

Ultimately, this was Kikome's curse of being a guardian of conflicting sides. You cannot protect and predict everyone, and you have to let your gut instinct control your actions. Sometimes the steps you need to take may seem farfetched or drastic, but deep down, you know it's for the greater good, even if it hurts them or you have to hurt them yourself. In the more extended scheme of things, it's for their own, and his own protection:

-Like torturing Sheek so as not to cause suspicion if any of Legacy's followers checked in on him, or even Legacy himself.

-Or risking killing one of Legacy's own scouts who was about to kill Sukari, hoping Legacy would believe the story that the scout died in 'conflict against the group'.

-Or painstakingly trying to keep Sheek and Sukari from meeting each other. It risked Kikome being compromised in his double life, and tonight was the proof.

On the outside, he was beaten and bleeding badly from what had been inflicted on him. On the inside, he felt conflicted. He had saved yet also failed others. He had to tell himself what had happened, has happened.

He had done everything in his power to keep to his vows, to guard and protect the lions he had or needed to. On his own life, he tried his best, so he wasn't to lay any guilt on himself. Anthi's injuries were severe, yet so were his own and out of his control. By the time he struggled and found another way back to the cave, it would be too late for Anthi. It would now take a lion with knowledge and experience of his unique skills to give Anthi his final chance.

With this thought, he lay still and rested on the grass, panting, and letting the rain clean and massage his torn-up pelt and neck. He needed a few more moments to himself before making his way to the cave. After all, he was no longer in a hurry. For Kikome's guard had ended this night, and it was now in the paws of another.

18. LULLABY

There was once a warm, bright morning. Back to the time when only a month had passed since Sukari had left the group, searching for a new beginning for herself and Anthi. She had simply taken refuge last night in some dense bush. It was a pleasant night, so there was no need for a hardened shelter. This place had also been found to house a decent-sized scrap of meat prior to using it. She questioned how it got there, and could've been many reasons. One most likely is whoever was eating the carcass got startled and ran. However, it was no longer worth pondering about as it now lay in her belly. A very much-needed meal for herself and also to keep her healthily producing milk for Anthi. Hunting had always been an alternate plan; however, this was risky for them both. She instead embraced scavenging, and she seemed to be quite lucky for that matter over the last month.

Sukari's eyes flickered in response to the rising sun that filtered through the bush, giving her a gentle warm embrace. The call of a buzzard that was perched somewhere, woke her up further.

Anthi was snuggled up and tucked in by her belly. His head was pressed against her, giving him the soothing sound of his mum's heartbeat. Anthi favoured here as this was the safest, softest, and cosiest spot to drift off to sleep. Conveniently, it was not too far to shuffle if he ever felt hungry too! Sukari took a deep breath and then slowly exhaled, taking in the fresh morning air that had cooled overnight. She peered through the gaps between the bush branches and gazed upon the distant lands that melted behind the horizon, which radiated a warm orange glow.

"*One day Anthi...*" she thought to herself as she hummed her lullaby. Not only she had used it on Anthi since their first night together in the burrow, but she also hummed it for herself. It gave her comfort in ways, regardless that bittersweet memories were still attached. Also, the gentle soothing melody matched that of this peaceful morning.

Her little fluffball soon disrupted her thoughts, wriggling around during his slumber. She slightly stretched out her body and moved her head towards him, taking a moment to gaze at her little creation and how sweetly he slept. He wore a faint smile on his muzzle with his nose twitching. His chest bobbed gently with a little flick from his rear leg, most likely dreaming of chasing a critter or playing. The sun had warmed Sukari's body this morning, but these little moments she shared with Anthi always warmed her heart.

As much as she didn't want to, it was time for him to wake up. They had to move while the morning was still a little cooler to make progress, resting later when the sun was at its highest. She gave Anthi a few nudges with her muzzle.

"You there, sleepyhead?" she whispered. Anthi replied with a moody growl from being disrupted, then simply tried to bury himself deeper under her belly. "No no, come now," she insisted, slightly firmer, rolling back to stop his hiding antics. Anthi groaned again in disapproval, rubbing his eyes and gradually opening them. His intention to keep sleeping was soon forgotten by the sight of his mum's exposed and welcoming teat. She watched and felt as Anthi latched on with ease to have his morning feed.

Sukari lay patiently for him, gazing out at the rising orange sun that painted a scene of beauty over the lands. Watching the sun she felt was a bit like watching over her cub; beautiful, calming, and sweet in the morning or evening, but such a pain and blinding during the day! She glanced back at Anthi, still feeding away with a little wiggle in his tail. From when she nursed him in the burrow of that cold and empty night, the strength of this bond between a nursing mother and cub never weakened or felt like a repetitive chore. It was an act of survival. Because of this, their bond was unbreakable. She loved him unconditionally.

Anthi started showing signs he was finished by getting rough and restless. A light disapproving pap on his head from Sukari's paw sorted that out. He grumbled in disapproval but was soon standing up, and with his short attention span, he started to stalk her tail as 'revenge'. However, she agreed with it, as it would wake him up further, develop future life skills, and put him in a good mood. A happy cub is a lot easier to control and put up with than a moodier one for the whole day. A smile widened across her muzzle as she flicked her tail from side to side, teasing his judgment of where it will stop, and watching in amusement as he either caught it a little or missed it.

Their little game ended when Anthi proudly latched onto her tail with both his paws and mouth, refusing to let go, showing his mum how much of an awesome hunter he will be when he grows up! This and also to 'teach her a lesson' - not to wake him from his comfy sleep or disturb a lion's meal!

“OK, OK Anthi,” she chuckled. “You win, you are definitely going to grow up strong, but for now, Mum is still stronger, ha!” she teased.

She grabbed him by his nape, and he relaxed his posture, yet reluctantly not wanting to let go of his 'kill'. Eventually, it slipped from his grasp as she pulled him forward. She placed him between her front legs and lowered her head in preparation for his morning bath, especially now he was a little dirtier from kicking up the dry ground after his 'hunting'. Just as her tongue was about to roll over his head, her ears flicked as she suddenly heard something that she had never heard before.

"I'm... stro... strong," Anthi murmured his first words, yet with a confident grin.

Sukari's Jaw dropped, her tongue left hanging out, her eyes wide open in shock yet amazement, and she just stared at him. This caused Anthi to reply with an amused giggle at how silly and funny his mum looked. Never mind the first word, Anthi managed two at the same time! Sukari flopped onto the ground and embraced Anthi with a tight hug, not without bearing a tear of joy that ran down her cheek.

"Yes Anthi... yes you are."

She closed her eyes tight while a deep tender rumble danced in her throat. During this, she could feel Anthi give her little licks and chirps in response. She never wanted this moment to end...

Suddenly a roar by Aramile thundered out. Sukari opened her eyes, snapping out of one of her fondest memories.

Her warm embrace of Anthi, and light from the sun, vanished from her mind. Replaced by the dark cold night, while being pounded by rain, her pelt was cold and soaked through to her skin. Her front legs were no longer holding her cub and instead were being used to keep herself moving. With the deep lacerations to her shoulder and bitten paw, she struggled to carry her weight after all that had happened, limping as she walked. She was in front, leading the group, she glanced behind towards Aramile, and he returned a nod with a reassuring smile from his roar.

"I replied to Kikome, signalling that everything is 'all clear'," he explained.

Sukari perked up her ears and looked downriver, which was quickly consumed by darkness.

"Kikome? Is he OK? What about Anthi and Tefnut? Sorry I was..." she panicked, but soon got interrupted by a reassuring hush from Aramile.

"Sukari, don't worry. Kikome sounded an 'all clear' from further downriver. Meaning everyone is safe."

Sukari had every faith in Tefnut's and Kikome's protection, and it seemed Kikome had this all planned out. However, she could not help but be worried for Anthi like any mother naturally would. The damage Anthi received from Legacy was severe; even though he was safe, she still was worried sick for him. 'Safe' doesn't necessarily mean he will survive his injuries. The sound of the crunch that came from his ribs continued to echo in her ears.

Sukari avoided looking at any water reflection on the ground as she continued to walk. She dared not see what she now looked like, and how she would be for the rest of her life. One side of her face continued to pulse with a numb throbbing, and a warm sensation of fresh blood trickling from her open wound circled it. Like Anthi, she knew she was safe now, but what if her injury caused further problems in the near or far future? She already knew she would be blind in that eye for life, but what if infection or disease developed?

Could she also live a comfortable and safe life with half of her peripheral vision gone?

She glanced behind again to see if Sheek and the lioness carrying him were OK. The lioness started to feel fatigued, so she lay Sheek down and switched with the lioness that had saved Sukari earlier. Sheek's eyes remained wide open and returned a gaze, but the life in them seemed gone. Sukari was getting worried not just about his physical well-being but also about his mental state. It's like his mind had blacked out.

Having the old group reunited once again and the threat of Legacy gone should have been a relieving occasion. One where they could all enjoy each other's company and look forward to the future, but the atmosphere was very much the opposite and quiet. They were all tired, battle-torn, soaked through and worried. Hopefully, when they got to the cave, they could all start to try to process the recent events while getting themselves dry, warm, rested and reacquainted. Sukari's priority though was just wanting to get back and see her son alive in the hope of making him better.

Over time, the group traversed through the long grass and hills before eventually reaching the summit of the Baobab tree hill. Sukari's pace had slowed as her energy was drained from the uphill struggle. She motioned to them to go ahead to the cave. The group walked ahead of her in subtle excitement about finally returning to their old home and out of the rain. Each member brushed their head over her shoulder as they walked past, making Sukari gain a faint smile. Legacy's lionesses lay down under the shelter of the tree. The lioness that was carrying Sheek was still standing.

"We will rest here. I'll take Sheek to the cave for you, then return here. You all need some privacy tonight to all get reacquainted."

Sukari then raised a concerned brow.

"But outside tonight is terrible. This rain doesn't seem to be stopping."

"The tree's shelter from the rain is luxury compared to what we are normally used to. Honestly, it's fine. There are more important things for you to take care of. We'll feel like we're just in the way if we go inside. Besides, we are used to keeping each other warm."

Sukari wanted to protest, but she knew logically that the lioness spoke wisely. She nodded in agreement, and the three made their way to the cave. The lionesses behind all shuffled up around each other, intertwining their bodies to keep warm. It was like a puzzle that they had mastered over time and experience. Sukari glanced back and saw them do this. It made her sympathise even more for them and how they adapted to their lives with Legacy.

As Sukari got near the entrance, she could see the blur of the group and the unique pelt of Tefnut inside. Their appearance was obscured by the water still falling from the top of the entrance. Her heart started racing; she didn't know what to expect inside. She took a deep breath and a hard swallow. She closed her eyes and made her way through the water.

Sukari shook her pelt and slowly opened her eyes, the remaining water blurring her vision but soon clearing. She then focused on Tefnut wrapped into a loose ball, cradling Anthi for warmth yet giving him enough room to help him breathe easily. Her paw was red, pressing on Anthi's bite wounds to stop the bleeding, which thankfully seemed to have worked. Tefnut gazed upon Sukari, letting out a gasp at seeing the side of her face and what remnants of her eye remained. Her shoulder and paw also showed significant damage. Tefnut went to get up, but Sukari quickly motioned her to stay still.

"Su... you are hurt..." she whimpered, deeply concerned.

Only Tefnut ever called Sukari by that nickname, and not even Sheek did. A glimpse of warmth flowed over her body momentarily from hearing it again. As lovely as it was, the current situation caused the cold to creep back.

"I'll be fine... I hope. How is Anthi? Are you hurt?" she squeaked as her throat tightened.

Tefnut hesitated. Her eyes immediately started to fill, and her lower jaw trembled. She looked down at Anthi, who was trying to pant, but his breathing remained shallow and hoarse. Her tears unavoidably dropped onto him.

"The bleeding has stopped, but his breathing

is getting worse. I tried everything I could... I don't know what else to do... I'm... I'm... sorry." her voice broke up and let out a whimpering cry. Sukari quickly leapt over, laying down next to her and Anthi to comfort them. She gave Anthi a few tender Licks on the top of his head while he was still in the legs of Tefnut. She then gave Tefnut a long reassuring muzzle on her cheek as it absorbed her tears. Tefnut then brushed her head along Sukari's shoulder, gently licking her wounds.

"Tef, you have done so... *so* much for us. Don't you *dare* feel you need to apologise for anything... not for one moment." Sukari reassured affectionately but firmly. She wanted to say so much more, but the worry for Anthi took over her mind. She poked Anthi's head with her muzzle, followed by a couple of licks. "Anthi... it's Mum. You there sleepyhead?" she gently said jokingly while fighting back her tears.

"And Auntie Tef," Tefnut added, giving him a playful nibble on his ear before lowering her muzzle onto the ground at Anthi's level.

The calming words from both of them echoed in Anthi's ears, making them flick. His eyes strained open with a groan croaking from his throat. He stretched out his paw, gently resting it on Tefnut's muzzle, making her smile affectionately. However, in Sukari's mind, this echoed his 'goodbye', like from the first time they left her.

"No no Anthi, no goodbyes, not now, stay with us... stay with us..." Sukari croaked. Meanwhile, the lioness carrying Sheek lowered him gently onto the ground before quietly turning to leave the cave. Sukari flicked her head around towards her, "Please... stay," she softly begged with her eye glistening. She didn't know exactly why, maybe because the lioness saved her life, and she felt they had made a connection. Sukari needed as much comfort as she could right now. The lioness returned the nod sympathetically before being surprised by Sukari's next question. "What's your name?"

The lioness took a step forward so she was next to Sukari, she hesitated a reply like she almost had to think about her answer. Under Legacy's command, she wasn't used to being addressed by her actual name.

"...Shujaa," she said, almost shying away, followed by a faint smile. To her, it felt good saying it again.

"Nice name," Sukari replied softly. She tilted her head with a bit of a realisation as a tear ran down her cheek. "The meaning behind your name, if you have ever questioned it, tonight you have earned it." She displayed a long respectful bow towards her. Shujaa went to bow in return but was stopped by Sukari giving her a soft nudge from underneath her muzzle, lifting her head back up. "You will never have to bow to me, dear Shujaa" she asserted affectionately.

Shujaa was at a loss for words, it had been too long since she was shown such kind affection, and she could only reply with a warm smile and a tear.

Sukari was too occupied to notice fully earlier, but Shujaa was a lioness that stood out, literally. She was quite tall and very muscular for a lioness; it made sense how she managed to reach and keep an anchored hold on Sukari's whole body weight from earlier. It also looked like she had been in her fair share of fights in the past, as her whole left ear was missing with only a heeled tuft of fur in its place. Various deep scars were buried in her chest, healed but still prominent. Her tall, tough, and rugged outer shell was such a contrast to her kind and well-hearted soul that lay inside.

Meanwhile, Aramile, Safila, Kisima and Anmani stayed quiet but close to Sukari. They didn't know what to say to make this whole situation any better. Still, they felt their presence was a softening comfort. They all approached closer and then lay down, either by her side or back, resting their heads against her. Mkuki and Mlinzi, though not personally as close to Sukari as the others, stood near the cave entrance guarding it. There was a slim chance of any undesirables coming in. However, it was their way of adding comfort for her. Sukari closed her eyes as she felt the warmth of her friends wrapped around her. She then felt a paw gently press onto her own. She looked up and half-opened her eye to see the paw was that of Shujaa's. Sukari then grew a trembling smile.

Meanwhile, Sheek lay motionless with his eyes still wide open, staring at the tender moments that unfolded, yet still himself not saying a word. Knowing what Legacy had done, Anthi had no chance of surviving, and Sheek had already mentally prepared himself for the inevitable. Anthi is just a cub, and he could no way survive the same injuries as Sheek; his little body isn't strong enough.

Regardless of Sheek's severe injuries and poor health, Sukari couldn't help but develop a fire in her belly in retaliation. She didn't approve of his current lack of actions or emotion. He was Anthi's father, and it was his duty to put his son before his self-pity!

"Sheek! I know things are tough, but your son is dying here for crying out loud! Isn't there anything we can do to save him? Or at least say or do something to comfort him! Put your self-loathing aside just for this one moment for the sake of him!" She growled but couldn't help it transform into a whimper.

Sheek simply then closed his eyes and turned his head away to the side.

"Sukari... I love you and Anthi more than you can imagine, but sometimes having too much hope makes things worse when it doesn't turn out the way you want." Sheek then curled up into a ball, letting out a few painful groans. "My father may be dead, but let's face it, he still won."

Sukari's jaw dropped in shock at Sheek's words. It's like he had just given up on Anthi's life and his own. She couldn't help but stare at him in disgust.

"If that's what you think, then fine! Continue wallowing, but at least say goodbye to your son. You owe him that much!" she growled, tears trickling down her cheek.

Shujaa pressed her head against the top of Sukari's in an attempt to calm her down and lead her head away back to Anthi. His breathing is now getting shallower with each passing moment, coughing and strained gasps squeezing through his chest. Sukari repeatedly stroked his head to comfort him.

"It's OK Anthi. It's OK. Stay with me, stay with us..." Sukari begged in a whisper.

Tefnut gave Sukari a nuzzle on her shoulder.

"Su..." is all she could squeak out before shuffling backwards, motioning Sukari to cradle Anthi instead. If this were to be his final moment, then it should be done so by his Mum; and his father if he came to his senses!

Sukari gently wrapped her paws around him. She turned her head to the cave entrance, took a deep breath, and then let out three unique roars – Kikome's signal, in desperation. The roars echoed around the cave before they fired out the entrance. Everything else then fell quiet, except the sound of the rain creating its tune as it splashed and dripped outside, and the roar echoing in the distance. She repeated the sequence as everyone looked on, not even beginning to imagine the pain she was feeling at this moment. The roars gave way to silence once again. With her mouth ajar, she pressed it against

Anthi's head, followed by a long mournful growl.

In the far distance, Kikome was still laying on the grass by the riverbank. He was conscious and felt as ready as he could be for his slow journey back. His ears flickered from an extremely faint sound deriving from a powerful roar, his signal. He was needed, but he knew he would be too slow.

"I'm sorry my dearest... I'm sorry..." he whispered to himself.

Regardless, he still struggled to his paws as his vows and personal responsibility for Sukari continued to surge through his body and mind. He took a deep breath before giving himself a majestic and proud shake, flinging torrents of water and mud everywhere. The long time spent soaking in the rain had melted and loosened away the earth from his fur and mane, along with that masking smell of dung.

This revealed his true colours of golden yellow and orange that had laid hidden underneath all this time, the very same colours that of Sukari... his daughter.

He knew her connection to him the moment he laid eyes on her all grown up. Her resemblance in looks and scent to himself and her mother was unmistakable. He couldn't tell her then, for the very same reason he left her just after she was born. He was a lone fighter in a plan to overthrow Legacy and get back his brother. His presence and connection to any collateral could not be known by anyone if he were to succeed in his plan, and it worked... mostly.

The only thing Kikome left Sukari with was a lullaby, a soothing tune he heard his partner hum while still pregnant with her. A few days before Sukari was born, his partner became seriously ill. Because of this, Kikome was present at the birth for the protection and care of her.

The moment Sukari was born, her mother fell unconscious. Kikome's paws instead were the first that cradled this tiny little fluffball he helped to create. He pressed his head against hers and hummed the same lullaby, welcoming her into this world. The sounds and vibrations resonated through her, just like they would have when she was still in her mum's belly.

After his lullaby, he left her in the care of a trusted friend who would stand in as her 'father'. His pride had nursing lionesses and their milk is the only thing now that would keep her alive, as her own mother had passed away.

Before Kikome left, he gave his tiny fluffball of a cub one last nuzzle...

"*Welcome to this land, my little one. You won't understand my words, but from a bereaved parent to their newborn cub, I just want to say... I'm sorry. I wish your beginnings started under brighter circumstances. However, I promise my unconditional love and protection, sacrificing anything to shield you, from what will lay ahead... alone.*"

In the years that followed, Kikome travelled all over the vast lands, mapping every tree, hill, rock, river, and valley in his mind. Whilst doing so, he relentlessly trained himself in every aspect of combat. All for one purpose, to replace Legacy and bring balance back to life, for all animals, lions, a brother, and especially for the future of his daughter.

Now with the threat of Legacy gone, he could reveal who he was. His eyes glinted with joy, something he felt was long lost. He could finally tell Sukari of her heritage and be the father to her he always wanted to be, making up for all the time they had lost together. Proving himself shouldn't be too difficult. If his true colours and the actual scent weren't enough, then reciting their lullaby would work. After all, he knew she had remembered it from hearing her sing it to Anthi a few months back at the burrow.

He just now wished with all his heart that his grandson, Anthi, would pull through too. If he didn't, then Kikome would be there for his daughter in her bereavement.

Until now it was always to be believed that Kikome had been leading a double life. One as Legacy's Successor and the other as a guardian. But in fact, it was a triple life. The third being a father, to a daughter that never knew who he truly was.

Back at the cave, silence fell after Sukari's mourn, which was then softly broken by Tefnut.

"Su... Kikome will be coming. He told me he would find a way back from the other side of the river," Tefnut spoke out gently, trying to reassure her.

"I need him! I need him NOW!" she wailed before taking an anxious deep breath. "He knows everything about Legacy's attacks, surely he knows how to survive one!" she cried out before burying her head, sobbing into Anthi's tuft of hair.

"Sheek survived! But it's clear he doesn't have a clue or cares how he did!"

Sukari was out of ideas, resorting to a final comfort for Anthi... her lullaby.

She began to let out a quiet hum from her throat, a tune that Anthi would know. It gradually got louder as Sukari calmed her breathing. It soon started to vibrate throughout the cave while everyone kept silent with expressions of sorrow and respect. Safila and Aramile leant on each other with tears flowing. Kisima and Anmani hugged each other tight, comforting each other. The hum continued, and Sukari's lullaby filled the cave with its melody. Sheek's ears flicked, and he half opened his now tear-filled eyes, gazing in the direction of Anthi. The harmonic tones suddenly dropped deeper as an additional voice joined in with the melody, that of Sheek. Sukari looked up towards him as he continued to hum, with tears in his eyes but bearing a plain expression, seemingly deep in thought.

Sheek knew the tune. Sukari once sang it to him for comfort when they were cubs. He had snuggled up to her after receiving a violent 'punishment' from his dad. Ever since whilst growing up, he sang it to Sukari for comfort too whenever she was hurt or upset. It was their little thing, and now it was passed onto Anthi.

Sukari felt Anthi react to her lullaby; his chest expanded larger and larger as he took the biggest breath he could manage. She looked down at him as his beautiful green eyes slowly opened wider.

"I'm... strong... but mum is... stronger." he wheezed before exhaling. His chest then froze, and it rose no more.

Sukari gave him a couple of small nudges with her muzzle but to no avail. She lifted his muzzle using her own, but his head just flopped back down again. She shook him a little, but his body just slightly shifted to a quick stop.

She tenderly latched onto his nape and dragged him over on his back to the warmth and comfort of her belly and curled slightly around, cradling him. She buried her head into him before letting out a long, heart-breaking howl that filled and echoed around the cave. Tefnut lay her head over Sukari's, then wrapped her paws around her shoulders. Her tears, in turn, absorbed into Sukari's fur.

"Yes Anthi... yes you were... and I will be... I promise," she murmured, taking long sniffs to clear her nose as she gently cradled him.

A few short moments passed, and Sheek approached, slumping down next to them with a quick hum in his throat. Sheek had seemed to have a change of heart and came to say goodbye.

He shuffled up close to Sukari, Shujaa

momentarily taking a couple of steps back to give him space. He placed his paw gently on top of Anthi's chest, feeling his warmth for the last time. He knew what would come next for Anthi. Dying from suffocation is not a nice way to leave this world, as he knew himself all too well. His paw on Anthi's chest started to tremble. He placed his other trembling paw on Sukari's own as tears continued to roll down his cheek. Although she appreciated Sheek coming to his senses, it was still a late sign of affection, and she disapproved of it. She momentarily retracted her paw while her face was still buried in Anthi.

"You're too late Sheek... he's gone!" she whimpered.

She then continued humming her lullaby once more into Anthi's ear as she felt him lifeless in her paws.

Sheek took a deep breath and exhaled slowly, on the verge of completely breaking down.

"Anthi... Sukari... forgive me."

19. Don't Look Back

It has now been two years since that night. That night where a lion who gave so much to the group and had touched many lives for the short time they knew him; had his life taken away too soon.

It was the first moment of dawn. Sukari lay under the Baobab tree, the Tree Of Life. She glanced over by the trunk and looked at the pile of rocks. Each one was placed by a member of the group and the lionesses, including the one that had little claw marks all over it. It was a memorial for him and his bravery.

Sukari slowly blinked before staring over the land as the rising sun started to peek from the horizon of the second hill. A beam of orange light flooded over the lands, painting the beauty of nature once again. This breathtaking scene felt timeless for her, and it would always bear bittersweet memories that she would cherish close to her heart forever. She closed her eyes as a gentle breeze brushed over her face, feeling her fur and whiskers massaged by the gentle wind. To her, it was a reminder that his spirit lived on.

A faint smile and hum from her throat started to develop, the melody was her lullaby for Anthi. This was intentional, being what day it was today. She slowly scanned the land while continuing her tune, taking in nature's charm. She now had to turn her head a little more to get a wider view, a reminder that she only had half of her peripheral vision. Thankfully, the wound had healed healthily over time without infection, thanks to Sheek's consistent cleaning and care. The scars ran from the top of her head, through her eye, and then finished below her cheek. She had learned to live with her appearance, afraid no more to look at her reflection, just like how Sheek had learned to live with his. She was thankful and felt lucky to get away with her life that night. However, her smile flattened when she soon remembered someone that hadn't.

Her hum gradually ended, not before the last few notes harmonised with a deeper hum behind her from Sheek. He had now gained back to a healthy weight with no sight of his ribs, now hidden and surrounded by a healthy layer of fat. His mane was now thick, full of colour and shone with life. Plus, it was very well-groomed! As the past couple of years progressed, so did his breathing. Time, food, patience, and a little loving company is the best healer in this land. He could now do physical activity without becoming dangerously out of breath or fear of collapsing. He knew he would never fully recover, and it now just felt as if he had aged twice as fast.

Sheek brushed his head against Sukari and then lay down beside her. He knew she liked her solitude in the early mornings and would usually join her a little later on. But knowing what day it was today, he wanted to give her some much-needed extra company.

"Morning..." he softly whispered with a quick lick on her cheek.

"Morning..." she replied, brushing her head against him. Her eyes were glistening, on the verge of breaking into tears.

"Thinking about Anthi?" he questioned softly.

Sukari nodded subtly in reply, wrapping her tail around him. They both silently gazed over the lands that were now their forever home. With Legacy gone and the support of the lionesses, this area was established as their territory, a pride's territory, and it was no longer a wanderer's abode.

Sukari changed her position, lying against Sheek to take the pressure off her abdomen. She snuggled her head into one of Sheek's front legs while he placed his other available paw over her, gently resting it on her extended belly. They were soon to be parents again.

With her size and the commotion she could feel inside, they knew they would have their paws occupied with more than one cub. This was soon reminded as Sheek felt a few rumbles under his paw, followed by an affectionate 'mew' escaping Sukari's muzzle. Sheek rested his head on her shoulder and gazed down at her belly. He had missed the time she was this far along with her pregnancy with Anthi, so every morning alone with her was special, noticing as their future sons or daughters gradually took up more space as they grew inside. He couldn't help but spoil her with unconditional love and affection because of the burden she bared. With past events carefully put aside and sticking together through a long and testing recovery of both their bodies and minds, their bond was unbreakable.

Sheek's heart skipped as he felt another prominent kick, the biggest he had felt and saw her belly twitch. Sukari took a small quick gasp from the weird sensation, followed by a wide, warm smile. Sheek buried his head in her neck, affectionately biting the nape.

"I think... it will be time soon," Sukari said softly.

Sheek's ears suddenly flattened from nervousness.

"I understand. You will be fine, and I will be waiting for you when you return with our new little furballs. Remember, they will never replace Anthi, he will always be our first, and always remembered." he tried to reassure her, but instead was panicking himself.

Sukari twisted her head and gave Sheek a tender lick on the underside of his cheek as he cradled his paw around the back of her head. Her smile flattened, though only slightly, as she felt his nervousness kind of adorable.

"No silly," she chuckled. "Our cubs are not ready... yet," she said while giving him another lick. "I mean to say our goodbyes."

Just then, a deep, dragged-out, groaning yawn was heard from behind them, it sounded like the grown lion had just woken up. He took a few more steps towards them while giving his body a good shake to perk himself up further. His mane danced around, ridding itself of dirt from last night's sleep.

"Replacing Anthi? Saying Goodbye? Gee... I know I'm leaving today, but I never knew my Mum and Dad to be so eager to get rid of me!" Anthi said sarcastically and grinning, now with a deeper and throatier voice.

"Aha, the young master has awoken!" Sukari returned the sarcasm.

"Mornin' son, yes, please leave, tired of sharing food with you now. You eat too much, not to mention your snoring vibrates the entire cave." Sheek muttered in dry humour, resulting in Anthi papping him on the head.

"*Oh gee, I wonder where he gets that from,*" Sukari thought to herself.

"Pfft, this is what I get for being the 'first' cub, as you called me just now. However, I prefer 'number one son forever'!" he grinned while puffing out his chest.

"Gee, how did we create and raise a lion with such a big ego?" Sheek murmured to Sukari, nudging her.

"Big ego? Ha!" Anthi scoffed. "Says the lion that never stopped reminding me how courageous he was at saving my life," he teased before tugging at his dad's ears with his teeth.

Anthi's mane flickered in the breeze with a majestic dance. Although not completely grown yet, it was already thick and prominent. His bodily physique looked more like a young adult, and his size was now almost the same as his father's.

Sheek growled and rolled over playfully. Sukari flopped her shoulders onto the ground, tilting her head and watching amused as father and son proceeded to have a small scuffle. She smiled warmly at the fact that as they had grown older, they still had that playful cub inside them. She chuckled to herself at the irony that she - literally does!

Anthi had temporarily pinned his dad in their antics, who looked at him with eyes full of life.

"I was proud that night, son, and let's not forget others that played just as an important part too." Sheek winked and warmly smiled, also being reminded of how strong and heavy Anthi had become.

"I'll never forget Dad. You know how thankful I am for what you did, and what everyone else did."

"Ha, I'm your dad. It's my job to look after my 'Number one Son'," he grinned before quickly pushing Anthi off with his rear legs. They both jumped at each other while darting around the tree for a short moment. Sukari still lay with a half-amused expression. Before long, she leant up and cleared her throat to get their attention. "*Gee, these males... please let all my cubs be lionesses...*"

Sheek and Anthi soon settled. Sheek lay behind Sukari, resting his head on her back, wrapping his front paw around, and placing it on her belly once more, embracing his future sons or daughters. Anthi lay down in front of her. She looked at her now handsome son with such pride that her eye glistened. You see something slowly grow up and change a tiny amount each day, and you never really notice until that one day becomes the last.

"My Son, My Anthi, my lion, all grown up. I'm going to miss you," she said with a slight squeak in her throat.

"Don't get mushy on me Mum," he chuckled. "Look how much *you've* grown," he said with his joking charm, motioning towards her belly. For that, he received a playful slap from his Mum's paw. "But seriously... I'm gonna miss you too, I'm gonna miss all of you, but we all know it's in my nature to leave," he said, but starting to choke up.

Sukari, Sheek and Anthi knew that another grown male lion could not stay in the pride. He is destined to leave, to start a life of his own, not to mention his younger brothers or sisters are due any day now, and he would just be in the way. Sukari knew he didn't want to stick around playing cub-sitter either, besides, he had his own pride to seek to create.

This is what today was all about. This was the day Anthi had planned to leave the pride on the anniversary of surviving his ordeal. It had been two years since Anthi had a second chance at life, and he found it a fitting day to go. Also, it had been two years since another lion who instead, had his life cut short.

Kikome never returned that night two years ago. His body was never found except for a large pool of blood that led to the water's edge. It's as if he knew he wouldn't survive his injuries. Their best guess was he let himself be taken by the river.

Sheek watched on, and his heart glowed as Sukari and Anthi shared a tender moment between mother and son. They nuzzled each other's shoulders and necks, their eyes full of love that spoke a thousand words to one another.

He trailed into the thought of his life-saving actions from that night, which made Anthi's survival possible.

Back then, he was in a dark place. He felt useless as he hardly contributed anything towards Anthi's or Sukari's rescue; the whole confrontation was resolved without him and Anthi lay dying. What could he say or do to make things better?

He had experienced the feeling of dying, both with loved ones surrounding him and another time completely alone. When you're at the end, it's nothing but waiting for darkness to consume you; either way, no one can make it better for you.

Surviving a near-death experience changes you forever. He was now immune to the fear, panic and emotion of it all, be it to himself or others. He could stare at it in the eye without a flinch. Just like he did with that young female cub. This made him come across as if he had the emotion of a rock and didn't care for his own life or Anthi's. This wasn't true. He just knew what was coming. It's a dark and lonely experience regardless of who is or isn't surrounding them.

However, when Sukari mentioned that he *did* survive an attack from Legacy, but didn't know exactly how; he had a flash of memory back to that moment. He vaguely remembered in his own darkness, taking his first strained breath and the sensation he felt before it. It made him wonder, what exactly *was* that sensation he felt when his chest cracked? He wasn't in the state of mind to think about it back then and soon forgot, but now he wondered... could it have possibly been a paw? Could it have pressed down hard onto his chest in the exact correct spot?

Sheek wasn't knowledgeable of this practice. He wasn't sure if it were true and would work. If he did it wrong, it might even kill Anthi quicker! However, when he placed his paw lightly on Anthi's chest and felt no signs of him ever going to breathe again, there was no guilt or risk in potentially killing him. He was going to die anyway. Sheek was immune to this fear of death, glaring at it confidently in the eye, but this time now on behalf of his own son. He was in control of his son's fate! His paws started to tremble as he heard Sukari snap at him, saying it was too late while holding Anthi limp in her paws. It was all or nothing now. What did he have to lose?

He took a deep breath.

He exhaled slowly with a tremble.

His vision tunnelled.

His mind was completely focused.

"Anthi... Sukari... forgive me..."

He delivered a hard, jolting press to the opposite side of where Anthi's chest had been crushed, followed by a loud crack. Anthi then, in turn, took a lifesaving gasp, followed by coughing up some blood that had settled.

"That's it Anthi... that's it, my son!" he said, surprisingly calm. "Come on Anthi... another breath... ANOTHER BREATH!" He began to cheer on, a tear running down his cheek, and in turn, Anthi took a long shallow wheezing lungful of air. Sukari's jaw immediately dropped with her ears and hair standing on end.

"ANTHI! Come on, come back to us!" Sukari wailed in hope while licking the blood away from his muzzle. Anthi again took another long-strained lungful of air before developing a steady breathing rhythm. It was shallow but survivable. Meanwhile, he was constantly being licked by his mum for comfort. Sukari then looked up at Sheek in complete shock with a tear-filled eye. "Sheek... I... I'm..." she croaked with a tremble. She broke down uncontrollably from relief, and Sheek lay his paw on hers, which she now instead grabbed onto tight.

Sheek's theory of his own survival was proven! A hard, educated press from a paw onto his chest, saved his own life that night. There was only one lion that came to mind, the only lion who was skilled in all forms of survival, the lion who swore to protect him. It was Kikome. He had saved Sheek's life. It was *his* blurred silhouette that Sheek had seen blend into the grass that night, not Aramile.

Sheek had now used the same technique to save Anthi. Luckily he did it in the right place, at the right angle, and the correct pressure was applied as he could remember. Kikome's guardian duties and influence had lived on, unknown to them at the time, even after his death.

Sheek came out of his past thoughts and back into the present. Sukari continued to cherish the moment with Anthi, as it would be the last for a long time. She felt his mane brush over her face. Even though she had watched him grow up into the handsome young lion he is today, it was still a surreal feeling how much he had changed. She was so proud of her son and how he had recovered from his injuries. Since they had happened to him when he was a cub, unlike his dad, Anthi's body managed to fully recover from Legacy's brutal attack, after being revived. He was now strong, happy and healthy.

For a while, the three no longer exchanged any words. They just stared out over the open lands as the sun grew a stronger presence on the horizon. The breeze gave them all a gentle massage, and both Sheek and Anthi's mane danced the same in the air, like-father-like-son. As Anthi's mane blew in the wind, it exposed two small, faded scars where Legacy had bitten him, the only lasting evidence of his near-death experience.

Sukari lay between Sheek and Anthi with a flick of her ear and a swish in her tail. She then felt a few little kicks from her unborn cubs, undoubtedly wanting to be part of this. With Sheek's paw wrapped around her belly, he felt it too, giving it a subtle affectionate stroke. She cherished every second of this wholesome moment, her family all here at once, one last time. They all continued to lay quiet, soaking up the ambience of this dawn. Before long, another voice was heard.

"Morning you three."

Shujaa appeared behind them before circling. She brushed against them in greeting, giving a little extra attention to Sukari. The two developed a strong friendship over the past two years since the night their lives entwined, and are now practically sisters. Shujaa was now the head lioness of their hunting party after showing bravery, strength, and determination.

"Good morning Shujaa," Sukari replied, brushing her muzzle along her shoulder. Shujaa then sat down next to her, with Sukari soon hooking her front leg around her tail.

Tefnut appeared and sat down beside the

three with a subtle smile and nod, which they returned. She had been around with them the last few days to visit, prior to Anthi's ceremony. Although she was a dear friend and family of Sukari and Sheek, she wasn't a permanent part of the pride. Now Sukari had the security of Sheek and their pride, Tefnut could come and go as she pleased. She could now enjoy the natural solitude that all leopards bestow by instinct, without worrying about the well-being of her family and friends. She knew though, there was always room for her in the cave when she visits.

Anthi lifted himself up, taking a few steps towards the hill's edge before sitting down again. He gazed at the endless lands he would soon cross and beyond to where he couldn't see. He stared at the natural display of beauty and tranquillity of the sunrise once more. His tail flicked with an odd slight spark of unknown excitement in what lay ahead. Yes, this endeavour still would not be without risk and danger, but he already had a considerable amount of experience in this. Besides, this was nature's law, and for Anthi, this will be the start of his life as an adult lion, seeking his place in the world.

Next to appear were Safila and Aramile, along with Dahlila, the lioness Aramile saved that night, and now they were a loving couple expecting cubs of their own. Safila, although grown-up, offered to stay with them both. Aramile had been her foster dad all this time, and she wanted to repay his kindness by helping to be a 'big sister' to the cubs. It would add strength and protection to the beginnings of their pride. This was proof again that brighter things had sparked from the darkness.

Along then came Anmani and Kisima, who were now fully grown adults and a couple.

Mkuki and Mlinzi then arrived and stood next to each other but just a little further away from the crowd. They had always been the ones that kept to themselves and shied away from being too social. However, Sukari had grown to respect and trust them. After all, they had been through a lot together, and she knew their hearts were large and loyal; they just didn't display it. It was just who they were, and she respected that. She saw them as friends just as much as the others. They both smiled and nodded towards her, she then returned the gesture.

All these lions and lionesses, at one point, were either wanderers, rogues, ex-pride members or orphans, all in fear. They had all now made lives of their own in their own territory or could now wander without consequences, possible now Legacy's fear over the lands had ceased to exist. However, they had never forgotten the 'family' from once they came, arriving back to their old 'home' the night before, ready for this day.

The rest of the lionesses who were saved from Legacy emerged from the cave, which was now their forever home. They now live a more promising and fulfilling life as a pride. They walked over and joined the rest of the group.

Everyone, pride lionesses and the group alike started to exchange greetings. They nuzzled and brushed against one another while talking about memories past and shedding tears of tragedies shared. Shujaa and Dahlila were especially happy to have a catch-up once again since Dahlila left.

After some time, they all quietened and settled down. Sheek, Sukari and Anthi then stood forward in front of everyone. They all then looked out from the summit of the hill where the Baobab tree stood. Sukari took a deep breath, expanding her chest, and stood proud.

“Today, we honour Anthi's day of becoming an adult, by his departure,” she announced, glancing over at him. “But before that, I want to add he would not be here today if it was not just for Tefnut's quick reflexes and Sheek's quick thinking, but all of you,” Her eye glistened as she motioned her head across everyone.

She took a trembling breath, “We all played our part in keeping Anthi and each other alive, plus finally never worrying about Legacy's tyrannous rule, making this land a safer place to live.” They all exchanged glances and nods at each other. “Unfortunately, one lion fell that night, and his body became one with nature.”

She paused to clear her throat while everyone else soon lowered their heads in respect. “He was brave, selfless, and proudly stood as our last line of defence as our guardian... and good friend. In the short time that we knew him, I feel he played a bigger part that we will never be able to comprehend. We cannot do so because his voice has now faded away,"-she wiped a tear away with her paw- "so let us carry it for him... in his memory!"

With her head held high and chest expanded once again, Sukari took a deep breath and then let out an incredible roar that shattered through the air. Sheek followed with his own powerful roar in a different tone. Anthi then finished off with his newly found staggering roar. In turn, the three roars formed the unique call of Kikome and his three-roar signal. It thundered over the lands, birds flew up into the orange sky, and small prey scurried away with their dancing shadows. Then, everyone repeated Kikome's roar in unison, the land and air being shaken once more. For this one moment, Kikome's spirit lived again.

For the past season, Sukari had polished Anthi's training in hunting and social skills, while Sheek did the same with fighting and self-defence. They could only do so much though, as the rest was up to him. Not everything can be taught, it has to be lived.

They had said most of their final heartfelt farewells last night to not make this morning as upsetting or painful. It was Anthi's wish not to drag it on and bring too much attention to himself. With this, he brushed his muzzle along his dad's cheek.

"Goodbye, Dad, don't go being a 'rogue' now. You'll soon have more cubs to look after... or scare." he chuckled, not without letting a softening sniff, clearing his nose.

"Goodbye, Son, try not to drown in a river again. You're too big to carry. However, dragging you from the river was... the best mistake of my life." Sheek grinned but with a tear in his eye. He then pressed his muzzle against Anthi's shoulder to hurry him onward towards his mum.

Anthi took a couple of steps towards her, pausing in front for a moment before lurching forward with a long emotional embrace. Sukari's tears were soaked up by his mane as his own dropped down onto her paws.

"When you leave, don't look back." she croaked.

"Who knows Mum, one day we may cross paths, and I can say that you're a grandma!" he teased, trying to lighten the tone. Another tear escaped his eye, before taking a short sniff to clear his nose.

"Gee, thanks, that won't make me feel old!" She scoffed. Soon seeing her son getting emotional, her heart started to ache, and she couldn't help but give him one last nuzzle. "This is it Anthi, time to find a new home and a new life." She croaked, then took a step back.

With this, everyone else started to crowd around him, exchanging their love, friendship, and farewells for his future endeavours. Sheek and Sukari took a proud step back. Anthi glanced at his mum and dad through the gaps in-between the commotion of all the lions and lionesses. His brows softened with a heartened smile. Sheek and Sukari gave him a confident nod, and he nodded in reply. His smile then turned into a confident grin as his brows hardened. He then let off another roar, then which everyone else joined in.

With that, he pounced and darted down the hill. Many of the original group and lionesses followed, running behind him, giving him one final send-off. Tefnut predominantly alongside him as she could easily keep up. Two years ago, Tefnut ran home with Anthi close to death on her back. Now she was running alongside him, away from home, all grown up. It was a special contrasting moment. Anthi turned his head slightly towards Tefnut as they both ran.

"Tef... I'm not gonna lie. I'm kinda nervous... I'm kinda scared." his voice trembled as he took deep breaths with his sprinting. Tefnut smiled deeply with confidence and gave him a reassuring shunt - shoulder to shoulder.

"Remember Anthi... scared is good, scared means you have a pure heart, and a lion with a pure heart is a force not to be reckoned with. You Anthi, you... are... strong." she exclaimed with confidence. Anthi let out a single chuckle and a confident grin spread across his muzzle with a single nod.

"Thanks Tef... that means... everything." With that, he let out a confident growl and continued his sprint up the second hill as Tefnut intentionally slows down behind. The rest of the group and the lionesses do the same until they all came to a stop.

They then watched on as Anthi ascended the second hill by himself. He paused for a moment at the top, wanting to turn his head around one last time to see them all. Instead, he continued one paw rhythmically in front of the other, soon disappearing from view over the summit.

Back at the Baobab tree, Sukari and Sheek sat next to each other paw in paw. They both gazed as Anthi and the mix of lions and lionesses ran into the distance. Anthi then soon paused at the summit alone of the second hill. He cast a large shadow that spread across the land with his body now a silhouette in the sun's orange glow. It then shrank behind the hill and vanished.

Sukari and Sheek faced each other.

"Sometimes, you take a step back and realise... we made that." Sheek sighed with a proud smile. Sukari hummed in agreement, her smile matching his own.

"And... there he goes, our little furball now turned lion." Sukari mewed, glancing over to the summit of the hill where she had last seen Anthi, with a glimmer in her eye.

"Are you worried?"

"Of course not!" she replied confidently, turning her head back towards him. "After all we have been through, I'll be worried for whoever tries to get in the way of him!" she huffed with a smirk. Sheek joined in with a short scoff before they leaned their heads on one another, with their tails entwined. Both then turned their gaze back over to the summit of the hill.

Suddenly, Sukari winced as her belly tensed for a short moment, along with a more than uncomfortable sensation wrapping around it. It wasn't the cubs kicking, but she had felt the same pain before when pregnant with Anthi. She knew what it meant.

"Sheek... talking of things being made... I think... it's now time."

Sheek nodded, shining with the proudest of smiles, though not without showing an unavoidable nervousness. This was it; their cubs were getting ready to come into this world. This meant Sukari had to leave and travel to her predetermined birth den. Of course, this meant he wouldn't see her for a while until she introduced the cubs back into the pride later. This didn't upset or phase him, as he had done far worse waiting in his life in the past, so this would be easy. This time he knew he would see her again, along with some new bouncing and mischievous furballs.

"Take all the time you need. I'll be waiting, with fresh leaves ready on the bed for our little ones," he said with a slight nervous tremble, but not without a proud glimmer in his eye.

They then shared a deeply intimate, warm embrace and nuzzle, which eventually turned into a playful moment of trying to nibble each other's ears, while subtly exchanging whispered laughs. After a few tender grooming licks of Sheek's mane to neaten it back up, Sukari then stood up and began to walk past him. Sheek brushed his head alongside her belly with a deep affectionate growl which she felt rumble through her. "Now, behave for your mum, furballs." he cooed. Sukari brushed her head affectionately across Sheek's back, then continued to make her way in the direction of her hidden den. It wasn't close by, but neither too far. Just enough distance to feel secluded.

Shujaa, who had joined the running send-off for Anthi, turned her head back towards Sheek and Sukari, seeing them still sitting under the baobab tree on the hill in the distance. She watched with a warm smile as she could just make out they were sharing a playful embrace before Sukari turned and left. She knew it could be happening soon, and it seemed now it was. Sukari was leaving to give birth to her cubs.

"Good luck, my dear sister. I can't wait to meet them," she whispered under her breath before her smile grew. She chuckled to herself, knowing she now had to put up with Sheek and his constant worry about Sukari's well-being. She didn't mind at all, and it was what being part of the pride was all about.

Sheek sat back down, turning his head in each direction. One direction was his lioness now on a journey to deliver new life, the other direction was his firstborn son now on a journey to make a new life for himself. As for Sheek, he was sitting under the Tree Of Life. He hummed a chuckle at how fitting the situation was. For a lion that at one point was broken, he now had never felt his life feel ever so complete.

Across the land, Anthi immediately felt a sense of solitude and loneliness as he passed over the hill. With the last words of his mum echoing in his mind and her tears still soaked into his fur, he bore a confident grin and looked ahead. A youthful chirp escaped his throat with an eager swish in his tail. His ears stood up with an excited yet nervous twitch.

"This is it Anthi, time to find a new home and a new life."

Anthi's search had begun, and Sukari's search was complete.

He didn't look back.

Epilogue - Life

Each morning before everyone had awoken, with the sun far from rising, this is where I came, my birth den. Each morning I would bring soft leaves or dried grass for my nest. I would even get the occasional tuft of Sheek's hair after I had groomed his mane, like from this morning. It bared his scent, a home comfort for myself and a scent my cubs would get accustomed to. I have arrived for my lengthened stay after saying goodbye to my now grown-up firstborn, Anthi.

I close my eyes, and I can picture him now, walking alone across the vast land with the sun on his shoulders. I can see him wearing that cheeky grin of his, with a spring and strut in his step, always being that little overconfident. We all have our quirks and wouldn't want him to change that for anything. After all, our quirks are what make us... us.

I lay here half curled into a ball away from everyone. I feel safe and secluded, away from all the commotion and attention from the pride. It's just me, my thoughts, and my little fluffballs causing all sorts of mischief cooped up inside. If this is what they are like before they come into this world, then myself and Sheek will be very occupied as they grow up!

I'm sure Shujaa won't hesitate to help. Though lionesses naturally help out with each other's offspring anyway, I'm certain she will be first in line to offer a paw. Be it keeping them occupied in play, giving them a groom or just being an all-around cub sitter while me and Sheek take a small break.

We have become best friends. It kindled from the night she saved me without knowledge or judgement of who I was. The moment she was no longer under the rule and fear of Legacy, she could be the lioness she always wanted to be inside. From these past two years, that kindling friendship has turned into a roaring fire, two hearts alight with a friendship and sisterhood that is now inextinguishable. It's ironic how a lion such as Legacy, full of such hate and evil, was the cause and effect of this now flourished bond.

As much as I miss Shujaa, my pride, and Sheek dearly, time alone here in this den is the best for my cubs and me. With this dense bush hidden away in the depths of a dried-out valley, I feel completely cut off from the world, and I kinda love it! I would've begun my solitude a couple of days earlier in this place, but for this one time, I fought against my instincts, staying with the pride until the anniversary of Anthi's chosen time to leave, and Kikome's passing.

As much as I want what is best for my cubs, I also wanted to be there for Anthi. After everything we had been through together, it's the least a mother can do. It wasn't *his* fault I chose to have more cubs... though indirectly, maybe it was?

Me and Sheek *did* send him on a long-distance patrol alone for the best part of a season as a lesson in self-survival, call it tough love so to speak. With my son 'gone' for a lengthened amount of time combined with several peaceful, almost romantic strolls alone with Sheek, going into heat was kind of inevitable. *Some* instincts I just cannot fight... heh.

Well, what is done is done, yet I wouldn't change it for the world. Anthi would *eventually* have to leave anyway. Me and Sheek always like to be kept on our paws too. If anything, it will only strengthen the bond between ourselves, our pride, and its future.

I'm not saying it wasn't strong to begin with. In fact, our bond is now more unique than no other. Because of our injuries sustained, we have adapted to help one another. I'm Sheek's nose, and he's my eyes; our weaknesses are supported by each other's strengths. Alone we may be more vulnerable, but together we are unstoppable in living an everyday life, regardless of what disabilities are bestowed upon us. Myself, Sheek and Anthi now bear scars from our past and with a unique reason for how we got them. They remind us that whatever story is behind that scar, we survived.

Being alone makes me feel more vulnerable, especially with only a single eye. Not seeing everything I typically could, I rely more on the protection and camouflage of my den. If anything happens, me and Sheek have already produced an emergency plan, so I have that reassurance. Speaking of one eye, this will be interesting as I literally will be trying to keep an 'eye' on my cubs! I have already placed brittle sticks around the enclosure; if any were to be stepped on, I would hear it. It's ironic, the first night alone with Anthi, I did this outside the burrow to hear anyone coming in; now I'm doing it to hear anyone getting out!

I won't lie. I'm kinda nervous and kinda scared. Carnivorous scavengers find cubs an easy meal. I have sacrificed my body and blood when protecting Anthi. I'll have no hesitation in doing it again! Though I prefer to not bear the pain again, any animal that tries to take my cubs away from me *will* come out from it a lot worse. You only have to look back to Legacy's demise to understand that.

Why am I also not concerned about other dangers like rival prides or felines? It seems news travels. Ever since Legacy was no more, we have not had any problems with prides or male lions challenging our own for dominance. At first, we questioned it, but then we realised that they were doing it out of respect. We didn't just set them lionesses free that night; we set the whole land free, without fear of Legacy and his tyranny, and with the natural law of territory restored.

Legacy still had scouts and followers spread throughout the land. Once his fear had gone, they had no one to fight for or nothing to fight with. Ironically they would now have faded into being wanderers, or as I like to assume, starting fresh new lives in prides or making their own.

My assumptions became even more apparent when two lionesses from a neighbouring pride visited. They had come to pass on a message of gratitude, thanking us for what we had done on behalf of their pride. Not only they were now no longer living in fear, but they had welcomed some of Legacy's ex-followers into their weakening and failing pride, giving them another chance at life. Both parties now merged and united, benefitting from each other. I'm now more confident this scenario is the same for prides everywhere.

I recognised these lionesses, and to my surprise, so did Sheek. It was the same lionesses whose cub was missing and had asked me for their help; the very same cub that Sheek refused to shelter. I knew he always had resentment and guilt over the matter. He used this opportunity to explain to them his whole story of what happened.

As upset as the lionesses were, they finally had closure and instead thanked him for his brave honesty. They knew it wasn't a lion's first instinct or nature to look after a cub from an unknown pride; they understood the laws of life and they saw the sheer amount of resentment in Sheek's eyes. Now though, they could live a life that myself, Sheek and our pride have made a little brighter now that Legacy is gone. They parted from us on neutral terms back to their territory. I noticed as they left the slightly larger belly of one of the lionesses who had lost her cub, she was now expectant again.

I cannot help but now laugh at the bitter realisation that if somehow I still joined them lionesses on the search for their cub all that time back, they would have unintentionally led me straight to Sheek! Though one path I couldn't pursue at the time, still met with the only path I could take. Life sometimes gives you the ability, and in some cases pure luck, to find your way.

As much as I love, care, and worry about Anthi leaving as any mother would, he knows he too will have to find his own place in life like all lions do, he needs to establish his own pride and territory. Just like the old group did when going their separate ways, and just as I did. Regardless of our help in ridding Legacy, the rules of a lion's territory still apply, and any lion would not hesitate to fight for its protection. Our victory doesn't give us a free pass to claim any land we please. If we did, we would just be as bad as Legacy.

It's now midday. Even though I am in the shade of the bushes and valley, it's still sweltering. I lay on my side, stretching out my rear legs and staggering out my front legs to minimize trapped heat. I pant heavily, not just to keep myself cool but to prepare myself for what is soon to follow. I feel pain wrap around my belly again, the strongest it's been. I wince and suck the air through my teeth, instinctively staying quiet with not a single growl escaping my throat. I cannot draw any attention to myself as to where I lay.

This is it. Although pressed against the ground, I close my remaining eye as my panting intensifies. My other eye is still open though staring blindly into nothing. The darkness giving me a sense of calm.

My little furballs are now making all sorts of commotion, and it's obvious they now want to see what all the fuss is about with this thing called 'life'.

Like my first son Anthi before them, me and Sheek won't pull the fur over their eyes. We will show them life head-on and teach them that there are always two sides. They will witness that life is a thing that can be cruel yet kind, challenging yet rewarding, dangerous yet thrilling... tough yet loving.

I can confidently say that combined, we have had an extraordinary amount of experience in every aspect of this. Now it's time for my cubs to enter this world and explore it for themselves.

As with Anthi, they are our future generation to carry their ancestor's voices in the wind. Because with any life, myself and Sheek's won't last forever.

You may feel you have choices in life, but the fact is, some have already been made. They were written the moment you were born. You just gotta live it out with the excitement of not knowing.

Welcome to this land, my little ones...

~Sukari

-The End

Acknowledgements

Firstly, thank you so much to you – the reader. You have spent your own time reading through this book, made by a first-time author who no one has a clue about, and have read it until the end. I really do appreciate it a lot, and I hope you enjoyed Sukari's journey. Thanks again, seriously!

~~~~

Next, I would like to thank Nathalie. P for her patience in putting up with my continuous tapping on the keyboard throughout the night. Also for supporting me in my project while dealing with boredom as I was in my own little bubble while writing it. It's not your kind of thing but you respected it throughout my endeavour. If that ain't love I don't know what is. Love you my squish!

Also, I want to thank Nathalie. T, a dedicated forum member who read this book as it was being written. You gave such lovely comments about how much you enjoyed reading each chapter as I released them. You even spotted some mistakes or gave constructive criticism which I deeply admire.
~~~~

You lead a busy life with other commitments but always found time to read this, and for that, I am so incredibly grateful. As you know as a gift of thanks, I wrote two of your characters into this story, it's the least I can do.

~~~~

Though this novel and plot were imagined and written solely by myself, it goes not without credit to the members of my forum. A roleplay within the forum was abandoned and forgotten in 2008, but it contained back elements and characters which inspired and gave me the drive to do this. This is one reason why I choose to publish this at the lowest price possible set by publishers (sometimes free). Not only I am a 'nobody' in the book writing world, but it also doesn't feel ethical to profit from something that contains characters by others, regardless of how long it's been. This was purely a passion project I wrote for myself and close friends, though it does not hurt to publish it to make my 'mark'. If in my wildest dreams, this gets a considerable amount of sales, these members will not be left out. I will also donate to animal conservation charities of my choosing.

~~~~

Contributing roleplay members are listed below:

Mark. W – Legacy, Mino, Pulsar, Anmani and Desmani. This man is to blame for creating such an evil character, it's all his fault! AFTER HIM! *raises pitchfork*. Joking aside, Mark was my right-hand man in managing the forum right from the start. We met online and have been best friends ever since. Even though we don't talk as much as we used to, as soon as we do it's like that time in-between never happened, the true sign of a strong friendship and have always thought of him like a brother. We both live our own busy lives but he would always be there for a chat if things got rough. I will always offer the same to you, my friend.

Kirsi. M – Tefnut. Such a unique character and was so much fun having the pleasure of including her in this story. Thanks for your kind words and feedback when I was drawing her, she has such a lovely design to work with! You were also a long-serving dedicated member and helper of the forum who injected fun and randomness into our community. Your drawings were an inspiration for my own. Thank you for your friendship.

Kaitlyn. P – Safila and Kisima. A veteran in the roleplay that help lay its foundations. You and your mother Gaewyn. P was at the heart of the community, you have done so much for members and not wanting or expecting praise, your service goes not without commendation. I wholeheartedly appreciate everything you have done.

Kristin. E – Jenna. You started the roleplay, so the oldest veteran in it, you again laid the foundations for it and helped around the forum. Even though the story turned into something completely different through the years, that's what makes roleplaying so fun! Thanks for planting the seed that turned into a forest of storytelling.

Andreas. K – Aramile. Although we haven't spoken for a good 15 years since the roleplay died down, your character was still part of it and cannot go without credit. I hope you are doing well in whatever you are doing and if you see this, enjoyed seeing Aramile back in action!

~~~~

The forum was created in 2005 and was quite active, nowadays it's more of a time capsule of what things used to be like. It existed before 'Social Media' was such a massive thing - which can ooze toxicity, shove adverts down your throats, and feels very impersonal. Our Forum is full of memories in friendship, creative writing, discussions and even silly games; all in a nice tight-knit community in our little corner of the internet. We could be ourselves without judgement and was our safe online 'home'. Activity on the forum isn't what it used to be, but that's ok. It may have run its course, but we all move on in life, we all take our own separate paths (just like Sheek, Sukari, and Anthi have done). Some of these members I still hold as dear friends and if you are reading this, you know who you are.

~~~~

I would also like to thank my medical diagnosis. Because of *you*, I needed something to concentrate on while I came to terms with living my life differently. I needed a form of escape and coping mechanism, and writing 'Sukari's Search' was exactly that. Although I hate you... thank you.

~~~~
~~~~

Finally, I want to say. In loving memory of my Auntie Gill, who passed away as I was editing this novel. You loved a good book and I wished I had a moment to share the manuscript with you, but you were taken away far too quickly and too soon, may you rest in peace. I'll never forget what you said in one in one of our conversations as you struggled with your own health, while I felt guilty complaining about mine.

"Adam, there is no hierarchy of who has things worse. I have my own issues and so do you, but nothing will stop one from becoming less important than the other, I'm here to listen."

POEM

I leave you with this, which was written and based on Chapter 7, when 'Rogue' has a spark of connection between himself and Anthi. It's one of my favourite chapters.

"Night of change"

I don't know you, cub!
Neither you know I.
Found you drifting, deceived as prey,
drowning and destined to die.

You're an inconvenience,
my heart is cold.
No care for other lives,
regardless how old.

I'm immune to sorrow,
of any lion's death.
I know from experience,
from my past 'final' breath.

I've been tortured and torn,
my soul ripped apart.
My own lioness and cub,
beating no longer in their heart.

I'm too injured to hunt,
no stamina to run.
No nose to even smell scraps,
my own death has slowly begun.

Then along you came,
my path you intrude.
Now acquainted to find your mum,
agreed with a promise of food.

I've brought you to my den for the night,
we will rest, sheltered from the flood.
It's been a journey for your short stubby legs,
and your body all covered in mud.

You're now asleep upon my paw,
a feeling of responsibility grows.
My heart feels warm, a long-forgotten sense,
by your peaceful and content pose.

I want to growl and shove you away,
I'm used to staying estranged.
Instead, I lay guard and let you rest,
tonight, I feel I have changed.

You've shown trust and faith in this sour old lion,
towards you, I've been nothing but mean.
One thing least I can do in return,
is bathe you until you are clean.

🐾x

Printed in Great Britain
by Amazon